"Delightful . . . [A] humorous tinsel-covered tale that made me laugh out loud even while keeping me guessing."
—Jenn McKinlay, *New York Times* bestselling author

"Witty writing, an unexpected solution, and truly likable characters ensure that the appeal of this holiday-themed series will last long past the Yule season."
—Kings River Life Magazine

"Delany has given us a story full of holiday cheer, an exciting mystery, wondrous characters all in a place I would love to really visit. Its charm just lit up my day. This is one mystery you shouldn't miss this holiday season."
—Escape with Dollycas into a Good Book

"I delved right into this story—it grabbed me in and wouldn't let me go."   —Socrates' Book Reviews

"Vicki Delany does a masterful job of creating an inviting fictional small town that is all about Christmas."
—Open Book Society

"Ms. Delany has started a promising new series with *Rest Ye Murdered Gentlemen*."   —Fresh Fiction

Berkley Prime Crime titles by Vicki Delany

REST YE MURDERED GENTLEMEN
WE WISH YOU A MURDEROUS CHRISTMAS

We Wish You a Murderous Christmas

Vicki Delany

BERKLEY PRIME CRIME
New York

BERKLEY PRIME CRIME
Published by Berkley
An imprint of Penguin Random House LLC
375 Hudson Street, New York, New York 10014

Copyright © 2016 by Vicki Delany
Penguin Random House supports copyright. Copyright fuels creativity, encourages
diverse voices, promotes free speech, and creates a vibrant culture. Thank you for buying
an authorized edition of this book and for complying with copyright laws by not
reproducing, scanning, or distributing any part of it in any form without permission.
You are supporting writers and allowing Penguin Random House to continue to
publish books for every reader.

BERKLEY is a registered trademark and BERKLEY PRIME CRIME
and the B colophon are trademarks of Penguin Random House LLC.

ISBN: 9780425280812

First Edition: November 2016

Printed in the United States of America
1   3   5   7   9   10   8   6   4   2

Cover art by Julia Green
Cover design by Sarah Oberrender
Book design by Tiffany Estreicher

Acknowledgments

To Joan Hall, beloved aunt, with love and thanks for all your support.

One of the joys of being a mystery writer is traveling to conferences all over North America and meeting marvelous readers. Among them, Arlene Vigne, who sat at my banquet table at Left Coast Crime and won a name placement in the book. I hope you like "my" Arlene, Arlene.

Another joy is the many friends I've met over the years in this wonderful community, high among them Cheryl Freedman, who read this manuscript and made valuable suggestions. Thanks, Cheryl.

Chapter 1

Decisions, decisions.

Did I want hearty, traditional winter fare or something to remind me of summers at the lake?

Prime rib with roasted vegetables or grilled salmon with rice pilaf?

"You have to make up your mind sometime, Merry." Vicky handed the waitress her menu. "I'll have the lamb shanks, please."

"That sounds good," I said. "Me, too."

"You always have what I have," Vicky said.

"That's because I can't decide for myself."

The waitress returned with a bottle of nice red wine and went through the ritual of opening and tasting. We were savoring the first sips when she came back, bearing an overflowing platter, and placed it on the table. Charcuterie: a selection of cheeses and paper-thin slices of cured meats with an assortment of pickles and nuts served with hunks of freshly baked baguette.

"That looks delicious," Vicky said, "but you have the wrong table. We didn't order it."

"Compliments of the chef," the waitress said with a grin.

"Nice." I picked a tiny knife off the tray and sliced myself a sliver of creamy blue-veined cheese. "I heard they hired a new chef. My mom says the food's improved dramatically. Is that why you wanted to try it? Wow, this is marvelous." I let the deep, sharp flavor linger in my mouth. My taste buds did a happy dance. Then I noticed the slight flush on my best friend's face. "Oh," I said. "I get it."

Vicky Casey and I were at the Yuletide Inn for a special treat of a fancy dinner. It was a Tuesday night in mid-December, and both of us were run off our feet at work, but Vicky had convinced me (without much difficulty, I will confess) that we needed a break in the midst of the madness of the Christmas rush. I own a shop, Mrs. Claus's Treasures, in Rudolph, New York, which we call America's Christmas Town. Vicky's the owner and chief baker of Victoria's Bake Shoppe. It was her idea to have a special girls' night out, to relieve some of the stress of the season. Judging by the high color of her cheeks, clashing dreadfully with the lock of purple hair falling across her forehead, Vicky had an ulterior motive.

"Evening, ladies," said the deep voice of the ulterior motive.

A man stood beside our table, dressed in a chef's uniform of white jacket and gray striped pants. The logo of the Yuletide Inn was embroidered onto the jacket, with his name written in script beneath. *Mark Grosse, Executive Chef.*

Every woman in town was gossiping about this man. For once the gossip was understated. He was tall and lean, with dark hair cut short, enormous brown eyes specked with bits of green, high cheekbones, and blindingly white teeth.

"Hi," Vicky squeaked. "Thanks for this."

"I hope you enjoy it." He smiled at her.

"Very nice of you," I said. I might as well not have bothered. Neither of them was paying the slightest bit of attention to me. Chef Mark was grinning at Vicky and she was grinning back.

"Oh, uh," Vicky said, remembering her manners at last. "Mark, this is my friend Merry Wilkinson."

He turned to me. His smile was dazzling. "So pleased to meet you, Merry. Are you a cook also?"

"I boil a mean pot of water," I said.

"I've got to get back to the kitchen," Mark said. "Nice meeting you, Merry. I hope you recognize the baguette, Vicky."

"Sure do," she said.

"Have a nice meal," he said. "Don't forget to save room for dessert. The gingerbread cake is fabulous." He hurried away, back to the mysterious depths of a top-ranked restaurant kitchen.

I broke off a hunk of baguette and popped it into my

mouth. Crunchy on the outside, soft and dense within. Delicious. "Yours?"

"Yup. As is the gingerbread cake."

"Does he get all his desserts from you?"

"Just the bread, mostly. As my gingerbread cake is a Rudolph specialty, he buys that from me, too."

I took a sip of wine. "Nice-looking guy."

"Is he?" she said, gulping down half a glass of her own. "I hadn't noticed."

I glanced around the dining room. It was full, and I knew Vicky only got a reservation because they had a cancellation for a table for two. Logs burned in the large, open fireplace against one wall. Next to it a tall, fat, real Douglas fir was weighted down with decorations and trimmed with delicate white lights. The tables were covered in starched white linen tablecloths, and crystal and silver glimmered in the gentle light cast by a single votive candle. The glass candleholders were trimmed with a piece of freshly cut holly. The room was full of light and laughter, warmth and wonderful scents, and that special something that was part of the season: Christmas magic. I settled back with a contented sigh.

"How's business?" Vicky asked.

"Mad. Absolutely mad. As they say in show business, any publicity is good publicity. All the attention the town received when that journalist was killed has helped draw in the crowds. Once they found the killer and Rudolph's reputation was cleared, anyway. I'm worried about running out of some of my stock before Christmas."

"That's a good worry," Vicky said. "Better than being stuck with stuff you can't move."

We wiped the charcuterie plate clean. When the waitress took away the empty platter she asked if we wanted another bottle. Vicky and I exchanged a questioning look before saying, "Sure!" at the same time. The lamb shanks arrived and they were delicious, served with delicate potatoes and grilled vegetables. We lingered over our meal for a long time, simply enjoying each other's company and the welcome chance to relax.

I've had more of Vicky's gingerbread cake than I can possibly remember, but I never get enough of it. I ordered that for dessert, and Vicky had the candy cane cheesecake. The gingerbread was served under a mountain of freshly whipped cream, and the cheesecake dotted with bits of crushed candy.

"My compliments to the chef," Vicky said as we rummaged for our credit cards.

The waitress was about fifty years old, but she giggled and blushed like a teenager talking about the captain of the football team. "Isn't he wonderful? We're so lucky to have him."

Vicky pulled out her phone and called for a cab. Neither of us was in any state to drive.

Then, stuffed to the gills and more than a bit tipsy, my best friend and I staggered out the restaurant door into the hotel lobby.

The lobby of the Yuletide Inn was also beautifully decorated for the season. The huge tree was hung with an array of antique (or antique-looking) ornaments; wooden soldiers stood to attention in the deep, stone windowsills; red stockings hung over the fireplace; terra-cotta pots overflowed with pink-flowered Christmas cactus and red and white poinsettias. Glass bowls of various sizes full of silver and gold balls sat on the large, round table dominating the center of the room. A charming Christmas village, complete with snow on the roofs and lighted windows in the shops and houses, was arranged on a side table.

"Hey, look who's here," a baritone boomed.

"Hi, Dad. Mom." Even though I'd seen them only yesterday, we exchanged enthusiastic hugs and kisses. My parents greeted Vicky the same way, and we shook hands with the couple with my parents. Jack and Grace Olsen, owners of the Yuletide Inn.

"Are you going through for dinner?" I asked. "It's late for you, isn't it, Dad?"

"We've just finished," he said, rubbing his round belly with a satisfied smile.

"I didn't see you in the dining room."

"We had a private room," Mom said. "It pays to know the boss." The two couples were close friends.

"Dinner was exceptional," Vicky said, patting her own firm, flat stomach. "The new chef is simply fabulous."

Grace and Jack beamed. "We're hearing nothing but good reports," Jack said. "And let me tell you, that's a relief, after the last guy." The side of one lip twisted up in disapproval. Jack was, for his age, a good-looking man with a strong, square jaw and dancing blue eyes.

"We're booked solid until New Year's Day," Grace added. "Some people have made next year's reservations already."

"Glad to hear it," Dad said. "What's good for the Yuletide is . . ."

"Good for Rudolph," we chorused.

Dad said, "Ho, ho, ho." My dad was born on December 25th and named Noel. He has plump red cheeks, a round stomach, a long white beard, a mass of curly white hair, and bushy white eyebrows. Even when he's not wearing the costume of red suit, black belt and boots, and pom-pom-tipped hat, Noel Wilkinson looks exactly like a storybook Santa Claus. And Santa he is, in our town, at least. Tonight he was dressed in brown corduroy slacks (circa 1980) and a red sweater sporting a reindeer with sprigs of holly entwined in his antlers and a big, red woolen pom-pom for his nose. I noticed people walking through the lobby giving him sideways glances, and their faces lighting up in smiles. It was late for small children to be around, but if they were, Dad would always give them a wink and a hearty, "Ho, ho, ho."

Vicky and I laughed and leaned against each other.

Always the more serious of the pair, my mother gave me a stern look. "You are not driving, I hope."

"We've called a cab, Aline," Vicky said.

"We can give you a lift," Dad said. "We're leaving now."

"Thanks, Dad, but the cab'll be here in a minute," I said. "We'll wait outside. Good night."

We headed for the front doors as Jack Olsen said,

"Did I ever tell you about the time I was in the navy, and Santa Claus visited the ship? We were in the Philippines, and he was the sorriest excuse . . ."

He broke off with a strangled cry. I heard a loud thump followed by a resounding crash. Grace screamed, my mom gasped, and Dad yelled, "Jack!"

I whirled around to see Jack lying on the floor. He'd knocked over the side table as he fell, and the lighted Christmas village display hit the ground. Many of the tiny buildings were shattered, and the town had been thrown into darkness when the electrical cord had been jerked out of the wall. Jack clutched his chest. His eyes were round and white, full of pain and fear. Grace dropped to her knees beside him. "He's having another heart attack. Jack, Jack, are you okay?"

He groaned.

"Call 911," I shouted to the woman at the reception desk, but she already had the phone in her hand.

My dad dropped to the floor beside his friend. Jack was dressed in a gray suit, white shirt, and striped tie. Dad ripped the tie open and undid the top two buttons. "Aline," he said, "give me your coat."

Without a word, Mom slipped her cape off. It was a gorgeous thing of black wool with an emerald silk lining and matching frog fastenings. Dad draped it over Jack. "Let's try to keep him warm. Hold on there, buddy—help's on the way."

Grace gripped her husband's hand and sobbed silently.

"They want to know if he's breathing," the reception-ist called.

A woman came out of the restaurant at a trot. "I'm a doctor. Let me help." She crouched over Jack, her eve-ning skirt spreading around her in a puddle of scarlet satin. "Get him sitting up."

Fortunately the Rudolph Hospital is located on the same side of town as the inn, and in minutes we heard the welcome sound of an approaching siren. I hurried outside to direct the EMTs to the patient.

A taxi followed in the ambulance's wake. "Nothing we can do," Vicky said. "We might as well go home."

"I'll be right back." I ran into the lobby. "Our cab's here. Do you want to come with us, Mom?"

She leaned into me, and I gave her a hug. Her body was trembling. "I'll stay with Grace."

"Call me as soon as you hear anything."

I jumped into the cab beside Vicky. "Do you think Jack's going to be okay?" she asked me.

"I don't know. Did you hear Grace say *another* heart attack? That can't be good."

"My brother died of a heart attack," the cabbie said, "and my father before him. Let me tell you . . ."

Vicky and I said not another word all the way home.

Even in the busy holiday season, midweek mornings are always slow in my shop. Which is a good thing, as it gives me a chance to reorganize the displays and restock the shelves. It was coming up on lunchtime and I was straightening the window displays when I spotted Mom heading my way.

My mom is always easy to spot. She's an opera singer, and at the height of her career she'd been nothing less than a diva at the Metropolitan Opera. She retired to Rudolph, my dad's hometown, to run a vocal school, but she still considered the limelight to be her natural environment. Today she wore an ankle-length black wool coat with giant red buttons, a black hat with red trim that managed to be both warm and elegant, red leather gloves, and red boots. My dad had called me last night when I was cuddling up with my bed partner—a Saint Bernard puppy named Matterhorn—to say Jack was being prepped for surgery and he and Mom would stay with Grace.

Mom breezed into the shop, not looking at all like a woman who must have been up most of the night. "Good morning, dear."

"Hi, Mom. Any news about Jack?"

"The surgery went well, and he's now, as they say, resting comfortably."

"That's good to hear. How's Grace?"

"Worried sick, poor thing. I'm going to the inn now, to pick her up and take her to the hospital."

"She said Jack was having another heart attack?"

"He had a minor one about a year ago. This one, last night, was not minor. He had a triple bypass."

"That'll mean a long recovery time," I said. "Is the hotel going to be okay without him running things?"

"I don't know, dear. Jack was very much involved in the day-to-day operation of the place. He's the manager, as well as the owner. Grace has told me many times that the hotel's getting to be too much for him. The constant stress of demanding guests, the endless hours involved in running a hotel, the worry."

"Worry? Is the inn not doing okay?"

"I believe it's doing very well," she said, "but when one owns one's own business there's no getting away from it."

"That's certainly true," I said, "as I've found out." I've owned Mrs. Claus's Treasures for only a couple of months, so this was my first holiday season. I specialized in locally sourced artisan crafts, but I occasionally bought pieces from farther away if they appealed to me. I trust my taste and buy only what I love and what I think others will love. I select everything I sell with great care and arrange it as I want. I love having this store. I love being my own boss and doing everything my way. It's a big responsibility, but I'm hugely proud of it. It's also a heck of a lot of work. "How's Grace going to manage? It would be hard enough anytime, but we're heading into the busiest weeks of the year."

"She called her stepson last night. The boy's from Jack's first marriage. He lives in California but said he'd be right out and will be able to stay as long as he's needed."

"I might know him. What's his name?"

"Gordon."

"Right, Gord Olsen. He was in school with me. He

left when his parents divorced and he moved with his mom to California. I remember him bragging about all the surfing he was going to do and all the movie stars he was going to meet." I also remembered how glad we all were to see the back of him. Gord Olsen had been a horrid boy. The worst sort of bully, who'd lie to a teacher's face and say it wasn't him, and then turn around and steal lunch money from a little kid. But all that was a long time ago, and I was sure he'd changed. "That's good to hear. If Jack doesn't have to worry about the inn he can concentrate on getting better."

"I'm driving Grace to Syracuse later to pick them up."

"Them?"

"I believe Gord's bringing his wife."

"Don't they have jobs or something?"

Mom shrugged her well-draped shoulders. Regular employment was not a concept she was familiar with. "Why don't you come to the inn around seven this evening to meet them? They'll need to get settled in and will want to meet the local businesspeople."

"I'll call Jackie and ask her to work tonight until closing. If she can, I'll come."

"Good." My mother left with a wave of leather-clad fingers.

The moment she stepped onto the sidewalk, Betty Thatcher, the owner of Rudolph's Gift Nook, the shop next to mine, pounced on her. Betty seemed to spend most of her day watching (and disapproving of) the goings-on at Mrs. Claus's Treasures. Assuming that news of Jack Olsen's heart attack had spread and Betty was on the hunt for gossip, I went back to work.

I phoned my regular shop assistant Jackie O'Reilly to ask if she'd mind doing a shift this evening. As I expected, she jumped at the chance to earn extra money. At one thirty I switched the sign over the door to "Closed" and trotted up the street to grab something for lunch. I'd been planning on teasing Vicky on the way home last night about the new man in town, Chef Mark Grosse. But with what had happened to Jack, never mind our cabbie's monologue about all the people in his family who'd been struck down with heart attacks, the mood for teasing had been extinguished as thoroughly as the lights in the hotel's Christmas village windows.

Now, I thought, heading for Victoria's Bake Shoppe, might be a good time.

I ran up the steps and opened the door. The delicious scents of freshly baked bread, warm pastry, ginger, and cinnamon washed over me. I took a deep breath. Heaven, I sometimes thought, must smell like Vicky's bakery. The lunch rush was dying down and the waitress was wiping down tables and clearing used dishes. "Hi, Merry," she said as I came in. "You here for lunch? There's not a whole lot left."

"Soup?" I peeled off my gloves and shrugged out of my coat.

"Only split pea. I can make you a croissant sandwich with ham and cheese to go with it."

"Sounds good," I said. I took a seat while I tried not

to look at the shelf above the counter. There, proudly displayed, sat not one but two giant trophies awarded for the Rudolph Santa Claus parade best float. There are two awards because we have a parade in midsummer as well as the main event the first Saturday of December: the town of Rudolph is promoted as *the* place for year-round Christmas celebrations. One of those trophies should have been mine. If my float hadn't been sabotaged by an individual out to destroy Christmas in Rudolph, it would have been. I was still bitter about that.

"I thought I recognized that voice." Vicky came out of the back, wiping floury hands on her long apron.

"Second thought, Marjorie," I raised my voice, "I'd prefer a baguette, if you still have any."

"All gone."

"Oh, that's too bad. I hope you had enough for the Yuletide Inn."

"If you must know," Vicky said, "I made the delivery myself this morning."

"How nice of you to make a personal trip and not send one of your lackeys. Was the head chef around, by any chance?" I wiggled my eyebrows.

"And isn't he a dream?" Marjorie, who's Vicky's aunt, put a steaming bowl of soup in front of me.

"As it happens," Vicky said as her face turned bright red, "he was. A top chef always wants to be on hand to inspect the goods when they're delivered."

"And much inspecting was done, I am sure."

Vicky looked as though she was thinking of making a sharp retort. Instead she burst out laughing. "Oh, all right.

You win. Yes, I like him, and yes, I think he likes me. And don't you dare tell my mom that, Aunt Marjorie."

"I never gossip about what happens in the bakery."

Vicky rolled her eyes. She dropped into the vacant chair at my table. "Although, about the last person I'd want to get involved with is a chef. They have absolutely killer hours." She pushed the single long lock of purple hair out of her eyes. The rest of her hair was its natural black, cut almost to the scalp. She always applied dramatic black makeup around her cornflower blue eyes, a tattoo of a gingerbread man cookie decorated her right wrist, and I knew she had numerous tattoos that were kept discreetly covered when she was at work. She had a heart-shaped face, and her smile was as mischievous as the youngest and naughtiest of Santa's elves. At five foot eleven and rail thin she had the body of a supermodel, rather than that of a woman who cooked delicious baked goods all day. I, on the other hand, barely reach five foot five and do not have the body of a supermodel.

"You keep the worst hours of anyone I know," I said. "Wouldn't that be a good fit?"

"A restaurant is the exact opposite to a bakery. I get up in the middle of the night to make bread, and we close midafternoon. He starts midmorning and sometimes goes until after midnight."

"You'll work it out," I said.

"You're getting way ahead of yourself, Merry. We haven't so much as had a cup of coffee together yet."

"Yes, you did," Marjorie called from behind the counter. "Before Thanksgiving."

"That was business. He came in to talk about placing a regular order. Don't you have work to do, Aunt Marjorie?"

"I can clean and talk at the same time."

"Judging by the way he was looking at you last night," I said, "you have nothing to worry about. Why, I bet as soon as the New Year's here and the holiday rush dies down, he'll be calling."

Her face brightened. "You think?"

"Totally. Then again, this is the twenty-first century, you know. You can call him."

"Yes!" Aunt Marjorie shouted.

I finished my lunch, nobly passing on a triple chocolate brownie that was one of the few desserts remaining, and headed home for my regular midday chore.

Somehow, without my quite knowing what was happening, a Saint Bernard puppy had wiggled his way into my life. And, I must add, into my heart. His name is Matterhorn, he's usually called Mattie, and he's just over three months old. One of Vicky's vast array of cousins breeds the friendly giants. Mattie's mother, a kennel show regular, managed to get herself "knocked up" by a dog without papers. To hear Vicky's family talk, it wouldn't have been any more scandalous if one of the Queen's grandchildren had run off with a punk rocker. As none of the kennel's customers wanted Mattie or his brothers and sisters, Vicky set about finding good homes for the puppies.

Against my better judgment, I said I'd consider it. I was taken to the kennels, and after one look at those giant eyes the color of melting caramel and one lick from his big pink tongue, I fell in love. Home with me he came.

The timing couldn't have been worse. It was the busiest time of year at the store, and because he was a hyperactive puppy and still basically untrained, he had to be left in his crate when I wasn't home. Which meant I had to keep popping out of the shop and running home to let him out to do his business. And then, at the end of a long day when I'd been on my feet for twelve hours or more, he needed a nice long walk.

Mattie greeted me with his usual unbridled enthusiasm and then bounded through the deep snow in the backyard for a while. I hadn't had much time to train him (although we were signed up for lessons beginning the week after New Year) but he was intelligent and eager to please, and I could usually get him back in the crate without too much pushing and shoving. He was going to be one mighty big animal.

Speaking of leaps, Betty Thatcher jumped out of the Nook when she heard me arrive at Mrs. Claus's Treasures after seeing to Mattie. Her store, Rudolph's Gift Nook, sells cheap, mass-produced Christmas stuff. I have no problem with that; we are not in competition. Betty, however, seems to think if I'd close up shop and slink into the night, my customers would be beating down her doors. "There you are!" she shouted. "If you want to run a business you can't be taking time off in the middle of the day, you know."

"I was out for lunch."

"That's no excuse. I never take a lunch break. I bring a sandwich from home. So should you."

"Yes, Betty."

"I'm not your social secretary, you know."

"Yes, Betty."

"People have been coming into the Nook for the past hour, wondering when you'll be open."

I glanced at the door. A paper clock hung there. It said "Back at:" and its hands pointed to two thirty. I glanced at my watch. Two twenty-nine.

"Where's Jackie?" Betty asked.

"She'll be around later," I said.

Betty harrumphed. "I've never liked that girl, you know. Too busy flirting with the male customers, in my opinion. Their wives don't like that."

"Thank you for the advice." I unlocked my shop door.

But Betty wasn't finished yet. "If you need dependable help, my Clark's looking for work."

Clark was Betty's son. He was always looking for work because he had an attitude problem—not that either he or Betty saw it that way—and couldn't hold down a job. I'd heard that he'd been hired at the Yuletide but that hadn't ended well, although I didn't know the details. These days he helped out at the Nook sometimes, but Betty never seemed to take a minute off.

"I'll keep that in mind," I said.

"You do that." She went into her shop, and I went into mine.

Traffic picked up over the rest of the afternoon, and it turned into a good day. Jackie arrived at six, and I went home to feed Mattie and take him for a walk before driving myself to the Yuletide Inn.

It was full dark when I pulled into the inn's long, curving driveway. The hotel was trimmed with white fairy lights, and colored bulbs had been strung between the trees lining the paths that meandered through the spacious gardens. In the summer the gorgeous grounds of the inn are one of Rudolph's prime tourist attractions. Even in the winter it's a lovely place for a stroll, to admire the sculptural naked branches of the oaks and maples, the snow-laden needles of pines and spruce. A man-made pond marks the heart of the gardens, and in the winter the hotel staff keep it clear for skating. As I walked up the stairs a family fell into step behind me. Mom, Dad, and two laughing kids, warmly dressed and pink cheeked from enjoying a walk in the fresh winter air.

"Merry Wilkinson, as beautiful as ever!" A loud voice greeted me as I came into the lobby. I was enveloped in a giant bear hug. "It's so great to see you." The man pulled back. Gord Olsen had put on a lot of weight since our school days. It didn't look good on his five-foot-six frame. His eyes were small and almost black, his lips thin, and his fair hair receding at a rapid pace. He must look like his mother, because the only trace of Jack I could see in him was the square jaw.

"Nice to see you, too, Gord," I said. "Any news about your dad?"

"'Stable' is the official word. I guess that's the best we can hope for at this time. Come over here, honey. Here's someone I'd like you to meet. Merry and I were in school together. Merry, this lovely lady is Irene, my wife."

I shook hands with Irene Olsen. She was taller than her husband, and, in boots with sky-high stiletto heels, not trying to hide it. She was about his age, meaning the same age as me, thirtyish. She looked stereotypically California: long blond locks, blindingly white teeth, a deep tan. She was slightly overweight, but who am I (an eager patron of Victoria's Bake Shoppe) to judge? She took my hand in limp fingers, and her smile didn't reach her eyes. "So pleased to meet you," she said, almost yawning.

I turned to Grace and gave her a hug. "You okay?"

"I'm as fine as can be expected. Noel and Aline have been a tower of strength."

I smiled at my parents.

"Now that we're all here, shall we go through?" Grace said.

At that moment I realized everyone else was dressed for dinner. Mom wore a tailored trouser suit, Grace was in a woolen sheath that showed off her slim figure, Gord in suit and tie, my dad in another one of his hideous (meaning absolutely perfect) Christmas sweaters, and Irene in a knee-length blue dress with gold jewelry.

I'd changed out of my work clothes to walk Mattie and had pulled on a pair of old jeans, a black T-shirt under a slightly ratty sweater, and heavy winter boots that were perfect for walking a dog in the snowy park. "I didn't know we were having dinner," I mumbled. "I'm not really dressed for it."

"Can't be helped," Mom said.

We were escorted into a small private alcove off the dining room. The lighting was soft and the Christmas decorations subdued. The moment we sat down, Gord ordered a couple of bottles of wine for the table. He opened his menu and studied it intently. "Prices are mighty steep, Grace."

"We have an excellent chef. He came here from the city, with the best of credentials. He gets as many of his ingredients locally as he can. Even at this time of year farms around Rudolph can supply much of what we need. The lamb, for example, is from a farm not more than half an hour's drive from here."

"It's really good, too," I said. "I had it last night."

"That's all well and good." Gord ignored me. "But the prices are too high."

"Step into the main room," Grace said. "We're full. We've been full almost every night this month."

"Sure," Gord said, "over Christmas. But when the holiday rush is over you won't get people here if it's too expensive."

"Jack," Grace said, her words clipped, "approved the menu."

"I'm sure he did, Grace," Gord said. "I'm simply pointing out where things could be done more efficiently."

"I'll try the lamb," Irene said.

The food was as delightful as it had been the night before, but the mood was not. I'd thought Gord had wanted to meet us to learn about the business community of Rudolph. Instead, despite the fact that he'd been here all of four hours, it seemed as though he'd made up his mind on what he wanted to do in his father's absence. Grace ordered the charcuterie plate for the table. When it arrived, Gord grabbed a slice of the baguette. He turned it over and studied it. He poked his finger into the middle and then broke off a piece of the crust and popped it into his mouth. "Where'd this come from?" he said, chewing.

"Victoria's Bake Shoppe," I said. "Best bread in Upstate New York."

"I bet it's expensive, too." Gord reached into the breast pocket of his jacket and pulled out his iPhone. His thumbs flew.

"The bakery's a Rudolph institution," I said.

"Plenty of large-scale operations around." Gord continued typing. I was seated next to him and managed a peek. He had the notebook application open. "I'll see what I can find," he said. "Bread is just bread, after all."

I glanced at my dad. His color was rising, and not in his habitual Jolly Saint Nick look. "Rudolph," he said, "is a community-orientated town. Christmas Town. In Rudolph we believe that a rising tide lifts all boats. Everyone here supports everyone else's business. Thus, we all benefit."

Gord laughed. "Sounds like that old Western town where folks made a living by taking in each other's washing."

I glanced around the table. Dad's face was beet red and a vein throbbed in his neck. Mom studied her napkin as if searching for the secret of life therein. Grace stared at her stepson in horror.

"That fresh tree in the lobby looks okay and all, Grace," Irene said. She seemed to be totally oblivious to the mood that had fallen over the table. "You should get a plastic tree that can be used every year. They come with decorations attached, so you don't have to bother with decorating it and then taking it down again. That must take time, and time is money. Am I right, honey?"

"Right," Gord replied.

"Ready to order?" The waitress arrived in the nick of time, as I was beginning to fear my dad would soon join Jack in the cardiac ward.

Grace and my mother were skilled hostesses. They managed to turn the conversation to the upcoming season at the Met and reminiscences of Grace and Jack's fall trip to Montreal. Gord spent the meal glancing around the room and typing notes into his phone. He might not have liked the prices here but, judging by the way he ate, he was certainly enjoying his meal. More wine was ordered, and not from the bottom of the price range, either.

After the main-course plates were cleared, the waitress put small dessert and liquor menus at each place. We all refused, except for Gord. He asked her what was good.

I said, "Everything is good. But you should try the gingerbread cake. It's a Rudolph tradition."

"Great. I'll have that. And a glass of port. Anyone else?"

"Decaf," Irene said.

The rest of us declined. I suspect my parents and Grace were, like me, desperate to make our escape.

The cake arrived. Gord took a bite. "Good," he said. He scooped up a forkful of the whipped cream. "Taste this, babe," he said to Irene. She leaned across the table, opened her mouth, and Gord thrust his fork into it. My mother's mouth hung open in shock.

"Yum," Irene said. "Real whipped cream."

"Of course it is," Grace said.

"That's what I figured," Gord said. "Whipped topping's cheaper. Most folks won't notice, not if the cake's made with more sugar."

The table rattled as Grace pushed back her chair. "I've had quite enough," she said.

"I can understand that," Gord said. "You must be tired. Nighty night. If you go to the hospital in the morning, tell Dad I'll be around later."

My dad and mom got to their feet also. I hurried to follow.

We left Gord to continue making notes on his cell phone while Irene topped up her wineglass.

Chapter 2

Most of the year, it's a mystery what dogs are up to. Seemingly out of nowhere they suddenly get furiously excited and head off full steam into the woods or walk in ever-decreasing circles with their noses to the ground. But in winter, you can see what only they can smell.

Mattie was circling a large patch of yellow snow, head down, nose twitching, butt trembling. Then he lifted his leg and made his contribution to the news of the neighborhood. When we'd come out of the house earlier, he'd charged straight across the yard, following a trail of rabbit tracks to the back fence. The rabbit had gone under the fence. Mattie tried to follow, but he hadn't entirely learned the limitations of his body.

Deep in my coat pocket my phone rang. I pulled it out, checked the display.

"Where are you?" Vicky said.

"In the park with Mattie."

"I'll pick you up in five minutes."

"Why?"

"Because it will do Mattie good to get used to being in different cars and going to different places—I told you that."

"Yes, but why now? And where are we going?"

"Surprise. Be waiting by the bandstand." She hung up.

Typical Vicky. She'd always been wildly impulsive and even after all these years of us knowing each other, she refused to believe that I am not. I thought back to the day we'd met. Our first day at kindergarten. She had walked up to me, put her hands on her nonexistent hips, and said I was now her best friend. She'd been dressed in a purple T-shirt and orange jeans with green socks, and her short black hair was standing on end. My mom had been away on tour, and Dad had taken seriously the responsibility of getting me ready for the first day. My hair had been brushed for all it was worth and pulled into a ponytail so tight my eyes were stretched upward. I wore a brown sweater over a brown dress with brown socks and black shoes. I'd looked up at Vicky—she was already taller than me—and said, "Okay," probably because I didn't know what else to say.

And we had been best friends ever since.

Mattie and I walked back toward the street to wait. It had snowed heavily overnight and the town park was a field of pure, untouched snow. A weak, white sun was only just touching the trees to the east, and to the north the vast reaches of Lake Ontario stretched dark and foreboding to the horizon. I switched my flashlight off as we approached the lights on the town's official Christmas tree beside the bandstand.

Next to the street and around the bandstand the snow was churned up by tracks human and canine, and I let Mattie sniff to his heart's content while we waited.

It was only a couple of minutes before Vicky drove up in the bakery's white panel van, the one she used for deliveries. Mattie and I jumped in. There were no rear seats, and the dog couldn't go in the back, among the bread, so I held him on my lap and tried to fasten the belt around us both. It wasn't easy. Mattie loved Vicky and he was determined to help her drive the van. I could only hope we didn't run into my archnemesis, Officer Candy Campbell. Candy would be more than happy to give me a ticket for improper seat belt use.

"Another week," I grumbled, trying to see over the dog's head, "of growth, and this isn't going to work."

"Enjoy them while they're young," Vicky said, pulling in front of a pickup truck, leaving it inches to spare. "That's what my mom keeps telling Rebecca, anyway. When one of the twins is throwing up her milk and the other is screaming for more, Rebecca has been heard to mutter, 'It gets worse?'"

"Spill," I said when the dog was finally settled in my lap and enjoying the view. "What's this about?"

"I'm making deliveries; thought you might want to come along. Give Mattie some exposure to the outside world."

"You're making deliveries? Is Ryan sick?" Ryan was one of Vicky's cousins. He usually drove the delivery truck on its morning rounds.

"No," she said. "I figured he needed to learn more about the business so he's helping Aunt Marjorie prep for breakfast."

She geared down, did a U-turn in the middle of the road, and we squealed out of town on two wheels. I tightened my grip on Mattie.

I was no detective, but even I could soon guess where we were going with these deliveries. "Why are you taking me to the Yuletide?"

"I told you, I thought you'd like the ride." Barely slowing down, she switched gears again and swung into the inn's plowed and sanded drive. I pressed my back into my chair and my foot into the passenger's seat footwell. "You don't have to help with the brakes," Vicky said.

"Yes, I do," I replied.

Mattie woofed.

We pulled into the lane, which curved around the back of the hotel, and parked beside the refuse bins and trash cans. A gleaming silver BMW sat next to a rusty compact missing part of the front bumper and a van with stick-on figures indicating a happy family lived there.

"Nice wheels," I said. "Must be lucrative being a chef."

"Oh," Vicky said. "Do you think that's Mark's car? I wonder what he's doing here so early."

"Vicky, why did you bring me along?"

She sighed. "'Cause I like him so much, it scares me. Okay?"

I reached over and touched her hand. "Okay."

The man himself came out to greet us. Mark couldn't have gotten to bed more than a couple of hours earlier, but he looked bright and alert. And very happy to see us. To see Vicky, I mean. I might as well not have been there. Mark was a touch over six feet, a good match for my friend. They grinned at each other like a couple of sixth graders discovering they liked members of the opposite sex after all.

I had to let Mattie out of the car. I couldn't get out otherwise. Never one to allow himself to be ignored, he ran toward Mark with a cheerful bark.

Mark tore his eyes away from Vicky. "Hey, there's a friendly boy." He crouched down and rubbed at the excited dog's head. "What a beauty. How old is he?"

"Three months," I said.

"Three months! He's going to be huge."

"Don't I know it."

Vicky beamed. I could almost read her mind. Car lover, dog lover, a man who could cook, and handsome to boot. If Mark Grosse wasn't her perfect match, he was darn near close. He gave Mattie a hearty slap on the rump and stood up. "I'm sure you have other calls to make. I'll help you carry your stuff in and you can be on your way."

They kept grinning at each other. "Why don't I do it?" I said at last.

"Oh, sorry," Mark said.

Mattie wasn't allowed in the kitchen, so I put him back in the van before helping to carry in trays laden with wheat bread sprinkled with a thick layer of seeds, flaky croissants, long, thin baguettes, plump gingerbread cake, and an assortment of Vicky's deservedly famous gingerbread cookies cut in reindeer shapes. The large industrial kitchen was clean and tidy; the stainless steel polished to a high gloss. Two waitresses were already at work, putting the coffee on and slicing fruit to arrange on platters. The scent of baking muffins filled the room. The restaurant was not open to the public before lunch, but it served a continental breakfast to guests. We put the trays on the island in the center of the room.

"Those look so good," one of the waitresses said. "We had compliments yesterday on the croissants."

"Morning, morning. Always nice to see people up and about bright and early and hard at work!" Gord Olsen came through the swinging doors leading from the dining room.

Mark's handsome face stiffened at the intrusion, and I assumed he'd met his boss's son already. Vicky didn't notice, and she stepped forward with a big smile. "I'm Vicky Casey, from Victoria's Bake Shoppe in Rudolph."

They shook hands.

"I was sorry to hear about your dad," Vicky said. "But they say he's going to be okay."

"Perhaps," Gord said. "The recovery will be long and slow. I'm glad I ran into you, Ms. Casey. I was going to phone you later. I was up late last night, still on California time, you know, trying to get up to speed on my dad's business. It can't be helped, I'm afraid. We have to consider what will happen if he's unable, or unwilling, to return to work." He paused for a solemn moment before continuing. "I have to say, your prices are very high."

"High? Not when you consider that all my baked goods are handmade in my own bakery. I use nothing but the highest-quality ingredients, all sourced locally where possible."

"Vicky's baking's the best," the waitress said. "Everyone says so."

"Yes, yes." Gord dismissed her with a wave of his hand. "That's all well and good, but if I'm going to implement some much-needed efficiencies, I've decided to start with the restaurant. We're going to have to negotiate your prices."

"Hey," Mark said, "the kitchen is my business."

"The *cooking* is your business," Gord said. "We'll get to your exorbitant salary later."

"I . . ." Mark said.

Vicky cut him off. "My prices are not open for negotiation. Or rather for renegotiation. All this was discussed with Jack and Grace when I first began supplying the inn. My prices are fair. I have a business to run, staff to pay, ingredients and supplies to buy, and rent on my premises."

"Not my problem," Gord said. "If you can't, or won't, reduce your prices by, let's say fifty percent, then I'll buy our baked goods elsewhere."

"Fifty percent! That's crazy. I might as well give it to you for free."

"Wow!" the waitress said.

Gord turned on her. "Do you two not have work to do? Your employment is also going to be under review."

The women snatched up laden platters and scurried into the dining room.

"It's out of the question," Mark said. "I don't serve mass-produced bread and desserts in my restaurant."

"Then maybe," Gord said, "it won't be *your* restaurant for long. I had a look at your contract last night, too."

Mark's body stiffened and Gord puffed himself up, trying to compensate for the substantial height difference. They looked like a couple of moose checking each other out before lowering antlers, and for a moment I expected the two men to come to blows. With a furious Vicky piling on. The doors swung open again, and Grace Olsen came into the kitchen. She was smartly dressed in a deep red trouser suit and her hair and makeup were perfectly arranged, but no amount of grooming could hide bags the color of winter storm clouds beneath her eyes or the fine frown lines radiating from her mouth. "What on earth is going on here?" she said. "I can hear you people out in the dining room. We'll be serving breakfast coffee and pastries soon."

"Nothing to concern yourself with," Gord said.

"I'll decide what concerns me," she replied.

"I totally understand, Grace. Let's let these people get on with their day, why don't we." He put his arm around her shoulders. She shrugged him off. "The inn is important to you," he said in a tone similar to one my dad used when a fractious two-year-old was plunked down on Santa's knee. "That's why I'm glad to be able to help you out here. But I suggest you remember that, according to the power of attorney my father drew up, I'm in charge now."

"You can't be serious," Grace said. "We won't be making major decisions while Jack's in the hospital. He'll be home soon and things can get back to normal. All you're needed for"—and her expression indicated that she was merely being polite, rather than saying what she really thought—"is to help with the day-to-day running of the place when I'm with Jack."

Gord sighed. "We can only hope Dad'll be okay, Grace. But until he's back in the saddle, I intend to do the best I can to honor the trust he's put in me. I'm doing it for Dad. And for you, of course. Are you off to the hospital? Tell Dad he's got nothing to worry about. I'm a quick study." Grace and Gordon began to walk away. Over his shoulder, Gord said, "Fifty percent, Ms. Casey. Let me know your decision before noon, so I can place tomorrow's orders elsewhere, if I have to. Plenty of places around here eager to do business."

Vicky's face was a study in shock.

The swinging doors closed behind Grace and her stepson. "What a . . ." I said, at a loss for words.

"I can't . . ." Vicky said.

"I know," I said.

"And you shouldn't have to," Mark said. "Your food's worth every penny. The day I have to serve Twinkies is the day I hang up my apron."

"Twinkies," I said, "with whipped *topping*."

"What?"

"Never mind."

The waitresses slipped back in. They threw Mark questioning glances. "Everything's fine," he said. I got the impression they didn't believe him.

"You have to get back to work," he said. "I'll walk you out."

"Can Gord do that?" I said. "Make changes willy-nilly?"

"I'll try to talk some sense into him," Mark said. "But I don't know if anything I say will be worth much. Let's hope Jack recovers quickly. I left a good job in the city to come here. Sold my apartment, packed up everything I own. I need this job, but I don't think I'm going to be able to work for Gord."

"I need this contract," Vicky said.

Mark gathered Vicky into his arms. She tucked her head into the crook of his neck. Mark threw me a glance.

"I'd better see to the dog," I said, fleeing the kitchen.

Vicky and I drove most of the way back to town in silence. As the van pulled up in front of my house, I said, "Will losing the inn's business hurt you badly?"

She shrugged. "It won't help. It's a good source of income in the shoulder season, when we don't have many tourists in town. It won't force me under, but if

Gord won't let Mark cook the way he wants, I can't imagine him staying on."

I patted her knee. "If you need anything, call me."

She gave me a strained smile. "I will. Thanks, sweetie."

Business had gradually built up over the course of the week. By Friday a steady stream of cars was moving slowly down Jingle Bell Lane, Rudolph's Main Street, and Jackie and I, as well as my part-time assistant, Crystal, were satisfyingly busy.

"Whatcha doin' for New Year's Eve?" Jackie asked as we prepared to open on Saturday morning.

"Heavens, I don't know. If I live until the day after Christmas, I'll make plans then." I had foolishly done something uncharacteristically impulsive and decided to host Christmas dinner at my place. I'd been thinking it would be only Mom and Dad, my brother, Chris, and me—easy to manage. I'd forgotten that my mom collected strays at Christmas. We were now up to a guest list of twelve. I didn't even own twelve plates. "By New Year's, I'll be ready to enjoy a quiet evening at home," I said.

"What! No date for New Year's Eve, are you kidding me? That must be awful."

"Thank you for your concern," I said with a sniff. "I've never believed there's anything special about New Year's. It's just a day on the calendar."

"Liar," she said. "Kyle and I are going to a party at Joanie's house. I guess you can come, if you want."

I couldn't think of anything I'd like less. Even if the invitation had been extended with something more than reluctant sympathy for my dateless state. Truth be told, I was feeling a bit glum when I thought of ringing in the New Year at home with the dog, dressed in my flannel pajamas and warm socks.

Last year I'd been living in Manhattan, and my New Year's Eve had been one for the record books. My almost-fiancé and I had gone with colleagues from the magazine we both worked for to one of the city's most fashionable restaurants. We'd dined on oysters and lobster and drank champagne, the real stuff. I'd forked out a thousand bucks for my dress and shoes and dropped a couple hundred on having my hair, nails, and makeup done. We'd gotten into such a good restaurant only because the owner of the magazine, Jennifer Johnstone, gifted the evening to my department as a bonus. Among our fellow diners had been the hottest couple in movies (with their numerous, surprisingly well-behaved children), several senators, and a former secretary of state.

How things change in a year. Jennifer had retired and new management had driven most of the creative staff out the door. My cheating almost-fiancé was now engaged to Jennifer's spoiled granddaughter. I'd quit my job, moved back to my hometown, and bought Mrs. Claus's Treasures. The dress was hanging in the back of my closet gathering dust; the shoes had hurt my feet so much, I'd given them to a charity shop. Instead of socializing with the glitterati, I was faced with spending the biggest night of the social year with the TV and a slobbering dog.

And Vicky. Nothing had been said, but I had sort of assumed that Vicky and I would be watching the ball drop in Times Square together. Now that she and Mark were giving each other expressive looks, I figured there was a good chance it would be just me and Mattie toasting each other at midnight.

Late Saturday afternoon, the bells over the shop door chimed, the door swung open, and two women came in. They were in their early fifties, both dressed in black coats and colorful scarves. Outside, snow was gently falling, and flecks of white dotted the women's hair and shoulders. One of them was short with soft, gentle curves and the other what my dad would call "a long drink of water." They smiled at me, and I smiled back.

"Welcome to Mrs. Claus's Treasures."

"Isn't this absolutely darling!" the short one said.

"This whole town is darling," the thin one said.

"Your first time to Rudolph?" I asked.

"Yes." The thin one thrust out her hand. "I'm Kathy Bowman. This is Arlene Vigne." Arlene nodded politely and edged toward the jewelry display. Kathy continued chatting. "I'm so glad we came. I was simply furious when Fred, that's my husband, announced out of the blue that he had to go away for a couple of days. Imagine, a business trip, right before Christmas. Well, that just wouldn't do. Not one little bit. Fortunately, the children—I have three, and they've given me five grandchildren—aren't due to arrive until Christmas Eve, but of course there's so much preparation to be done. The little ones, and even the older ones, expect my traditional Christmas cookies and cakes to be on hand. I was not pleased, let me tell you, but when Fred told me he was coming to Rudolph, New York, America's Christmas Town, I said, 'Fred, I insist you bring me with you. Think of the shopping I can get done!' Isn't that right, Arlene?"

Arlene muttered something that might have been "yes" and picked up a pair of delicate silver earrings formed into the shape of snowmen. They'd been made by my part-time helper Crystal, who was planning on going to New York to study art and design next fall. "And then," Kathy continued, "when Fred relented and said I could come, he told me Jim was coming, too, so I called Arlene right away and suggested we make a holiday out of it." Kathy beamed at me.

"How nice," I said.

"I'm so glad we did. This is such a wonderful town. I adore Christmas. Can't get enough of it, can I, Arlene?"

"Can I try these on?" Arlene asked.

I made a move to go and help her, but Jackie beat me to it. Leaving me trapped in the tornado that was Kathy's stream of conversation. "We're staying at the Yuletide Inn. So charming. We were awful lucky to get rooms, weren't we, Arlene? They're totally full up, but they had a cancellation. Nice to see the place is so popular."

Which reminded me that I should give Mom a call to check up on Jack. My parents reported that Jack was recovering well from his surgery, and Grace was cautiously optimistic he'd be home before Christmas. As he'd promised, Gord had canceled the regular order from Vicky's. The town's rumor mill reported that yesterday Gord and Mark got into a giant blowup when a truck from a national bread chain arrived at the inn. Mark had threatened to quit, and Gord had dared him to go ahead.

"Of course," Kathy droned on, "if the inn wasn't so popular, Fred wouldn't be wasting his time looking at it."

That caught my attention. "Why's your husband here? What sort of business is he in?"

Her flat chest might have swelled a fraction. "He's the manager in charge of expansion for Fine Budget Inns, of course. If we take over the inn, why, we can come here all the time. That would be so darling."

"Kathy!" Arlene dropped the earrings on the table. "You can't be telling folks that! It's secret."

Kathy's eyes widened in horror. "Oh gosh. I forgot. I got so carried away with myself. Fred always says I'll dig my grave with my tongue one day. You won't tell anyone, will you?"

"Uh," I said. I glanced at Jackie. Her mouth was a big O.

"Fred will be absolutely furious." Tears welled up in Kathy's eyes. "He didn't want me to come. Said I can never keep my mouth shut. But I so didn't want to be left alone at home again! Not with Christmas coming. Ever since Rhonda, that's my youngest, got married, the house seems so lonely."

"Kathy," Arlene said firmly, "have a look at that train set on the table over there. Isn't Jamie's birthday in January? Wouldn't it be a great gift for her?"

Kathy scurried across the room.

"It's handmade by a local artisan," I said. "True craftsmanship, made with love and careful attention to detail."

"My granddaughter would love it," Kathy said. And the shopping frenzy began.

At last, Kathy and Arlene left, laden with Mrs. Claus's Treasures' bags.

"Was she ever a motormouth," Jackie said once the door had closed behind them.

I was so deep in thought, I didn't reply. So, people from a hotel chain were considering buying the Yuletide Inn, were they? Gord Olsen certainly wasted no time. I wondered if Grace knew about this.

"I have to go out for a while," I said to Jackie. "You can mind the shop."

I never drive to work as I live only a few blocks away. Today, I wished I had. I pulled out my phone as I broke into a run. "Dad, where are you?"

"Council offices. I'm about to go into a meeting with the budget chief."

"Cancel it. I'll pick you up in fifteen minutes."

"It's an important meeting."

"Believe me, this is more important."

I ran down Jingle Bell Lane and took a shortcut

through the park, past the bandstand and the huge decorated tree, toward my house. The snow was picking up, turning the world into a soft white blur. I live in one half of the second floor of a grand old Victorian built in Rudolph's heyday when the town was an important Lake Ontario port. I belted up the driveway and galloped upstairs. Mattie was in his crate, his ears up, eyes bright, and tail wagging at the sound of my key in the lock and my footsteps on the stairs.

"Sorry, buddy," I said. "No time."

I grabbed my purse with my driver's license and car keys and headed out again. I tried to ignore the dog's plaintive whine when he realized he was being left behind. He couldn't have sounded more disappointed if he'd found coal in his stocking Christmas morning.

Dad was waiting for me at the steps of the town council offices when I pulled up. "What's this about, Merry?"

"Gord Olsen is in negotiations to sell the Yuletide to Fine Budget Inns."

"How do you know this?" It says a lot about my dad's trust in me that he didn't even say, "Are you sure?"

"A chatty woman came into the store. She and her friend are staying at the inn with their husbands. I gather the husbands don't normally take them on business trips, but as this came up suddenly and it's Christmas in Rudolph, they did this time. She couldn't stop herself from spilling the beans."

"Jack's still in the hospital, and his son's selling his business out from under him. I can't imagine Grace approving of this."

"There's more. I was at the inn on Thursday morning with Vicky when Gord told her he's not going to be using her to supply bread. He can get cheaper products from an industrial facility. Mark, the new chef, threatened to quit, and Gord basically told him to go ahead. If the inn is sold, that means the restaurant will go with it."

"Not good," Dad said. "Fine Budget Inns aren't bad, but they are budget. We have plenty of reasonably priced accommodations in and around Rudolph. The Yuletide Inn attracts the better-heeled crowd, and its restaurant, as well as A Touch of Holly in town, feeds the special-occasion and fine-dining guests. We need all income levels coming to Rudolph."

"What do you want to do?"

"I'm going to talk to Grace. She needs to know. If she knows, and approves, then there's nothing we can do. But if Gord's acting behind her back . . ."

I slowed as we approached the inn. "Why does Gord have Jack's power of attorney and not Grace?"

Dad sighed. "They didn't want it to be common knowledge, but Grace had a bout of cancer a couple of years ago. A fairly serious type, not that all cancers aren't serious. She's in remission and doing very well, but they felt that if the cancer came back, Grace wouldn't be in a position to manage the hotel's affairs."

I slowed as we approached the inn's festive sign and turned into the long driveway. Three cars were pulled up at the side of the road, and a small group of people were standing at the edge of the gardens. Gord and Irene were talking to two men. As we drove by, Gord gestured to the open expanses around them. Gord didn't notice us, but Irene did. She did not smile or wave.

"Do you think those might be the guys from Fine Budget?" Dad asked me.

One of the men was a tall, well-built, middle-aged African American, the other a white guy who couldn't have been any older than me. "I can't see them being the husbands of the women I talked to earlier. Although," I said, "I suppose I don't really know."

"Isn't that your mother's car over there?"

It was, and we found my mom having tea with Grace. The Olsens lived on the property in a charming cottage tucked behind the inn, overlooking a patch of woodland.

"Noel, Merry. This is a surprise," Grace said when she answered the door. "Although a pleasant one. Come on in. We're having tea, but if you'd like something stronger . . ." We followed her into the living room. A fragrant balsam filled one corner, soft white lights burning, decorations shining. My mother was sitting in an elegant wingback chair upholstered in a fine blue fabric. A matching chair was on the other side of a gas fireplace in which a fake log was glowing cheerfully. Candles with the slightest hint of vanilla burned in two sturdy iron candlesticks beside a china tea set laid out on a side table. French doors led to a spacious deck, now empty of furniture and covered in a blanket of untouched snow, an enclosed garden, and dark woods that marked the borders of the hotel property.

"I'm fine, thank you," Dad said. A look passed between him and my mother, and I saw Mom go instantly on alert. They had a way of speaking without words that always drove me and my three younger siblings absolutely nuts.

"How's Jack?" Dad said.

"Well enough to have been moved out of the ICU," Grace said, taking her seat. "The doctors are very pleased. It's amazing how quickly patients are released from the hospital these days. The doctor told me that, if all continues going well, Jack can come home on Monday."

"I'm glad to hear it," Dad said. "Grace, I realize this is none of my business, but I hope you'll allow me to be frank."

Her hand went to her cheek and her lovely gray eyes opened in fear. "Is it about Jack? Do you know something the doctors aren't telling me? I've been visiting regularly, but I'm finding him very lethargic. That worries me. The doctors say it's to be expected, but they don't know Jack. Usually, I find his enthusiasm exhilarating, if not exhausting."

"No," Dad said quickly. "I don't have any information about Jack. It's not about him. You know how the Rudolph rumor mill works. I've heard the inn is for sale."

All the tension left Grace's face. She fell back in relief. "What a silly idea. Jack and I aren't even considering selling the inn. It's his life, you know, and he's always said he'll only leave in a wooden box. Gord's helping out now, but Jack will be back on his feet soon. The doctors say he should be able to resume some work in six weeks or so. When he's better, I'm determined to

try and talk the old fool into hiring a proper hotel manager, which will take some of the day-to-day responsi-
bilities off his shoulders and allow us to take a vacation
that lasts longer than three days."

"Why are you telling us this, Noel?" my mom asked.
She knew that if my dad was repeating it, it wasn't idle
gossip.

"Two of your hotel guests are from Fine Budget
Inns."

"The executive in charge of expansion is one of
them," I said.

Grace waved her hand. "That means nothing. We get
lots of guests here, Noel." She laughed. "I can well understand why someone from Fine Budget would prefer
to vacation at the Yuletide."

"Perhaps," Dad said slowly, "you should ask Gord if
he invited them. As you say, they might just be enjoying
a vacation, but you need to find out. I'll talk to Gord if
you'd prefer."

"Mark Grosse is threatening to quit," I said, "if Gord
keeps interfering with the way he runs the restaurant."

"He can't quit. We only just hired him. He has a
contract."

"Contracts can be broken," Dad said, "by both sides."

Grace reached for the phone beside her chair. "Let's
get to the bottom of this."

My mom started to stand.

"No," Grace said sharply. "If Gord's putting his nose
where it isn't wanted, I'd like you to stay."

She said a few words and then put the phone down.

"They'll be right here. Now, I for one have had enough tea. Noel, pour me a scotch, will you? It's in that cabinet."

We made polite conversation while waiting for Gord to join us.

"Do you have plans for tomorrow night, Grace?" Mom asked. "Noel and I are driving to Rochester in the morning. We have tickets for the opera and then dinner reservations, but I'm sure . . ."

"Thank you, Aline, but I have some work to do getting the house ready for Jack to come home. I'm looking into hiring a private nurse to stay with him for a few hours a day, so I can spend time at the inn without worrying that he's here alone."

A loud rap and then the sound of the door opening were followed by Irene calling out, "We're here."

"You could wait for me to invite you in," Grace muttered under her breath. She plastered on a smile.

"Whoa! Having a party?" Gord laughed, stamping snow off his boots onto Grace's shining wide-planked hardwood floors. He kept his coat on and didn't take a seat. "What's up? I've got company. Told them I'd be right back."

Irene said nothing. She stood in the doorway, her eyes fixed on Grace.

Grace smoothed her skirt. "Your father is ill, but expected to make a full recovery. We will not be making any changes around here in his absence."

Gord's eyes flicked toward me. "Merry, you were here the other morning with that bakery girl."

"That highly accomplished baker and small-business owner," I said.

"If you say so. It's time to make some changes around here, Grace," Gord said. "Streamline the operation, cut unnecessary expenses."

"Sell to Fine Budget Inns?"

A twitch started above Gord's right eye.

"Who told you about that?" Irene said.

Grace shrugged. "Irrelevant. Are you going to tell me what's going on?"

"No need to get upset," Gord said. Far from being upset, I thought Grace was acting so calmly she might have had ice flowing through her veins. "I'm not planning to sell the business to Fine Budget Inns."

"That's good to know," Grace said, visibly relaxing.

"It'll be a franchise operation," Irene said.

"What!"

"We . . . I mean you'll . . . still own the inn, but Fine Budget will . . . help with management. We can take advantage of FB's nationwide advertising campaigns, of their practical expertise in years of hotel management, of . . ."

"No," Grace said.

"It's a win-win, Grace," Gord said.

"I won't hear of it."

"Actually, Grace," Irene said, "it doesn't matter one bit what you want or not. Gord has his father's power of attorney."

"As long as Dad's unable to act on his own behalf,

I'm prepared to make some hard decisions," Gord added.

"Decisions," my dad said. I thought he showed admirable self-control in not giving Gord a piece of his mind before now. "Sell a man's livelihood out from under him the minute he's laid up, you mean."

Gord turned to Dad with a smile that did nothing to lessen the hostility in his face. "I'll take my father's wishes into consideration at every step."

"I don't think . . ." Dad began.

Grace lifted her hand. "One moment, please, Noel. I'd like you to explain that statement, Gord."

Gord grinned at her. I realized that he was enjoying this. "I told Dad my idea yesterday morning. He said to go ahead."

"I don't believe you," Grace said.

"We figured you'd say that," Irene said. "So we had a nurse come in and be a witness. Show her, honey."

Gord reached into his jacket pocket. He pulled out a piece of paper and unfolded it with great ceremony. "Signed and witnessed. Dad instructs me to make all necessary decisions regarding the property and the business."

"He didn't mean selling it!" Grace's cool composure was beginning to crack.

"Not selling. A franchise deal, as I said."

I spoke for the first time. "Jack hired Mark Grosse. He contracted with Vicky Casey to provide bread and pastries for the restaurant. You can't change all that on a whim."

He turned that grin on me. "I don't have to explain

myself, or my father, to you. But I will anyway. When I showed Dad that we could make a lot more money by implementing efficiencies, he agreed. He told me I had a free hand."

"Jack loves this inn," Grace said. "Doesn't that mean anything to you?"

"Does he?" Irene said. "Or is it you, Grace, who loves it the way it is? Fancy hotel, fine dining, important and wealthy guests." She glanced around the room, taking in the tea service, the blazing fire, the good furniture, the expensive art. "Quite the lady of the manor, aren't you?"

"That," my mother said, "is completely uncalled for."

Irene snorted. "I don't think Aline Steiner, the celebrated diva, would be drinking tea with the wife of a Fine Budget franchise owner, do you?"

"Enough," my dad roared. "Grace, I'd be happy to take you to the hospital. You need to talk to Jack himself."

"Not so fast," Gord said. "I insist on being with you if you're going to discuss business. I'll tell my associates to come back later."

"I saw you showing them the gardens," I said. "They didn't look like horticulturalists to me."

"All that property, just lying there covered in snow. Must be worth a fortune. It needs to be put to good use. If there's one thing Rudolph's lacking, it's a big-box store."

My dad choked, and I threw him a worried glance.

"We invited some folks from Mega-Mart to have a look," Irene said.

"Are you insane?!" Dad shouted.

"No," Grace said, "simply greedy."

"I'm a practical businessman," Gord said. "You're not making much of a profit the way the inn's being run now."

"We're making enough to provide an income for us and employment for many people," Grace said.

"The gardens alone could be sold and . . ."

"Those gardens, this inn, the restaurant, are a vital part of Rudolph," my dad said. "Of what we are proud to call Christmas Town."

"Now I get it," Gord said with a snort of laughter. "You're Santa Claus. Go back to the North Pole, old man."

Mom gasped.

"I won't have you destroying this town," Dad said. "Ruining everything Rudolph stands for, turning us into another soulless, dying rust belt town. I will stop you. One way or another."

"That sounds like a threat," Irene said.

"Take it however you want it," Dad said.

"Threats or not," Gord said, "there's nothing you, or my stepmother there, can do about it."

Chapter 3

"So there," Irene said.

She and Gord walked out, leaving a shocked group behind them.

"I'll take Grace to the hospital," Dad said.

"That's not necessary," Grace said.

"I think it is," Dad said.

"Did Jack say anything to you this morning when you visited?" Mom asked. "About the business and the property?"

Grace shook her head. Her hands trembled. Her face was shockingly pale, and I remembered she was in remission from cancer. "He didn't say anything at all. He seemed listless, so uninterested in everything going on around him, I mentioned my concerns to the doctor. He assured me it isn't unusual for patients who've had a close encounter with their own mortality to be withdrawn. I tried telling him that wasn't Jack, but he brushed my concerns off. You know Jack, Noel, Aline. So full of life and fun." She burst into tears.

"What sort of business is Gord in?" Mom asked.

"I don't really know. Something he calls 'consulting.' Helping companies buy and sell other companies, Jack told me once."

"He moved mighty fast," I said. "He probably already had contacts in Fine Budget Inns and Mega-Mart."

"And knows how the game is played," Dad said.

"Gord's never liked me," Grace said. "His mother's influence, I suspect. He rarely visits his father, and when he does they argue. Jack left Gord's mother to marry me. I didn't break up their marriage, it was already broken, but that's not the way Karen saw it. When Karen died two years ago, I'd hoped Gord and his father would get closer, but it didn't happen."

We headed for the front closet and donned coats, gloves, hats, and boots.

"Why don't you let Merry drive you home, Aline?" Dad said. "I can bring Grace back here after we've been to the hospital, and pick up your car. That okay with you, Merry?"

"Happy to," I said.

Snow was spilling out of a dark sky. The lights in the hotel and the gardens glimmered with holiday magic, but none of us were in a particularly festive mood.

"I'm going to cancel our hotel and dinner reservations for tomorrow," Mom said. "I'm sure I can find someone to give the opera tickets to."

"Are you sure?" I said. "Maybe it'll all get cleared up."

"If Jack does come to his senses and tells Grace he isn't going to let Gord sell the place out from under them . . ."

"A franchise opportunity," I said.

Mom huffed in disapproval. ". . . Gord will be furious. I don't want Grace to be alone. I don't trust that man." She pulled out her phone and pressed buttons. "Your father is with her now, and I'm going to make a dinner reservation at the inn for tomorrow. Rumors will be circulating and Grace will want to put up a brave front. Are you seeing Russell this weekend?"

"Why would I be doing that?"

"You two seemed to be hitting it off recently. He's handsome, eligible, gainfully employed. And you are over thirty, dear."

Russ Durham was the new editor in chief of the *Rudolph Gazette*. As well as the virtues Mom listed, he was charming and flirtatious and had expressed an interest in me. But I was hesitant, unsure. I suspected Russ was the sort of man who flirted as easily as he breathed.

Then there was Alan Anderson, our town's toymaker. Alan was a highly skilled woodworker, and he crafted everything from furniture to jewelry, from decorations to toys, much of which I stocked in Mrs. Claus's Treasures. He often played Santa's helper and delighted the children in his toymaker getup, using a feather-topped pen to write their gift wishes on a long scroll of paper. Alan and I had dated briefly in high school, but after graduation we went our separate ways. Now that I was back, I sometimes thought I'd like to pick up where we left off. But he was quiet and shy, and I didn't know where we stood.

Perhaps I was afraid of finding out we didn't stand anywhere.

"If you must know," I said to my mom, "I have no plans to see Russ. Or anyone else."

"What are you doing, then?"

"The shop's open late tonight, and tomorrow I'm planning a quiet Sunday evening at home alone. Get caught up on some things."

"You can come to dinner with us."

"I don't . . ."

But Mom was already speaking into her phone. "I'd like to make a reservation for tomorrow evening, please. We'll be five. Oh, I see. Perhaps you could check again. This is Aline Wilkinson calling, and Grace Olsen will be among our party. Yes, eight o'clock will be fine." She hung up.

"Five?"

"Noel and I. You and Grace. I thought I might invite Alan to join us. He spends too much time alone in that workshop of his."

I took my eyes off the road and looked at my mom. She was staring out the window, her face deep in thought.

Betty Thatcher scurried into Mrs. Claus's Treasures the moment I stepped foot across the threshold. I'd dropped Mom at home and headed back to the store to help

Jackie until closing. Jackie immediately asked me if it was true the Yuletide was going to be demolished for a big-box store, and Betty heard her. "He's selling the inn!" she screeched.

"Not selling it," I said. "Looking into a franchise opportunity. And that remains to be seen."

I don't think she even heard me. "The Yuletide's a valuable Rudolph tradition. What's Rudolph without the Yuletide?"

"They say the new chef has been fired." Jackie pouted. "I didn't even have a chance to properly introduce myself to him yet. He's super hot. I wonder what it's like dating a man who can cook."

"Who cares about some cook," Betty said. "I can't believe Jack would sell the inn. Tell your father to do something, Merry."

"It's not up to my dad to do anything," I said. "Anyway, it's not Jack but his son, Gord, who wants to sell. And he's not selling the inn itself, but some of the property. And he hasn't fired the chef, either. At least not yet."

Betty glared at me. "That miserable lowlife. I remember Gord Olsen well enough. He was always up to no good. Like boy, like man."

I couldn't argue with that. "Sorry, Betty, I don't have any more information."

"Your parents are close to Grace and Jack, aren't they?"

"Yes."

"Could you let me know, Merry, if you hear anything more?"

"Sure," I said.

Betty struggled to force the words through her lips, but I waited patiently and at last she managed, "Thank you."

"Why do you suppose she cares?" Jackie said after the door had slammed shut behind Betty. "Fine Budget Inn or Yuletide, it should be all the same to her."

Community spirit was not Betty's strong point.

"Maybe her feelings go back a long way," I said. "She's the same age as Jack, her son, Clark's around the same age as Gord. The families probably knew each other. Betty obviously doesn't like Gord, even all these years later." I glanced at my watch, wondering what was happening at the hospital. The chimes over the door sounded, and this time, instead of a furious Betty Thatcher it was, thankfully, a group of eager shoppers.

For the rest of the day, Jackie and I went about our business, helping customers, ringing up sales, smiling, and being friendly. We were too busy for me to spare any thought about the goings-on at the Yuletide.

I was standing at the door, waving off the last group of stragglers, about to flip the sign to "Closed" when I spotted other business owners coming out of their own shops and heading my way. No one was smiling, and their faces were dark as they muttered to one another.

I wondered what was up, and then, to my considerable surprise, they streamed into Mrs. Claus's Treasures, demanding to know what was going on at the Yuletide. Word had spread that I had the inside scoop.

Which, come to think of it, I did.

"Two men came into my place for lunch," Andrea Kenny of the Elves' Lunch Box said. "They wore business suits and sunglasses. They looked totally out of place."

Rachel McIntosh from Candy Cane Sweets nodded. The look on her face was a sharp contrast to the necklace made of real candy canes bound with red ribbon that was part of her work uniform. "Mark my words, they're up to no good."

"I don't like the sound of that." Sue-Anne Morrow, a town councillor and our acting mayor, had seen the delegation heading my way and popped in to find out what was going on.

Two men having lunch in a friendly diner in a small town on a Saturday afternoon shouldn't be terribly suspicious, but Andrea and Rachel did have a point. Rudolph was a family-friendly destination. We catered to women in shopping groups, families with kids who wanted to see Santa Claus and his helpers, and even honeymooning couples finding the Christmas atmosphere romantic. But men, on their own?

"Maybe they wanted to get a break from their shopping wives," I said without much conviction.

"They had," Andrea said, "briefcases and papers and iPads, spread out all over the table. They talked in low voices and made lots of notes. I just happened to be bringing their sandwiches to their table when I overheard the words, 'no competition.' They clammed up the moment they realized I was standing there. What do you think of that?"

"Mega-Mart," Rachel said with a shake of her head that had the candy canes clanking. "People are saying they're from Mega-Mart. Is that right, Merry?"

"My aunt's the bookkeeper at the inn," Jackie said. "She told my mom she's really scared. If Fine Budget takes over, they'll bring their own staff in and fire people who've been working at the inn for years."

"They had a fancy wedding there last week," Rachel said. "I supplied all the favors and the table decorations. I made the centerpieces out of candy canes, my chocolate snowmen were at every place setting. Vicky baked an elaborate wedding cake and she provided gingerbread cookies for the favor bags. No other place in Rudolph can host that sort of big, extravagant wedding."

"Young couples with money to spend won't be having their weddings at Fine Budget, I can tell you," Jackie said. "I've been thinking of having my own wedding at the Yuletide. I'm going to have it in the spring, when the gardens are at their best."

"You're engaged!" The women squealed. I refrained from rolling my eyes.

"Well, no," Jackie admitted with a grimace. "Not officially. I'm expecting Kyle to pop the question any day. Of course, when he does, I haven't decided what I'm going to say. I'm not ready to . . ."

"The gardens," Rachel moaned. "They're so popular, and not only for weddings. In summer, folks love taking a tour of the gardens and then popping into town for an ice cream."

"Never mind the gardens." Jayne Reynolds, owner

of Jayne's Ladies Wear, was next through my doors. "I can't compete with a Mega-Mart! I try to keep my prices reasonable, but they'll drive me out of business. Sue-Anne, surely the town can do something."

Sue-Anne shook her head. "There isn't much we can do. The property is zoned commercial. As long as no one's talking about putting a housing development or a factory there, it's out of our control."

"Hold on here," I said. "You're getting ahead of your-selves. It might never happen. Grace doesn't want to sell, and that has to mean something. You know she and Jack run the inn together, although she pretends he's in charge."

The women nodded.

"Now," I said, "I need to be heading home."

One by one they left, muttering to themselves. Soon only Jackie and I remained in Mrs. Claus's Treasures. "Leave the vacuuming until tomorrow," I said. "I'm bushed." I went into the back, switched off the lights, powered down the computer, and got my coat. The main room of the shop was lit only by the lights on the tree, which would stay on all night, a night-light behind the counter, and the subtle decorations in the window. Jackie was a dark shape staring out into the now-quiet street.

For the first time ever, I didn't find my shop at night to be a warm, comforting place. I had tried to sound optimistic and cheerful in the face of the women's concerns, but when they left they took my jolly mood along with them. "Go home, Jackie," I said, more sharply than I had intended.

She turned to me. "You'll be okay, won't you, Merry? My job's safe, isn't it? I mean, you sell nicer stuff than they do at Mega-Mart."

"Sure," I said. "Not to worry. It's all a misunderstanding. My dad went to the hospital with Grace to sort it out."

Jackie gathered up her own things and left. I locked the door after her and set off home. The sidewalks were empty and lights were being switched off in all the shops. As Jackie had said, I was in a better position than many shop owners to face competition from Mega-Mart. I sold mostly artisan goods. My merchandise wasn't cheap but it wasn't overly expensive, either, and I catered to mid-level spenders. Betty Thatcher's Gift Nook, on the other hand, would likely be one of the first places to close. She sold the same inexpensive, mass-produced goods Mega-Mart did. And they'd sell them at a cheaper price.

Mrs. Claus's Treasures wouldn't be immune from the fallout from the big-box store, though. There was nothing worse for business than a Main Street of boarded-up shops.

"Merry! There you are." My landlady, Mrs. D'Angelo, greeted me as I trudged up her neatly shoveled sidewalk. She lived on the ground floor of the house, and I lived in an apartment on the second floor. Mrs. D'Angelo's mission in life was to know every single thing going on in Rudolph, New York. And that included everything going on in the lives of her tenants. I suspected she'd been lurking at her front window waiting for me to arrive. Enveloped warmly in a shawl, she'd come out to stand on the big wraparound porch. "My phone's been ringing off the hook all day." She waved a thin, sleek, latest-model iPhone at me. Technology was Mrs. D'Angelo's lifeline. "What is going on, Merry?"

"I don't know," I said.

"My brother's brother-in-law's uncle owns the Carolers Motel. He says they'll never be able to compete with Fine Budget, not with their national advertising campaigns."

I buried my head into the collar of my winter coat.

"Tell your father I said he has to do something," she shouted to my disappearing back. "I've been trying to get Noel all day but it keeps going to voice mail. And now his voice mailbox is full!"

My dad, I knew, also loved technology. He was particularly fond of the caller ID display.

As usual, my mood lifted the moment Mattie heard my footsteps on the stairs and let out a joyous, welcoming woof. I let him out of his crate and allowed myself to be enveloped in exuberant leaps and a barrage of slobbering licks. I wiped drool off my face and followed the bouncing dog back down the stairs. I snapped his leash on and we went for a long walk in the park. Fresh, untouched snow crunched under our feet. It was well after dark, and the night was clear. A silver sliver of a moon hung over the dark waters of Lake Ontario, stars filled the sky, and the lights of the town's Christmas tree and the gaily decorated houses sparkled in the distance.

I stood in the park, closed my eyes to feel the sting

of fresh, cold air on my face and to listen to the silence broken only by the snuffling and panting of my dog.

It was Christmas in Christmas Town, and there was nothing I loved more. When I'd lived in New York City, realizing my dream as a deputy style editor at *Jennifer's Lifestyle* magazine, I thought I'd achieved everything I wanted in the world. I loved the whirl of Manhattan, the shops, the restaurants, the always-on-the-go social life. I loved working with the movers and shakers of the magazine and decorating industries. But something had always seemed off, something was missing. I'd put it down to nerves about my career, worries about my relationship with my boyfriend (worries which turned out to be well-founded, the cheating rat!). Only when I'd quit and moved back to Rudolph did I understand that this was where I was meant to be. In this charming, quirky, Christmas-obsessed little town on the snowy southern shores of Lake Ontario.

When we got home I fed Mattie and pulled a frozen pizza out of the freezer for my own dinner. I noticed the message light blinking on my apartment phone. It was my dad, and when I called him back, my happy Christmas mood once again disappeared in a flash.

At the hospital, Dad and Grace had found Jack listless, not wanting to talk. Grace tried to explain that Gord was moving too fast, making decisions that could not be undone once Jack had a chance to go over them in detail. Jack had merely waved his hand and said, "Let my son do what he wants to do. I don't care anymore."

Whereupon he closed his eyes, turned his head, and pretended to fall asleep.

"The word is obviously out," Dad said. "My phone's been ringing nonstop with people wanting to know what's going on. All I can say is 'Nothing has been decided at this time,' but folks aren't content with that. Dan Evans, the butcher, dropped in to visit Jack before Grace and I got there, and he started shouting at Jack, made such a fuss security was called and he was thrown out of the hospital. The hospital's put a family-only visiting order on Jack's room. I only got in because I was with Grace."

I'd never known my dad to sound so upset. He loved Rudolph. He was a former mayor and still sat on the town council. The whole Christmas Town thing had been his idea in the first place. Under his guidance the town was thriving and the residents prospering. The Yuletide Inn was an important part of Rudolph's year-round-Christmas image. Not only that, but Jack and he had been friends for many years. When Jack married Grace, Mom and the new Mrs. Olsen had bonded instantly.

"He's going to come to his senses one day," Dad said over the phone, "and look around him and see that his son has destroyed everything he worked for."

"Not everything," I said, trying to be optimistic. "He still has Grace. And their home. Gord's not planning to sell the cottage, I hope, along with the gardens."

"Gord did have enough sense to assure her they'll be

able to keep the cottage. Although, come to think of it, it was Irene who said that."

"What about Irene? Maybe you and Grace can talk to her?"

"I suspect Irene's behind all this, Merry. She's supporting Gord if not outright encouraging him. They stand to make a lot of money from the sale of a good chunk of the property as well as the deal with Fine Budget."

"Not to mention implementing efficiencies," I muttered.

"Any money gained will be Grace and Jack's, of course. But Gord's Jack's only child and Grace has no children of her own. Jack's had two heart attacks and Grace has had cancer . . ." Dad's voice trailed off.

"The hotel will still be there, just under a new name." I was trying to sound optimistic. It wasn't easy.

"Fine Budget Yuletide," Dad said. "I can't wait."

He hung up without saying good-bye.

Chapter 4

No matter how good the food promised to be, I was not looking forward to another meal at the Yuletide Inn.

I could only hope Gord and Irene had the presence of mind to stay away from our group, although diplomacy and respect for other people's feelings didn't seem to be Gord's strong suit.

I arrived precisely on time. I'd decided to make up for my sartorial faux pas the last time I'd dined here and dressed carefully in one of the few remaining outfits from my earlier life among the big names in the New York City magazine world. I wore a red knee-length dress with sleeves cut to the elbow, a deeply scooped neckline outlined in black, and a thin black belt. I added a rope of pearls that had been a birthday gift from my ex-almost-fiancé (the cheating rat!) and matching teardrop earrings. As I was driving directly to the inn, and I knew the walkways would be sanded and shoveled, I slipped on a pair of black shoes with killer heels rather than practical, but ugly, winter boots. I'd bought the shoes in Manhattan in a mad splurge after I'd found out my boyfriend had gotten engaged to another woman. I'd needed to do something to make myself feel attractive and desirable, not like the dumped, ex-girlfriend I was. The shoes cost way more than I could afford and they hurt my feet like crazy, but they sure did make me feel good.

Then, ignoring Mattie's plaintive whines (and that wasn't easy), I sailed out the door. My stomach was in knots, whether at the idea of encountering Gord and Irene or having dinner with Alan Anderson, I didn't know. Mom had said she was going to invite him, but I hadn't heard if he'd accepted.

The parking lot of the inn was satisfyingly full. I switched off the engine and sat in my car for a few moments. The inn was such a perfect picture of Christmas, it could have been used in a backdrop to a Currier and Ives print. The wide, sweeping driveway was lined by snow-covered pines, a huge fresh wreath hung on the front door, lights glimmered in the gabled windows and shone on piles of fresh snow while smoke rose from the stone chimney. This view was regularly featured in ads promoting Rudolph. Couldn't Gord see what a prosperous, successful place this was? Why did he have to change it?

Maybe that was it. Maybe it wasn't about implementing efficiencies or turning a larger profit, but about wanting to undo his father's legacy. Maybe Gord just thought he could do better.

I got out of the car and turned at a man's shout.

"Merry!" Russ Durham, the editor in chief of the *Rudolph Gazette*, was loping across the parking lot toward me. He looked particularly handsome tonight dressed in a good suit and perfectly knotted tie. Russ was on his own. I figured he must have let his date out at the restaurant doors.

"Are you here for dinner?" I said with a tinge of what I refused to think might be jealousy.

"Yup. Good timing, too. I can escort you in."

"I'm meeting my parents."

"I know. Nice of your mom to invite me."

My heart dropped into my stomach. "She did?"

"I called Noel for a statement about rumored changes at the Yuletide and your mom yelled at him to let me know they were dining with Grace Olsen tonight. I decided to take that as an invitation."

"A statement?"

"The whole town's talking about nothing other than Gord Olsen, mysterious visitors speaking in subdued tones and carrying briefcases and laptops, and other mysterious visitors with hard hats and surveying equipment, measuring the property." Russ shook his head. His deep, slow and sexy Louisiana accent gave his tone extra weight. "I don't have to tell you, Merry, the whole town's in an uproar."

"What did Dad have to say?"

"That the affairs of the Yuletide Inn are for Jack and Grace Olsen and their heirs to discuss as they see fit. Same thing he's been telling everyone who expects him to do something. In the absence of a mayor, everyone's looking to Noel for leadership."

"Dad didn't run for mayor again because he didn't want the responsibility anymore."

"He's got it, whether he wants it or not." Russ took my arm. "And whether Sue-Anne Morrow wants it or not. Let's go in. But first, can I say you look absolutely breathtaking tonight? Love the shoes." He winked.

The others were already seated when Russ and I arrived. Alan got to his feet with a smile. The smile faded when he saw Russ, who'd momentarily stopped to greet a group of diners, catch up to me. I wasn't sure if it was because he thought Russ was my date or he just wasn't feeling friendly toward the newspaperman. It was a toss-up between Alan and Russ as to who was the handsomest. They were both tall and fit and lean. Alan had sparkling blue eyes, curly blond hair, and slow, gentle mannerisms. Russ was darker with short-cropped black hair and serious hazel eyes that were always watching everyone and everything. Tonight Alan wore a wool sweater in shades of oatmeal over a blue button-down shirt. My dad greeted me with a kiss on the cheek. His sweater this evening was red with a Santa face appliquéd to the front and numerous multicolored lightbulbs, battery operated, sewn into Santa's hat. I guessed Mom had ordered him to switch the light display off in the restaurant.

My mother did not go for ostentatious displays of holiday ornamentation. She was, as usual, a knockout in a simple (although not simply tailored or priced) black suit.

My mother directed me to the chair between Russ and Alan.

An embarrassment of riches.

To my surprise, and relief, the evening went well. As I have said, Mom and Grace are excellent hostesses, and they managed to control the conversation so it stayed away from gossip about the future of the inn. Grace had only a light salad, but Mom and I dug into the delicious seafood pasta. Russ and Alan each had a plate of ribs, and Dad's steak was served bloodred, the way he liked it.

The waiter was clearing our entrée plates when Grace tapped her lips with her napkin and laid it beside her place. "I'm sorry," she said, "but I am dreadfully tired. Will you excuse me if I leave before you're finished?"

I had to admit, she didn't look well. The strain of the past week was showing in the delicate skin of her face.

The three men pushed back their chairs and leapt to their feet.

"Not at all," Dad said. "I understand how exhausting all this must be for you. Let me walk you to your door."

"You don't . . ."

"No," Dad said, "but I'd like to."

Grace stood up. "That would be nice. Please, everyone, stay and finish your dinner. You'll want coffee, and I'm sure Mark has something wonderful on the dessert menu."

"Won't say no to that," Russ said with a smile.

My dad took Grace's arm and they walked out of the

restaurant. Grace's back was straight and her head high but she was leaning on my dad's arm for more than appearances.

"She's a strong woman," Alan said.

"She's going to have to be," Russ said. "I hear Jack's being released from the hospital tomorrow. He's still showing no interest in what's happening with the inn and the property?"

"No," Mom said with a sigh. "Grace is simply beside herself. It's as much her business as Jack's, although because she married him after it was a successful operation she has no legal claim to it."

"She has a moral claim," Alan said.

"Unfortunately, morality has no place in business," Mom said. "Gord and that wife of his have dollar signs dancing before their eyes. I'm not going to have dessert, but you gentlemen please go ahead. I'm going to indulge in a brandy this evening."

We opened our dessert menus. Gingerbread cake was noticeably absent from the list of choices. Alan ordered the candy cane cheesecake and Russ asked for old-fashioned plum pudding with brandy sauce. I didn't want dessert, and, as I was driving, I had only a coffee.

My cup was empty, the dessert plates had been scraped clean, and Mom was taking her last sip of brandy when her sequined evening bag began to sing the "Drinking Song" from *La Traviata*. A text from Dad.

"Excuse me. Terribly rude, but I need to see what Noel wants." Mom pulled out her phone and glanced at the screen. She let out a long sigh.

Russ's and Alan's eyebrows rose.

"What's the matter?" I asked.

"Your dad's gone home. He wants me to continue to enjoy my evening and have you drop me off. He must have had a talk with Grace and found it upsetting."

"Sure," I said.

"I hear," Alan said, "the Muddites are excited about the potential transformation of the inn into a second-rate hotel."

"Why?" Russ asked. "They have a handful of cheap motels over there, but nothing to rival the Yuletide."

"To the Muddites," I said, "everything is a zero-sum game. If we lose, they win."

The neighboring town of Muddle Harbor was our archrival. At least that's how they saw it. As far as the Muddites were concerned, if Rudolph failed, all those shoppers and hotel guests would flock to spend their money in their miserable, run-down, hardscrabble town.

Mom stood up abruptly. Alan and Russ scrambled to follow. They spoke at the same time.

"Are you okay to drive, Merry?"

"Let me take you and your mom home."

I grinned at them both. "I'm fine. Thanks."

It was getting late, and the restaurant crowd was thinning out. The lobby was empty, and outside all was quiet.

"Good night," Mom said as we stood on the front steps. It had stopped snowing and the fresh fall shimmered in the warm lights of the hotel.

"That was a lovely evening, Mrs. Wilkinson."

"Thank you for inviting me, Aline."

We headed across the lot toward my car. Mom and me and our two charming escorts. I'd noticed the men giving each other suspicious sideways glances. *Rivals for my affections?* It was a nice thought.

"I have always loved these gardens. Your father and I had our wedding reception here." Mom's voice was soft and dreamy.

"I know that."

"It was in winter. A night as beautiful as this one. It would have been nice to have had a Christmas wedding, but I was singing *Tosca* at La Scala all of December. We had the ceremony in January. It was a small wedding. My parents and sister, some of my friends from the opera world. Your dad's family and his close friends."

"It sounds lovely," Russ said.

"It was. It was. We stayed here, at the inn, on our wedding night. Jack was married to Karen then. I never liked Karen much; she had a poisonous tongue in her mouth. Whether spreading the muck about the guests at the inn or snapping at Jack for some supposed slight, she never had a kind word to say about anyone. It was widely rumored he was having multiple affairs over the course of their marriage. Eventually, Karen left and Jack married Grace. I feared the pattern of infidelity would continue, but there's never been so much as a whisper. They've been very happy together.

"As have Noel and I. After our guests had left or gone to their own rooms, your father and I went for a walk in the gardens. On a night just like this one." Mom drifted away. Russ and Alan and I exchanged glances and followed her. My Manhattan revenge-shopping-spree shoes were hardly suitable for walking in the snow, but the paths meandering through the gardens had been recently shoveled. Colored lights dusted with snow sparkled in the trees. From the parking lot, we heard a woman laugh, car doors slam shut, and an engine start. The car drove away. Then all fell as wonderfully quiet as it can be only after a fresh snowfall.

My mom turned and faced us. Flakes fell from the branches of the trees onto her dark hair. Her eyes danced and she looked thirty years younger as memories flooded over her. She lifted up her arms and threw back her head. I glanced at the two men on either side of me. They were both smiling. No one had said a word since we passed our cars.

A shout broke the silence of the winter night.

It was followed by a single cry, cut short, and then a low moan. I heard the sound of footsteps breaking through hard-packed snow and saw a dim, wavering light moving rapidly away from us.

"What's happening there?" Russ called.

"Is everyone all right?" Alan shouted.

Silence.

Two iPhone flashlight apps switched on, flooding the path in white light.

"We're going to have a look," Russ said to me. "Merry, you and Aline wait here."

The men stepped off the path. I followed them, and my mom followed me. Snow spilled over the rims of my high-heeled shoes. We passed through a small grove of oak trees, the naked skeletal limbs reaching for our faces, branches poking through our hair. I shivered. Mom took my arm. In a few steps we emerged into a small clearing. A marble statue of a woman, draped in classic stone robes, stood at the center of the glade. In the summer she poured a bucket of water into a small pool at her feet. In the winter, she wore a crown of holiday lights with additional lights wrapped around her long, graceful neck. Russ stopped walking so abruptly I crashed into the back of him. My mom squeezed my arm and let out a soft cry.

"What the . . . ?" Alan said.

Russ moved and I could see. The statue stood still and serene, no water spilled from her pail, and the surface of the pool was covered in a blanket of snow. But tonight this was not a place of peaceful contemplation. The lights adorning the statue showed a man lying on his back in the pool, a patch of green holly dotted with red berries resting on his dark jacket. As my eyes became accustomed to the shifting light, I could see that the red wasn't berries but rapidly spreading liquid. The handle of a knife protruded from the center of the ring of holly.

It was Gord Olsen and he had been stabbed through the heart.

Chapter 5

Alan jumped onto the surface of the frozen pool while Russ dialed 911. My mom and I stood together, watching, feeling completely useless.

"I think he's dead," Alan said. "Tell them I can't find a pulse."

"Ambulance and police are on the way," Russ said. "The operator is telling us to be aware of our surroundings."

Mom gasped and we clutched each other.

"Aline and Merry, get back to the hotel," Russ said.

"No," Alan said. "Whoever did this might still be out there. We need to stay together until help arrives."

Mom squeezed my hand so hard I thought it might break. I glanced around. The dark trees, the falling snow, the deep shadows. The empty eyes of the watching statue were cast down, her cheerful holiday lights so dreadfully out of place.

"The operator says not to try to remove the knife," Russ said.

I felt my mom sway. "Mom needs to sit down," I said.

Russ whipped off his coat and spread it out on a carved stone bench. I guided my mother to it and helped her sit, giving Russ a nod of thanks.

Alan, Russ, and I looked at one another. Then Russ hung up on the 911 operator and began taking pictures with his phone.

"What are you doing?" I shouted. "Don't you dare take a picture of me or my mom."

"A good reporter's always working," Russ said, leaning over the pool to snap a shot.

"Freakin' ghoulish," Alan said. "If I'm in one of those pictures I'll sue you for all you're worth. I am Santa's toymaker, you know."

"Give me some credit." Russ swung the phone toward me.

I shrieked and covered my face with my hands.

"Just kidding," he said.

"Not laughing," I replied.

We let out a collective sigh of relief as the sound of sirens fast approaching reached us. Soon, strong lights were coming through the trees, and Russ, Alan, and I shouted, "Over here!"

Two uniformed officers broke into the clearing. They were followed by EMTs laden down with equipment. One of the paramedics climbed over the low stone wall into the pool while the other spoke into her radio.

"VSA," the first one called to his partner. Vital signs absent.

"Officer," I said, "I need to take my mother inside. Can we leave?"

"Wait in the hotel," he grunted. "All of you. The detective's on her way. She'll want to talk to you."

"Okay." I helped my mother to her feet.

"Campbell," the cop shouted. I wasn't particularly happy to see the round, pale face of my old high school nemesis, Officer Candice Campbell, pop out from behind a tree. "Take these people to the hotel. Find them a private room. They're to talk to no one until the detective sees them. And no talking amongst yourselves, either."

"I'll stay here," Russ said. "Freedom of the press and all that. *Rudolph Gazette*."

"You'll come with me," Candy snapped. "Like you've been told."

"I guess that'll be all right," the other cop said. "For now."

"Right," Candy said. "For now." She shone her Maglite into my face.

"Someone has to tell Irene and Grace what's happened," Mom said.

"Who are they?" the cop asked.

"Wife and mother-in-law of the . . . deceased," Mom said.

"You know who this is?"

"We all do," I said. "It's Gordon Olsen. His parents own this hotel."

"I don't want you talking to anyone. Let the detective handle it." The cop nodded to Candy.

"Let's go," she grunted in her pretending-to-be-a-tough-guy voice.

We emerged from the gardens into a scene totally different from the one we'd left only minutes earlier. Police cars and an ambulance lined the driveway, throwing flashing blue and red lights onto the snow. An officer was stringing yellow crime scene tape between the trees and bushes. A crowd had gathered on the hotel steps, some of them dressed in pajamas and slippers, wrapped in the hotel's fluffy white robes. A large police officer stood at the bottom of the steps, his arms crossed and his face set as if daring them to cross the invisible line he'd created.

I scanned faces quickly, but didn't see Grace or Irene. Grace and Jack's bedroom was at the back of their cottage, which was behind the hotel. Quite possibly she'd gone to bed and hadn't heard the uproar.

Escorted by Candy, we climbed the steps and passed through the crowd into the hotel. Everyone stared at us, and someone called out, "Merry, what's going on here?"

"We need a private room," Candy snapped at the wide-eyed, openmouthed receptionist. "Stat!"

"No need," my mother said. "We'll be quite comfortable over there." She pointed to the collection of chairs arranged around the fireplace.

"I was told . . ." Candy protested.

"Whatever," Mom said. "You can join us, if you wish." She smiled at the receptionist. "Could you ask the kitchen to prepare us a pot of tea, dear? When they have a moment." She settled herself onto the sofa, the rich brown leather cracked and worn with age. Alan and I took the chintz-covered wingback chairs on either side of her. The chairs were arranged around a low coffee table. Real logs blazed in a huge stone fireplace, and beside it the live Douglas fir glowed as if lit from within. The pretty illuminated Christmas village Jack knocked over when he collapsed had been replaced with a poinsettia.

I leaned back in my chair, closed my eyes, and stretched out my legs. Heat washed over me as the logs burned and spat. The crowd murmured, and Candy might have sworn under her breath.

A sharp pain tore through my right foot. Followed by another. My eyes flew open and I looked down. Only now that they were warming did I remember I was wearing high-heeled pumps and panty hose. My legs were soaked up to the knees. Rapidly melting snow filled the shoes. I kicked the ruined footwear off, consoling myself at their loss by thinking that it served me right for indulging in such a useless bit of extravagance, and stared at the sodden stockings.

"Here." Mom unraveled her pristine white scarf. "You'd better dry those feet off before you get frostbite."

"I can't use that," I said. I struggled to stand. My feet didn't seem to want to hold me up, and I tottered. Alan leapt to his feet and grabbed my arm. "Go to the ladies' room, Merry. Run those feet under warm, but not hot, water."

"You have to stay here. Where I can see you," Candy said.

"If she loses her toes to frostbite, do you want her suing the police department?" Alan asked.

I doubted I was in that much danger, but Alan's threat served its purpose. "Don't you talk to anyone in there," Candy shouted after us. With Alan's help I managed the few steps down the hall.

No one was in the ladies' room for me to talk to, had I been so inclined. I stripped off my hose, tossed them into the trash, and soaked paper towels in warm water. I sat on one of the stools at the vanity and draped the wet towels around my lower extremities. While the warmth soaked through my skin, I glanced around. The room was decorated like a traditional powder room with rose-patterned wallpaper and upholstered chairs in shades of soft pink. I imagined the ladies of *Downton Abbey* fixing their hats in such a room. A display of garish holiday decorations ruined the ambience somewhat. Silver tinsel had been draped across the tops of the mirrors, and plastic red and green balls were suspended from the ceiling by gold ribbon. Grace liked to support all the shops in Rudolph, and she'd probably bought these things at the Nook and stuck them away in the bathrooms, where they wouldn't get too much attention. I stopped criticizing the decor and checked the damp towels on my feet. They felt much better, and after a few minutes I flexed and wiggled my toes. The pain had gone and I was able to stand.

The door opened and Detective Diane Simmonds

came in. "You okay, Merry? Officer Campbell said something about frostbite?"

"Just cold, wet feet," I said. "I'm fine now. Although I have nothing to wear." I held up the sodden shoes as evidence. They didn't look all that sexy anymore.

"I've been given to understand that you found the body?"

"So it is a body, then. He's dead?"

She nodded.

"I was with my mom and Russ Durham and Alan Anderson. We'd had dinner here, in the restaurant, and Mom wanted a walk in the gardens before going home. There we found . . . you know."

"The officer who was first on the scene said you know the deceased."

I nodded. "His name's Gord Olsen. He's from California, and he and his wife came here when his dad, who owns the inn, suffered a heart attack last week."

"Had you seen this Gord Olsen earlier this evening?"

I shook my head.

"Did you see anyone else in the garden? Hear anything?"

I tried to remember. "We heard a shout, and then footsteps that might have been someone running away, but they were muffled by the snow. A cry of pain, of fear, maybe." I lifted my hand to my mouth. "I bet that was Gord."

"Did you see anyone?"

"Not from when we left the hotel until we came across Gord."

"This shout you heard? Male, female? Might you have recognized the voice?"

I shook my head again. "There were no words. Just a sort of strangled yell. And that was all. It could have been either a man or a woman."

"Thanks, Merry. I want to speak briefly to your mother and Mr. Anderson, and then you can leave. I'll get a full statement from you tomorrow."

"Sure."

Hotel guests and staff were still standing at the doors and windows watching the activity, but no one had approached the circle around the fireplace. No doubt Officer Candy Campbell, hand on the butt of her gun, face set in determined lines, deterred anyone from asking Mom or Alan what was going on.

Simmonds spoke briefly to my mother and Alan. They answered in low voices, and then Simmonds said we were free to leave. Alan glanced at my bare feet. "Let me see what I can do," he said.

He spoke to the receptionist; she went into the office and a few minutes later came out with a pair of pink plastic boots covered with purple flowers. "Lost and found," she said. "Never claimed. I suppose it'll be okay if you keep them."

The boots were a shocking contrast to my red dress, but what the heck. Better than losing toes to frostbite. I sat down and pulled them on. They were about three sizes too big.

"Has anyone told Grace what's happened?" Mom asked.

"Grace is Gord Olsen's mother?" Simmonds said. "I was going to call on her now."

"Not his mother, but his stepmother," Mom said. "His father's in the hospital recovering from heart surgery. Gord is his only child. This is going to be a terrible blow."

"His wife's named Irene," I added. "They're staying in the hotel."

"Did you see Irene Olsen this evening?" Simmonds asked.

"No."

"Grace is a dear friend of mine. I will accompany you to break the news to her," Mom said. "As Merry's driving me home, she can come with us."

"I can . . ." Alan began.

"Thanks," I said. "But I'd like to stay with Mom."

"Let's do it, then," Simmonds said. "We'll speak to Grace Olsen first, as you're here now. Then I'll look for Irene."

The crowd of onlookers parted to let us through. I saw more than a few people I recognized and knew that tomorrow morning, once again Mrs. Claus's Treasures would be the spot to gather to hear the latest gossip.

I clomped behind Mom and Detective Simmonds in my giant boots, struggling to keep up. Along the driveway and in the gardens, emergency vehicles and personnel came and went.

"Did your husband not dine with you this evening?"

Simmonds asked Mom, her voice drifting behind her in the cold, crisp night air.

"Yes, but he and Jack are old friends, and Noel's worried about Jack, and all that's going on here at the inn. He wasn't in the mood to socialize. He left the table early, at the same time Grace did."

"Hey!" I sprang forward, tripping over the toes of the boots. I grunted as I stumbled, and my arms windmilled to keep me from falling flat on my face.

Mom and Simmonds turned to check that I was okay. I might have tripped by accident, but I did manage to stop my mom from talking anymore. Detective Diane Simmonds didn't engage in small talk. My dad and Grace had left the dining room early. Either one of them might have been wandering through the hotel grounds alone at the time in question. Dad would want to help the police if he'd seen anything, but I figured it would be better if he called Simmonds of his own volition.

"I don't know if you know this," I said, once I'd caught up to them. "Gord Olsen was not a popular man."

"What do you mean?" Simmonds asked.

"You'll have more luck finding someone in Rudolph who wanted to be rid of Gord than anyone who didn't. He had plans to turn the inn over to a budget chain and sell the gardens to a big-box store. That didn't make a lot of people in town happy."

"Is that so?" she said.

"Everyone was upset, and some people were down-and-out angry. Of course," I hastened to add, "those were just words. No one in Rudolph would actually kill someone to stop a Mega-Mart."

"I wouldn't be so sure," Simmonds said. "Can you name some of these people?"

Vicky's enraged face flashed before my eyes. "No one in particular," I said with a casual wave of my hand.

"How about Mrs. Olsen herself?" Simmonds asked. "What did she have to say about her stepson taking over the business?"

"Grace was happy he'd come to help out," Mom said quickly, "leaving her to concentrate on her husband's recovery."

Simmonds gave my mom a long look. And then the detective said, "I guess we'll just have to ask her, won't we."

So much had happened since we left the restaurant it should have been the middle of the night, but when I glanced at my watch, I saw it wasn't even ten yet. Lights were still on in Grace and Jack's home.

Simmonds marched up the steps and rapped loudly. I recognized the large wreath on the door. Made of circles of brightly colored balls, it had been bought at my shop. Mom and I exchanged nervous glances.

The door opened, and Grace peeked out. She was ready for bed: face scrubbed, jewelry removed, wearing ivory satin pajamas and a matching dressing gown. She looked questioningly at Simmonds and then saw us. "Aline. Is something the matter?"

"Mrs. Olsen, I am Detective Diane Simmonds of Rudolph PD. May I come in for a few minutes?" She made the request sound like a question, but I knew it wasn't.

Grace's hands flew to her chest. Her eyes opened in fear and she took a step back.

Mom read her friend's face. "Jack's fine. We're not here about Jack."

The flash of panic faded, and Grace lowered her hands. "Come in, please. Has something happened at the hotel? A theft from one of the rooms? It has been known to happen, although not very often." She led the way into the comfortable living room.

Simmonds didn't pause to take off her Uggs, and Mom didn't remove her ankle boots, so I clomped after them in my pink and purple boots. Melting snow on her hardwood floors would be the least of Grace's concerns tonight.

A single lamp burned behind a chair. A cup of tea, steam rising, and a hardcover book sat on the side table. The white lights of the tree glowed in a corner, the gas fireplace burned cheerfully, and a Christmas choral concert was playing on the Bose speakers. The curtains across the French doors were closed against the night.

We stood awkwardly in the center of the room. "Would you like . . ." Grace began.

"You have a stepson by the name of Gord Olsen?" Simmonds said.

"Why, yes. Jack's son by his first marriage." Grace looked at my mom, her face a picture of confusion. "Aline, what is going on? Is Gord in some sort of trouble?"

"I have to tell you, Mrs. Olsen, Gord was found dead earlier this evening," Simmonds said.

"Gord. Dead?"

"Yes."

"What happened?"

"That's still to be determined," Simmonds said.

"Grace, dear, I am so sorry," Mom said.

"I'd prefer it if you leave it to me to break the news to my husband," Grace said. "He's in the hospital recovering from heart surgery. I'll visit first thing tomorrow and let him know."

"We can do that," Simmonds said.

Grace gathered her dressing gown around her and sat down. She took a sip of tea. "Is there some question of the hotel being at fault?"

"Not as far as I'm aware at this time," Simmonds said.

"Thank you for coming to tell me," Grace said. "You can show yourselves out."

"Grace!" Mom said. "Didn't you hear what the detective said?"

"I heard her perfectly well. Gord is dead. I'm surprised you think I'd be upset, Aline. You know I don't believe in false sentiment. He was a thoroughly nasty little man. My only concern right now is for Jack, and it's too late to go to the hospital. Jack loved his son very much, despite all his faults. This will come as a terrible shock. I assume Gord had a heart attack? Quite ironic when you think of it." She took another sip of her tea.

"Not a heart attack, no," Simmonds said. "Although his heart did stop beating. Your stepson was knifed, Mrs. Olsen. Murdered. Not all that far from this very room. Do you have anything to say about that?"

The blood drained from Grace's face in an instant. Her teacup hit the floor, and liquid spread across the hardwood. "Murdered! You can't be serious. Who would do such a thing?"

"You didn't like Gord very much," Simmonds said. "As you made quite plain."

"I didn't like him, but I certainly didn't kill him. I hope you are not implying . . ."

"I never imply," Simmonds said. She was cut off by a ringing from her coat pocket. She pulled her phone out and checked the display before answering. "I'll be right there." She hung up. "I have to go. I'll want to talk to you again in the morning, Mrs. Olsen."

"I'll be at the hospital as soon as visiting hours begin. I can speak with you after. Right now, I'm going over to the hotel. A murder on the premises isn't good for business."

"I didn't say he'd been killed on the premises," Simmonds said.

Grace raised one perfectly sculpted eyebrow. "Don't think you've tricked me into a confession, Detective. I simply assumed that, seeing as how Aline and Merry are with you and you said Gord was killed not far from here. Now, I'm going to get dressed and go up to the hotel."

Before we could move, the front door flew open and

Irene Olsen ran into the living room, followed by Candy Campbell. "You!" Irene shrieked. "What have you done?"

"I assure you I've done nothing," Grace said coolly.

"Sorry, Detective," Candy said. "Someone saw the body being loaded into the ambulance and told this lady here. I said she was to wait for you, but she wouldn't listen to me."

Simmonds stepped in front of Irene. "Mrs. Irene Olsen?"

"Yes? Who are you?"

"I'm Detective Simmonds of the Rudolph police. Why don't you let Officer Campbell take you back to the hotel? I'll be with you shortly."

"My husband has been murdered, and you want me to go back to bed and forget all about it!"

"We are investigating," Simmonds said, her voice calm and in control. "I need to talk to you about your husband's movements tonight. But this isn't the place."

"I'll walk back with you," I said, trying to be helpful. Irene's face was clear of makeup and very pale. Her feet were stuffed into unlaced boots, and a shawl had been thrown over her white nightgown. I reached out, intending to give her a comforting pat on the arm.

"Keep your hands off me," she snarled. "You did it. I know you did. You and your father."

"Huh?" I said.

Irene turned to Simmonds. "I heard him myself. In this very room. That foolish man who pretends he's Santa Claus, her father, he threatened my Gord."

"That's ridiculous," Mom and I shouted at the same time.

"I wouldn't be surprised if you were all in it together. I heard him. You heard him, too." Irene lowered her voice into what, I had to admit, was a good imitation of my dad. "*I will stop you. One way or another.*'

"I demand you arrest that fake Santa Claus."

Chapter 6

started to laugh. One glance at Simmonds's face and the laughter died in my throat.

"That's ridiculous," I said again. Mom dropped into a chair.

"I understand you and Mr. Wilkinson left the restaurant early?" Simmonds asked Grace.

"Yes, we did. I wasn't feeling in a social mood and wanted to be alone. Noel kindly walked me home."

"Did he come in?"

"For a short while. We talked about Jack, reminisced about the good old days. Noel left and I prepared for bed. I was intending to read for a bit before turning in when you arrived."

"Mr. Wilkinson was alone when he left you?"

Grace hesitated. She glanced at my mom.

"Answer the question, Mrs. Olsen," Simmonds said.

"Yes. But people are around all the time. This is a busy place, particularly in the weeks leading up to Christmas."

"Did he say where he was going?"

"Back to dinner, of course," Grace said. "His wife and daughter were waiting for him."

Simmonds looked at me. Her eyes were unreadable. "But your father didn't accompany you on your walk in the garden?"

I shook my head.

"Why not?"

I glanced at Mom. She took a deep breath but said nothing.

"He phoned Mom to say he was going on home ahead of us," I grudgingly admitted. "He . . . wasn't in the mood to come back to dinner and make small talk. He asked Mom to get a ride back to town with me."

"So you didn't see him again after he and Mrs. Olsen left the restaurant?"

"No, but . . ."

"What time would that have been?"

"I can't say. I didn't check my watch."

"When he left with Mrs. Olsen, he was intending to return to dinner, though?"

"I don't know what he was intending to do," I said.

"I wonder what, or who, Mr. Wilkinson saw that caused him to change his mind," Simmonds said.

"I resent your implications." Mom slowly rose to her feet and straightened to full diva posture. She had a way of making herself look larger than life, of projecting to the corners of the room, whether a packed opera house or a crowded living room.

"As I might have said," Simmonds said, "I never imply. Before this goes any further, I'm going to have a talk with Mr. Wilkinson." She pulled out her phone, and to my horror she ordered an officer to go around to my parents' house. He was to pick up my dad and take him to the station.

"You can't be serious!" Mom cried. Irene smirked.

"I can assure you I am," Simmonds said. "I take threats of this nature very seriously. Particularly when someone ends up dead."

"Don't worry, Mom," I said. "Everything will be cleared up soon. The idea is preposterous."

"Before I go," Simmonds said to Irene. "You appear to be ready for bed, Mrs. Olsen. When did you last see your husband?"

"Yes, what were you up to tonight, Irene?" Grace demanded. Mom put a restraining hand on her friend's arm. Irene looked as though she were about to spit. Instead she lifted her head and stared directly into Simmonds's face. "Gord and I ate dinner in Rudolph. At the something-or-other holly. One of those ridiculously childish names they stick on everything in this town."

"A Touch of Holly?"

"Yes."

"Why not eat here? I've heard the restaurant is excellent."

"Gord's the sort of man who is always working, always paying attention to detail. If we had dinner here, at the hotel, he'd be concentrating on analyzing the quality of the food, not enjoying himself."

Making notes about the prices, more likely. I kept my own face impassive.

"You're staying here, at the inn?" Simmonds asked.

"Of course we are. Gord needs . . . I mean, he needed, to be close to his father at this time. Regardless"—Irene threw a poisonous glance at Grace—"of what *she* thinks about it." Irene pulled an overused tissue out of her pocket and dabbed at her eyes. I myself hadn't noticed a touch of moisture in their depths. "We got back to our room around nine or so. I wanted to relax and watch some TV, but Gord said he needed to do one last round of the hotel. Make sure everything was running smoothly. He didn't"—she paused and took a deep breath—"return."

"Thank you," Simmonds said. "I'm heading into town now, but I will want to speak to you again."

Irene threw another look at her stepmother-in-law. "I may not be welcome here, but I'm not going anywhere."

"Officer Campbell will accompany you back to your room," Simmonds said. "And wait with you until we can talk."

Irene left, followed by Candy, who looked as though she was not pleased at playing babysitter instead of being involved in the questioning of suspects. Grace went to her bedroom to change before going to the hotel to attempt to calm frightened guests. Simmonds left to—*shudder!*—question my dad.

Mom and I drove back to town in silence. Only when

I'd dropped her off at the police station, and she'd ordered me to take myself home, did I check my phone messages.

Call me if you want to talk, Alan had texted me.

You OK? said the message from Russ.

I was not okay and I did not want to talk.

But it was nice to know they'd been thinking of me.

I didn't get much sleep that night and woke feeling groggy and confused. It was still dark. I called my mom immediately, not much caring if I woke her up. I did, but she said she was glad I'd called. Then she passed the phone to Dad.

"Nothing to worry about, Merry," he said in a very worried voice. "I'd been overheard threatening Gord, and as I didn't have an alibi for the time of his death, Simmonds had a few questions for me. I assured her that as much as I didn't approve of the man's plans for his father's business, I wasn't about to kill him over a Mega-Mart." Dad's laugh was about as fake as the snow we used to decorate the town's Christmas tree in July. "You have a good day, honeybunch." And he hung up, leaving me not feeling a whole lot better. I could at least console myself with the thought that he hadn't spent the night in the slammer.

I walked Mattie through the dark streets as lights came on in the houses and people emerged to shovel their sidewalks and scrape snow off their cars. My thoughts kept returning to last night. I hadn't liked Gord one bit and I'd been horrified at his plans for the

Yuletide Inn, but the man didn't deserve to die. Grace's indifference to Gord's death had been, frankly, shocking. Then again, was it wrong to not pretend to grieve for appearance's sake? It would certainly make things easier, for the police most of all, if we went around saying what we thought all the time. Grace had Jack to worry about, and the news of his only son's death to break to him this morning. I hoped it wouldn't bring on another heart attack.

Unwillingly, the image of Gord's dead body came to mind. I saw the sprig of holly laid out on his chest, the knife through it. Holly wouldn't have been difficult for the killer to get his—or her—hands on. It was a common decoration in Rudolph. It had to have some significance. Did the killer mean to emphasize that Gord had to die because he threatened to destroy Christmas Town?

Or was it an attempt to make the killing look as though it was perpetrated by someone in Christmas Town?

Was someone trying to frame my dad? The idea was ridiculous. Everyone loved Dad. He was the very personification of Christmas.

Well, not entirely everyone. The Muddites weren't exactly fans of Dad or of Christmas Town itself. Sue-Anne Morrow was worried Dad would be persuaded to make another run for mayor. And, if he did, she had to know he was almost guaranteed to win.

I pulled Mattie away from his inspection of a line of rabbit tracks and set off home. The police would no doubt find the killing had nothing to do with Rudolph. It had most likely been a random attack. That was not an entirely comforting thought, either. The last thing we needed one week before Christmas was for word to get around that a crazed serial killer was stalking visitors.

Gord's enemy might have followed him here from California. That had to be it. Irene had been mighty quick to point the finger of suspicion at Dad. Was she trying to deflect blame from herself? I considered paying a condolence call on the grieving widow later, but soon dismissed that idea. She was unlikely to take a visit from one of Grace's friends kindly. She told Simmonds she'd been in her room when Gord had died. Meaning she had no alibi. How stable was their marriage anyway? Her reaction to the news of her husband's death was more an attempt to point fingers, than actual grief.

Then again, different people reacted to shock in different ways. Perhaps Irene was the sort to do her grieving in private.

I took Mattie home and settled him into his crate before heading to the shop. As long as I was up and restless I might as well get some paperwork done. I stopped at the Cranberry Coffee Bar to pick up coffee and a muffin. They were busy with people heading for work, and I joined the line.

Everyone, it seemed, was talking about Gord Olsen. If there's one thing the residents of Rudolph, New York, love almost as much as they love Christmas, it's gossip.

"I hear you found the body, Merry," the assistant librarian said. "How awful for you."

"Was he, like, dead already?" a town hall clerk asked, an unpleasantly curious gleam in her eye.

"Multiple stab wounds, I heard," said the guy who operated the snowplow. "Must have been blood everywhere."

"No. It was quite peaceful," I lied. I tried not to shudder as I remembered the scene.

But they weren't really interested in hearing how peacefully Gord had gone. When I placed my order, I caught the teenage girl behind the register checking my fingernails for blood residue.

"They say Noel Wilkinson was taken in for questioning in the middle of the night," I overheard a real estate agent say.

"That's ridiculous," the kindergarten teacher said.

"It's true," he said. "Ask Merry here."

"Only because my dad was at the hotel last night. He might have seen something important without realizing it."

Most of the people surrounding me nodded in agreement, but some looked doubtful.

"Lots of people at the hotel last night," the real estate guy continued. "They weren't all brought in for questioning."

I opened my mouth to protest, but the assistant librarian beat me to it. "This town has no stronger supporter than Noel Wilkinson."

"Right," I said.

"If Noel took one for the team, good for him," said Rachel McIntosh. "Someone had to get rid of that Gord Olsen."

"Hey!" I said. "My dad didn't have anything to do with it."

They all smiled at me. Rachel patted my arm. "We understand, dear." She winked. "Our lips are sealed."

The barista passed me my coffee. I grabbed it with so much force, I spilled about half of it on the counter. I snatched up my muffin and stormed out.

My phone rang as I was putting my key in the shop door. I balanced a half-full cup, the small paper sack, my iPad bag, my key ring, and dug the phone out of my pocket. "Hold on," I said, twisting the key in the lock. I dumped everything on the first available counter. "What?" I growled into the phone.

"Everything okay?" Vicky asked.

I let out a long sigh. "Yeah. I guess. I've just been to Cranberries, and the talk is all about Gord Olsen. Some people have the nerve to be hinting my dad killed him to save the town."

"Why did you go to Cranberries? You always say my scones are the best in town."

"And they are." I didn't add that Cranberries' *muffins* were slightly better than Vicky's. "I'm at the shop, and they're on my way."

"Just make sure you come here for lunch."

"Don't I always?"

"Not always."

"Okay, today I will. Why are you calling?"

"Because I heard about what happened last night. I've been told you and your mom found the body. Is that right?"

"Unfortunately, yes. We went for a walk in the gardens after dinner, and there he was." I shuddered at the memory.

"Are you handling it okay? Want to come around for dinner and talk?"

"I'm okay—don't worry. It was unpleasant, but not grisly or anything. It was good that Russ and Alan were with us."

"Russ *and* Alan? What were they doing there?"

"My mom invited them to dinner."

Vicky let out a peal of laughter. "Trust Aline. The two most eligible bachelors in Upstate New York, each one of them handsomer than the other."

"She was being friendly."

"She's hearing wedding bells, Merry. Or she wants to. Trust me, I know all about it. Once a woman passes the big three-oh her relatives figure it's time for them to intervene. Last week we had a bunch of guys going ice fishing in here for breakfast, and Aunt Marjorie had the nerve to get me out of the kitchen on some silly pretext to meet them." I could almost hear Vicky's eye-roll over the phone. I laughed and felt my spirits rise. I always did feel better talking to Vicky.

"Talk to you later," I said.

"Offer's still open for dinner. We can order in a pizza or something."

"Let's see how the day goes. I'll call you later."

The shop was busy all morning. I overheard shoppers talking about police activity at the inn the previous night, but they seemed to think a man had either died from a heart attack or fallen asleep in the gardens and frozen to death, probably a combination of both. I suspected Grace and the hotel staff (not to mention the townspeople) had been hard at work spreading those rumors. When Jackie arrived she had a copy of today's *Gazette*. The story was on the front page, but small and beneath the fold. The picture of a cruiser and police tape cordoning off the gardens could have been taken at just about any crime scene anywhere. Russ had laid out the facts without sensationalism and with plenty of quotes from Detective Simmonds about it being an "ongoing investigation" and that the police hoped to be "close to an arrest soon." Most tourists didn't read the local paper, and the report of a single murder in our out-of-the-way town wouldn't get much space in the larger papers. Not today, anyway, as the online news on my iPad was all about a fifty-something congresswoman found last night in a highly compromising position with an eighteen-year-old male escort during a routine police traffic stop. Speculation was rampant whether or not her ultrawealthy octogenarian husband would "stand by his woman."

It was midafternoon when the shop door almost flew off its hinges as my mother stormed in. She carried a newspaper in her hands, and it wasn't the *Gazette*. "Have you seen this outrage?" she yelled.

The shop happened to be busy at that moment, and everyone stopped what they were doing to look. Mom waved the paper at me. "I'm going to sue."

I grabbed her arm. "Whatever it is, not here," I whispered. I dragged her into what in my more prideful moments I think of as my office. It is, in fact, a room with a desk, a computer, overflow storage, staff coat closet, and the place where we keep cleaning equipment. I slammed the door behind us.

There isn't room for more than one chair in my office/broom closet, and I gestured to my mom to take it. She dropped into the seat and thrust the paper at me. It was, as I had feared, the *Muddle Harbor Chronicle*. The entire top half of the front page showed a grainy black-and-white picture of my parents. My dad had his head down, beard buried in his chest, while Mom scowled at the camera. She had been caught in the act of lifting her hand, but too late to block the shot. If you squinted, you could make out the words "Rudolph Police Station" over the door in the background. Dad looked like a New York City street person arrested for panhandling, and Mom could have been about to go onstage to sing one of the witches' parts in the opera version of *Macbeth*.

As awful as the picture was, the headline was worse: "Rudolph's Wilkinson Questioned in Brutal Murder."

"Oh dear," I said. If a photographer from the *Chronicle* had been at the Rudolph police station in the middle of the night, someone had to have tipped him off.

"This is a disaster!" Mom wailed.

"Pay no attention to the *Chronicle*," I said. "No one reads that rag."

"Someone might," she moaned. "I am having nightmares thinking of more than one of my rivals pinning that picture to mirrors in their dressing rooms and enjoying a good laugh."

"I'm sure they've had unflattering pictures taken of

them, too. Never mind that. What happened last night? They let Dad go, right? So that's good."

She sighed. "That odious Detective Simmonds was ensconced in the interview room with your father for a long time. They made me wait in the front lobby and wouldn't let me so much as pop in to tell him I was there. Everyone who came in and out of the police station pretended they didn't recognize me. It was quite possibly the most humiliating experience of my life. Other than that incident when the stagehand at Covent Garden . . ."

"Mom! Stick to the point."

"The point. Yes. All Noel would tell me when they finally let him go home was that Detective Simmonds made him admit he had threatened Gord, as Irene said he had. Noel assured her it was nothing but words. Everyone says things like that at some time or another when under pressure. I've been known to do so myself. All I can say is, it's a good thing that Covent Garden stagehand didn't turn up dead the following morning, I can tell you."

"Moving on, Mom. Simmonds must have had some other reason for wanting to . . . talk to dad. . . ." I avoided using the word "interrogate." My mom might seem flighty sometimes, not to mention self-absorbed, but my parents' devotion to each other was rock solid. She was dressed as perfectly as always this afternoon in a black wool coat, black faux-fur hat, black boots, and red leather gloves, but her deep red lipstick had slipped at a corner of her mouth, and she'd forgotten to apply mascara to one eye.

"Simmonds was interested in hearing every detail of his movements last night. Noel told her he walked Grace to her door. The normal number of people, staff and hotel guests as well as diners, were about. Grace offered him a drink, but he refused as he was driving home. They chatted for a few minutes, and he left. The conversation with Grace about the future of the inn had depressed him, and he didn't feel like coming back to dinner with us and making polite conversation. He decided to simply go on home, knowing I could get a ride with you."

"Did something happen in the talk with Grace?"

"I asked him. Grace told Noel that Gord threatened to destroy everything she and Jack had built. Not everyone knows this, but Grace is very much the one in charge at the hotel. She lets Jack pretend he's the boss, but all the important decisions are made by her. The business has grown by leaps and bounds since she's been doing so. You can imagine how upset she was when this . . . interloper shoved his way in and told her she's not needed."

I could imagine, all right. I said nothing, but my mind raced. Might Grace have followed Gord into the garden? Maybe she'd phoned him after my dad left and suggested they meet to talk things over. She would have had time to change into her nightclothes and pretend to be relaxing before we showed up at her door. I couldn't see Grace throwing my dad under the bus, though.

"Don't even think it," Mom said.

"Think what?"

"That Grace killed Gord."

"I wasn't," I squeaked. *How did she do that?* Like the time I was only *thinking* of snatching a cookie off the baking tray and she smacked my hand. "I don't suppose Dad can prove he went straight home when he said he did?"

Mom shook her head. "Not unless someone specifically saw him driving away from the hotel."

"Look, if Simmonds doesn't have anything more on Dad than that, there's nothing to worry about. Half the town of Rudolph wanted Gord dead. Simmonds will have more than enough suspects. It's just that Dad's name came up last night, that's all."

"I wouldn't be surprised if that miserable Irene did it herself. She seems like the type to me."

I wasn't sure what type that was, but I didn't bother to ask. "The best thing you and Dad can do now is go about your business. Pretend everything is A-OK. By the way, do you know you're only wearing one earring?"

She screeched and lifted both hands to her head. Finding one earlobe empty, she slipped the lone gold hoop out and dropped it into her bag. "My mind was elsewhere this morning."

"It'll be okay, Mom. You'll see."

"Simmonds told Noel he isn't to leave town."

That didn't sound good, I thought, but didn't mention it. "What did Dad have to say to that?"

"He has no plans to go anywhere. Where else would Santa be at Christmas than in Christmas Town?"

"He said that to Simmonds?"

"Yes."

"He isn't really Santa Claus, you know."

"I am aware of that, Merry. And so, I can assure you, is your father. I believe he was making a joke. Detective Simmonds doesn't seem to have much of a sense of humor."

"Go home, Mom. Try to relax. Don't worry, everything will work out fine."

She gave me a small smile as she got to her feet. "That's what I keep telling your father."

"I have one question." I pointed to the newspaper. "Who took that photo?"

Mom shook her head. "Some lowlife member of the fourth estate, I would imagine. I didn't get a look at him. It was dark and then a blinding light hit my eyes."

"It was a man?"

Mom thought. "I don't know that it matters, but I think so. He hurried away after taking the picture, and he had that wide-legged slouched way of walking young men these days have. No doubt because they can't keep their pants up." She sniffed in disapproval and left my office.

I heard Mom say good-bye to Jackie, and the chimes over the door tinkle. Only when I was sure Mom was gone did I drop into my chair and put my head in my hands. What a mess.

Diane Simmonds was new to Rudolph. She'd been a cop in Chicago for a long time and apparently wanted to give small-town life a try. I'd seen her working before, and thought she was intelligent and competent. But I didn't know how police minds worked. If she had a suspect—meaning my dad—how hard would she try to find other suspects? To find, I reminded myself, the *real* killer. My dad was as kind, gentle, and loving as you'd expect from someone known as Santa Claus. He didn't even kill flies that got into the house, but guided them back outside.

I tried to look at the situation from the police perspective. Means, motive, opportunity. Wasn't that what the cops looked for in mystery novels? My dad seemed to have had all three. Means: a knife. Insignificant. Anyone could get hold of a knife. Motive: Dad was furious at Gord. Also insignificant: So was everyone else in Rudolph. Opportunity: In that one Dad stood out. He'd been at the hotel around the time Gord died, wandering the grounds by himself.

My dad hadn't killed anyone, and if Simmonds thought he had, then it might be up to me to prove him innocent. Dad was so cheerfully optimistic he probably thought *helping the police with their inquiries* meant just that. Being a good, helpful citizen.

I thought back over the events of the past week since Jack's heart attack and the arrival of Gord and Irene. Problem was, I had too many suspects. I glanced at my watch. It was coming up to three. I hadn't even had lunch yet.

"I'm going to Vicky's," I said to Jackie. "Want me to bring you back anything?"

"Peanut butter square," she said, not bothering to look up from her magazine. The store was empty. All the shoppers who'd been here when Mom made her theatrical entrance had left, as if they were extras called to stand onstage at the right moment. Even a week before Christmas, Mondays were slow in the store. I expected business to pick up throughout the week, culminating in the big children's party the town had planned for Saturday and Sunday. There'd be skating on the bay, a snow sculpture contest (judged by age group) in the park, a concert at the bandstand, clowns and magicians in the streets, and hot dogs and hot chocolate served outside the shops on Jingle Bell Lane. Santa would be in attendance with a full accompaniment of high school kids playing elves and Alan Anderson in his toymaker persona.

I'd gotten in extra orders of Alan's wooden soldiers and train sets, hoping the parents would be inspired by their kids' love of Christmas to get one last gift.

Maybe two.

And something for themselves while they were at it.

I headed up Jingle Bell Lane toward Victoria's Bake Shoppe at a rapid clip. They closed at three, but Vicky could usually be persuaded to find something in the back of the shelves for me. Thick gray clouds hung low in the sky and the wind was sharp and cold. I buried my gloved hands deeper in my pockets. Everyone in town was keeping an eye on the weather. The forecast for Friday, the day before the children's party, was for increasing temperatures, and on Saturday they were calling for—horrors—freezing rain.

I ran up the bakery steps. The sign had already been flipped to "Closed," and I could see Marjorie inside sweeping the floor.

I knocked. She looked up, scowled, and tapped her watch. I put on my pleading face. She put down the broom and unlocked the door.

"Whew!" I said. "Just made it."

"We're closed. And we're all out."

"You must have something left over." I scanned the rack of shelves behind the counter. Clean, bare wood eyed me back. "Soup? A muffin or scone?" I sniffed unobtrusively. The scent of pastries baking and soup bubbling lingered in the air, but only as a faint residue. The countertops were scrubbed clean and the floor swept. Chairs were upside down on the tables. I glanced at the clock on the wall. Two minutes to three. "Why are you closed early? Where's Vicky?"

Marjorie let out a long puff and jerked her head toward the back.

"What's going on?"

"That detective woman'll be here soon. Vicky thought it best to close up."

"I am expecting," Vicky said, coming out of the kitchen, "a visit from the police shortly. Simmonds was, thank heavens, polite enough to call and make an appointment, so I wouldn't have to talk to her in front of a room full of customers." Vicky'd taken off her apron and wore baggy jeans with numerous holes and patches and a summery blue T-shirt. Her spiky black hair was freshly brushed, the long front lock of purple falling over her right eye. The rows of silver earrings through her ears caught the light.

"Why?" I asked.

"I do not want to find out. I can only imagine it has something to do with Gord Olsen. No loss to anyone."

"That seems to be the common sentiment."

Vicky shrugged. "I don't know what it has to do

with me. You might as well go home now, Aunt Marjorie."

"I'll stay, dear. In case you need moral support."

"Thanks, but I'll be fine."

Marjorie tried not to grimace. Moral support, to Vicky's relatives, meant reporting back to the family. She went to get her coat, and when she left the bakery, Marjorie passed Diane Simmonds coming in.

"You again," the detective said to me.

"Me again."

"You seem to always be at the heart of things in Rudolph, Merry. Like your father."

"What does that mean?"

"Your dad's a big man around here. The unofficial mayor, everyone tells me. Number one mover and shaker. Santa Claus."

"My father plays Santa Claus on occasion." I rushed to his defense. "People respect him. And so they should. My dad's the one who saved this town from falling into a postindustrial slump like so many others around here. He had the idea of taking advantage of the name of Rudolph and becoming a year-round Christmas Town." I didn't bother to give her a history lesson—how the first plan for the revitalization of Rudolph had centered on the War of 1812 heroics of the founder of the town. That idea had quickly been shelved when researchers discovered he'd been a British spy all along.

"With a name like Noel and that beard and belly and those twinkling blue eyes, who better to be Santa?" Vicky said.

"The town's important to your father," Simmonds said to me.

"Yes, it is. I'd say . . ." Just in time I saw the trap opening up in front of me. "I'd say it's no more important to him than it is to anyone else who lives here. If you must know, my parents are thinking of moving to the city in the summer. Mom's had an offer to teach voice lessons at a school of dramatic arts, and . . ."

"Really?" Vicky said. "I hadn't heard that. I can't imagine your dad ever leaving Rudolph. All those years your mom was on tour or singing at the Met, he stayed here and raised you kids and . . ." Finally, Vicky noticed the frantic signals crossing my face. She snapped her mouth shut.

We smiled at Detective Simmonds. She had the grace not to smile back, but if she had I'm sure it would have resembled the cat who found the cream pitcher left out on the kitchen counter. "I haven't forgotten that I need to talk to you, Merry. I'll come around to your shop when I'm finished here."

"I'm here now," I said helpfully. "Why don't you speak to Vicky and me together? Save you wasting your time on two interviews."

"It's my time to waste." She opened the door. She did not smile.

"Call me as soon as you're done," I said to Vicky.

"Will do."

I left.

I never did get lunch.

Rachel McIntosh waylaid me when I passed Candy

Cane Sweets. "Merry, what's happening? I saw that awful policewoman going into Vicky's."

"Routine inquiries," I said.

Rachel shook her head. "I don't know about routine. I heard your father was arrested."

"He was not! Who told you that?"

"I don't remember. Might have been Sue-Anne."

I ground my teeth. That blasted Sue-Anne. My dad didn't even *want* to be mayor again, but she simply wouldn't believe him. "He was at the hotel last night at the time in question. Naturally Simmonds wanted to talk to him, to ask if he'd seen anything out of the ordinary. That's all."

Rachel nodded. "They say Gord Olsen was murdered. Stabbed."

"So they say."

"What do you think's going to happen with the inn? I mean, the deal with Fine Budget and Mega-Mart?"

"Gee, Rachel, why are you asking me? I have no idea."

"Everyone's talking about it, Merry. People need to know." Rachel threw a quick glance up and down the street. No one was approaching us. "My money's on Grace. And I don't blame her one little bit, the way that Gord marched in and began taking over."

"I hope you aren't telling people that," I said. "Particularly not the police."

She sniffed. "Just my opinion. I'm only telling you because you were there. Or so they say."

"So they say." I continued walking.

* * *

"Are you expecting someone, Merry?" Jackie asked.

"No! Why are you asking?"

"Because you jump every time the bell rings and you keep looking out the window, that's why."

"Oh. Detective Simmonds said she might pop around later this afternoon to talk to me about the events of yesterday."

"That's no reason to be nervous. Unless you did it." Jackie laughed uproariously at her own joke. I did not join in.

It was coming up on four thirty. As well as peeking out the window, I kept checking my phone in case Vicky called. That she hadn't must have meant she was still ensconced with Simmonds.

"You can leave now," I said to Jackie.

"I'm scheduled to work until five today."

"My treat."

"Wow, a whole half hour off. Are you not wanting any witnesses or something when the cops arrive? Wouldn't you be better off if I stayed? Kyle figures it was some sort of gang thing. The mob's big in construction, you know. Maybe Gord did something they didn't like, tried to cheat them or something."

"That's a possibility," I said, cheering up. "Kyle should mention it to the police."

"Kyle tries to have as little to do with the cops as possible."

That didn't surprise me. But I had no time to reflect on what differences Jackie's chronically underemployed boyfriend and the officers of the law might have. My phone chirped to tell me I had a text.

Vicky: *Incoming. Call me when she's done.*

A minute later the chimes over the door tinkled merrily, and Detective Simmonds herself walked into the shop. "I'm sorry I didn't get around to you earlier, Merry. It's been quite a day."

"This morning's paper said you were about to make an arrest," Jackie said. "Who is it?"

Simmonds gave her a cool look. "The papers say a lot of things. Occasionally they even get it right. But not often. Shall we go into your office, Merry?"

"There's not much room in there. I'll close the shop early. We finish at five on Mondays anyway, and it's almost that now. Good night, Jackie."

Jackie seemed to take a particularly long time getting her outerwear on and preparing to take her leave. Simmonds browsed through my shop. "As I've noticed before, you have some lovely things here."

"Thank you."

She studied a train display on the toy table. The tiny tracks, engine, cars, and caboose were made of wood, lovingly handcrafted by Alan Anderson. She picked up the bright red caboose and turned it over. "Nice."

"Yes."

"You sell a lot of locally made goods."

"I try to. Some things I bring in from the city but I source locally whenever I can. I want to support the town, and that's what the visitors to my shop want to buy."

"Would I be right in guessing you're not too worried about a Mega-Mart opening a couple of miles down the road?"

"They wouldn't be competition for me, if that's what you mean, but it would be bad news for many other shops."

"Like the one next door?"

"You mean the Nook? Probably. Mega-Mart would stock the same stuff Betty does and sell it cheaper."

"Betty is Betty Thatcher, owner of Rudolph's Gift Nook?"

"She wouldn't be the only one in trouble," I said. "Most of Jingle Bell Lane, like Main Streets all over America, is threatened by big-box stores."

Simmonds moved on. She studied the jewelry display. She picked up a pair of Crystal's earrings. They were silver, the delicate threads forming a triangular tree shape. Simmonds read the price tag and let out a low whistle. "Forty-five bucks."

"Handmade."

"No competition from Mega-Mart, but turning the Yuletide Inn into a Fine Budget might cut down on the sort of customers who can afford to pay almost fifty bucks for seasonal jewelry."

"So what?" Jackie said, coming out of the back and pulling on her gloves. "Business is business. One store closes, another opens."

"Some people might not see it that way," Simmonds said.

"Whatever. Kyle thinks a Mega-Mart would be great. He's going to apply for a job with the construction firm if it goes ahead. See you tomorrow, Merry."

We watched Jackie leave. Simmonds turned to me. "Apparently not everyone in Rudolph is opposed to Gord Olsen's plans."

"Apparently not."

"Tell me about last night, Merry. Everything you can remember from the time you finished dinner until the police arrived."

I rounded the counter and plopped onto Jackie's stool. Simmonds stood in the center of the floor with her feet planted and arms crossed. I spoke slowly and chose my words carefully. I'd left the restaurant with my mom, Russ Durham, and Alan Anderson. Mom wanted a stroll in the gardens. We heard what sounded like an argument, someone shouted, someone else cried out, and we heard a person running away. We found Gord and called 911. That was all.

"Last night you said you couldn't tell if the people you heard arguing were men or women, and you didn't recognize the voices. Is that still the case?"

"Yes."

"You heard two distinct voices?"

"I think so. I can't really be sure. Have you spoken to Alan and Russ?"

"I have. As well as your mother."

"What did they say?"

She didn't grace that question with a reply, but cocked her head at me. "Did you make out any of the words?"

"No."

"Did you see anyone else in the vicinity of the hotel gardens?"

"No. Not a soul."

"But a lot of people go there?"

"It's very popular, even in winter. Grace does a beautiful job of decorating it for the holidays. Family groups like to skate on the pond and make snowmen on the lawns. Hey, I bet you got footprints, right? Nothing like snow for leaving footprints. What'd they tell you?"

"That a lot of people walked in the garden since the last snowfall. You and your friends, I hate to say, trampled the area up thoroughly."

"We were trying to help a man."

She lifted one hand. "Just saying. We took several good impressions leading away from the statue where you found Olsen. Winter boots, mass-produced brand, the sort both men and women wear. Average size."

"Is that going to help you?"

"Impressions are meaningless with nothing to compare them with."

"Where did the prints lead you?"

"Into the parking lot. Where they completely disappeared amongst all the traffic coming and going, both vehicular and foot. The owner of the boots might have gotten into a car and driven away. They might have taken a shortcut to the paths to the hotel, which are well shoveled. I'm going to show you something, Merry. Please tell me if you recognize it."

She reached into her bag and pulled out a plastic

envelope containing a photograph. I braced myself, expecting to see Gord Olsen's dead body. But I need not have worried; it was only a picture of a knife. A perfectly ordinary-looking knife, the sort you'd find in any kitchen. I swallowed. "I assume that's what was used to murder Gord."

She said nothing.

"I didn't notice the one that . . ."

"Take your time, Merry."

"That killed him. But I'm pretty sure I've seen that knife before. One like it, I mean. In the dining room of the Yuletide Inn. My . . . someone at our table had a steak. He . . . I mean they . . . were given a knife just like this one."

"I know your father ate steak for dinner, Merry. So did a lot of other people, not only last night, but many other nights. Not to mention we found a kitchen drawer full of knives exactly like this one."

"I happened to notice," I lied, "that my dad's knife was on his empty plate when the table was cleared."

Was a liar supposed to look one directly in the eye or glance away? I couldn't remember. I had no doubt, however, that Simmonds knew. She gave me a long look.

"How well do you know Mark Grosse?"

I blinked at the sudden change of topic. "Not well at all. He's new in town. He's the chef at the hotel. I've only met him twice. He's nice."

"Your friend Vicky Casey seems to agree."

"What are you saying?"

"Nothing. I understand you were witness to an

altercation between Gord Olsen and Mark Grosse and Vicky Casey over sourcing bread and pastries for the hotel."

"Come on, Detective. Everyone in town must have told you Gord was talking about making changes to the hotel. Big changes. Not many people were happy about it, Kyle Lambert not withstanding."

"True. But some people stood to lose a lot more than others. Vicky Casey's business depended on that order."

"No, it doesn't. She can manage fine without it. It's a nice-to-have extra, that's all."

"Mark Grosse gave up a good job in New York City to work at the Yuletide. And then there's Grace Olsen herself. Furious at what her stepson was planning to do to her hotel."

"You can't go around accusing people like that," I said.

"Can't I?" she replied.

"Did you get any fingerprints off the knife?"

"No," she said. "It had been wiped clean. At this time of year a person wearing gloves goes unnoticed."

"What about the sprig of holly?"

Simmonds glanced around the room. "I notice you don't sell fresh flowers or greenery."

"Not my line. There's a florist who takes care of that."

She nodded. "There's no shortage of poinsettias, Christmas cactus, or holly in this town. Even the dispatch desk at the police station has a vase of red and white carnations and holly branches on it."

"That's Rudolph," I said.

"A length of holly appears to have been taken from one of the arrangements in the Yuletide Inn. It was snapped off and its broken end matches the piece found on Olsen's body."

"That proves the killer was in the hotel recently. Not much of a clue. Lots of people go to that hotel."

"As you say, a good many people pass through their doors. There's no security at the entrance, people are free to come and go as they like. As well as staff and guests, there are tourists having a look, families needing a restroom after skating on the pond, diners, tradesmen. But it does help narrow things down. I'd like to get the pair of earrings we were looking at earlier for my sister for Christmas. Can you put them aside for me? I'll come back tomorrow to pick them up."

"Why not now?"

"I never mix business with pleasure," she said. "And shopping is always a pleasure, isn't it, Merry?"

The moment the door closed behind Detective Simmonds I grabbed my phone and texted Vicky.

Home and Mattie first. I sure hope you have lots of wine.

Chapter 7

Mattie knew his way around Vicky's house, and the moment we were through the front door and I'd snapped his leash off, he made a beeline for the kitchen, where he inhaled the last of Sandbanks's dinner. Sandbanks was Vicky's ancient golden Lab. When I'd asked Vicky why she wasn't taking one of the unwanted Saint Bernard puppies, she explained that poor Sandbanks's old heart wouldn't be able to survive living with a rambunctious, enthusiastic, not to mention gigantic, new friend. Looking at the old dog now, who managed only to lift one eyelid and mumble a protest at the theft of his supper, made me realize Vicky had a point.

"Oops," Vicky said. "I forgot to pick up the bowl."

"Too late now," I said as Mattie sniffed in corners, hoping to come across some tidbit dropped and forgotten. I handed Vicky the bottle of white wine I'd grabbed from my own fridge, and she took two glasses out of the cupboard.

We carried our drinks into the living room. I curled up in the love seat, and Vicky flopped onto the couch.

We took a sip of wine, sighed with pleasure, and then said in unison, "How'd it go?"

We laughed. "Maybe we spend too much time together," Vicky said. "Next we'll be finishing each other's . . ."

"Sentences. We already do that."

"I'll talk first. It went dreadfully. Simmonds almost accused me straight out of killing Gord Olsen because he'd cut my business."

"Do you have an alibi?"

"Unfortunately, no. I told her I went to bed at seven, alone, read for a bit and had the light out by eight. Whereupon, I slept the night through. I don't think she believed me."

"Why wouldn't she?"

"What sort of single, thirty-year-old woman goes to bed at seven o'clock?"

"One who gets up at four, seven days a week to work twelve or more hours," I said.

"I told her that." Vicky held her wineglass up to the light and watched the liquid swirl around inside. "I'm worried more about Mark than me."

"Why?"

"Simmonds was asking all sorts of questions about him. Like, did I think he has a temper and what will he do if he's let go from Yuletide. One of the kitchen staff at the hotel told her about that scene the other morning when Gord threatened to void Mark's contract. I got the feeling she might have exaggerated the argument more than a little bit, wanting to make herself sound important." She sighed. "Mark called me first thing this morning. Asked me to play down the argument if I was asked about it. He sounded really worried."

"You don't think . . ."

"Of course I don't. But I don't like that Simmonds thinks he's a good murder suspect. First attractive eligible man I've met in ages." She tossed back the contents of her glass and reached for the bottle.

"They're centering their investigation on the inn." As she poured, I told Vicky about the holly taken from a meeting room, and the steak knife, probably stolen from the restaurant. I didn't add that the knife might have been taken directly from the kitchen.

"Who do you think did it, Merry?" Vicky asked.

I threw up my hands. "I have no idea. Who didn't want to kill Gord Olsen? He was a thoroughly unlikable man. He hadn't changed one whit since he was a horrid kid at school. He seemed to almost delight in rubbing our noses in the changes he wanted to make. If he'd simply gone quietly about it, we might not have even noticed until it was too late. All I know is who didn't kill him. My dad, you. Me."

"Grace?"

"Grace had motive, all right. But I saw her later, not long after we found Gord's body. Calm and composed, relaxing before going to bed. I'd say her shock when she heard the news was genuine. She didn't try to pretend to be mourning the guy, and wouldn't she think she had to do that if she'd killed him? I can't say the same for Irene, though. I don't know her well enough to judge. She was upset, but she seemed to be angry at Grace rather than grieving for her husband. What do you think?"

"I'm thinking the Muddites need some investigation."

"Why? Wouldn't they be pleased? The enemy of my enemy is my friend and all that?"

"Maybe they want the Mega-Mart for themselves. They don't have much of a downtown shopping area for it to destroy." She downed the last of her wine and put her glass firmly on the table. "Rain check on that pizza. Time for you to be going. I'll go in early, get the baking started, and leave Marjorie to open up. I'll pick you up at seven."

"Why?"

"We're going to Muddle Harbor."

"We were run out of that town so recently our tracks are barely dry. I suspect our pictures are still hanging on the wall at the post office."

"Seven o'clock. Sharp."

I groaned. "Suppose I say I don't wanna go?"

"Then I'll go by myself."

"I was afraid you'd say that."

For once Vicky was late. Punctuality is one of her most annoying features, at least to the chronically late me, and I'd decided to indicate my disapproval of this trip by being ready exactly on time.

But Mattie and I were waylaid by my landlady, Mrs. D'Angelo, the moment we rounded the corner of the house, and this time I couldn't pretend I was in a hurry to get someplace else.

Mrs. D'Angelo had recently bought a pouch and belt to carry her iPhone so she could be instantly reachable at any moment. Standing on the porch, with the contraption strapped to her waist over her dressing gown, and her feet shoved into high-heeled mules, I thought she looked like the tough widow who was standard in old Western movies. Instead of a six-gun, she had her weapon of choice close to hand: a smartphone.

"Merry Wilkinson," Mrs. D'Angelo demanded, "what is going on in this town? Annabelle Watson told me that her grandson, who works at the garage that services the police cars, says your father was arrested for murder! The very idea doesn't merit discussion." She went on to discuss it at much length. I told her that her information wasn't accurate, and she nodded sagely and said she never did put any store in gossip. For the briefest of moments I considered getting revenge on my worst enemy (my only enemy), Betty Thatcher, by telling Mrs. D'Angelo I'd seen Betty running away from the dead body wild-eyed and spattered with blood. Mrs. D'Angelo was the fastest draw in Upstate New York. She'd have that phone out and the news spread all over town in no time. But I couldn't do that even to Betty. Worse, I could imagine what Simmonds would have to say if she heard the false rumor had come from me.

At that moment Vicky pulled up and tooted the horn,

saving me from the evils of temptation. The last time Vicky and I visited Muddle Harbor she'd borrowed her great-aunt Matilda's ancient Mercury. Today she was driving the bakery's delivery van.

"Where are you two off to this early, Merry?" Mrs. D'Angelo asked.

"Vicky and I are eloping together," I said. "I'll send someone around for my things."

I jumped into the van and settled Mattie into my lap after he extended effusive, and very wet, greetings to Vicky. "We're not incognito today?"

"No point. Not after that incident the other day when you made such a scene."

"Me? I only wanted to eat my breakfast."

We drove out of Rudolph. The sun was rising, but it was hard to tell. Heavy gray clouds hung over the lake, wrapping everything in gloom. "It's supposed to hit thirty-three degrees tomorrow," Vicky said. "And then get even warmer."

"All our lovely snow," I said sadly.

"Not to mention the ice on the bay. Marjorie told me Kevin told her they're talking about making a skating rink in the park in case the lake's too soft. Can't have the little tourist kiddies falling in."

Mattie woofed in agreement.

Muddle Harbor isn't far from Rudolph, but it might as well be on another planet. They're struggling to keep their Main Street vibrant, but too many of the storefronts are boarded up. Those that are still hanging on had holiday decorations in the windows, but to my experienced eye they looked halfhearted, as though no one had sufficient energy to care anymore. There were few cars on the streets, and the occasional pedestrian had their back bent and their head buried into their collar. It might be gray and gloomy in Rudolph this morning, but in Muddle Harbor everything seemed grayer and gloomier. Then again, that might have been nothing more than my imagination working overtime.

We drove past the Muddle Harbor Café, the lone bright spot on that depressing street. Several cars were pulled up to the curb outside, and yellow light shone inside, giving the place a warm and inviting glow. The big front window was outlined with red and green lights and fake snow frosted the glass.

Vicky slid into a parking spot.

"I hope I can enjoy my breakfast this time," I said.

"That's why I brought you. As we can't be undercover anymore, we need an excuse to visit. Your desire for artery-clogging grease, factory-produced eggs, and industrial bread has to be satisfied."

"There are places like that in Rudolph, you know," I said. "The Elves' Lunch Box isn't exactly up for an award from the American Heart Association."

"Do they give awards to restaurants?"

"Not that I'm aware of. I am simply making a point."

"And an excellent point, I am sure. Mattie will have to stay in the van."

I struggled to get the dog off my lap and wiggle

myself out of my seat without letting him leap into the street. "I'll bring you a treat," I said, giving him a pat as I slammed the door. "A piece of bacon, perhaps."

"I won't let you poison that animal," Vicky said.

"He's a dog. He thinks cat poo is a delicacy."

We went into the café. The strong scent of frying bacon and sausages, warm toast slathered in runny butter, and fresh coffee filled the room. The place was busy this morning. A few old-timers lingered over their breakfasts, solving the problems of the world; high school–aged kids slouched in chairs, putting off the time when they had to leave, and young mothers chatted while babies squirmed on their laps.

The big round table in the center of the room was full. Six men, two of them in business suits, three in business casual, and one in overalls and steel-toed boots. Papers and iPads were spread on the table among the full coffee cups, empty plates, and used cutlery.

The waitress began gathering up their dirty dishes. "Be with you in a sec," she called to us over her shoulder. Then she turned and saw us. "Oh. It's you two," she said. The men glanced up at the tone of her voice.

Randy Baumgartner, mayor of Muddle Harbor, scowled at the sight of us. I gave him a cheerful wave. He did not return the greeting.

"We're back," Vicky said. She headed straight for the long counter and dropped into a red vinyl stool. I could do nothing but follow. The café was decorated like a '50s-style diner. I figured it wasn't so much retro chic as the fact that the decor had never changed as the decades passed. But it was clean and the coffee was strong and hot. The laminated menu was tucked between the salt and pepper shakers and the napkin dispenser. I pulled it out and opened it to the page of breakfast specials.

"I'm surprised you two would show your faces here again." The waitress wiped her hands on her apron before placing them on her ample hips and glaring at us. Her eyes were like shards of ice.

"My friend insisted we come," Vicky said.

"I did? I mean, I did. I . . . had to come here for breakfast again. Janice, isn't it?"

The ice in her eyes melted fractionally. "Yes."

"It was sooooo good. I couldn't resist. I own a shop in Rudolph. The other day some of my customers asked where the best breakfast place was, and I sent them here. Did they come? Middle-aged couple?" I had done no such thing. There were plenty of restaurants and cafés in Rudolph to suit all tastes and price ranges. Whenever a customer asked me for a good place to eat, I sent them to Victoria's Bake Shoppe or the Elves' Lunch Box for lunch or breakfast, to the Hearthside if they wanted a casual dinner, or to A Touch of Holly across the street from me for something fancier. If they looked to be well-heeled or just wanting a special night out, I suggested the Yuletide.

Janice wasn't about to say my customers hadn't shown up. "Yes, I think they did."

"That's great. I believe in helping everyone out. A rising tide lifts all boats, right?"

"Right. Let me grab the coffeepot while you decide." She bustled away.

"You don't have to go that far overboard," Vicky said under her breath.

I gave her a smile. "Your idea."

Janice came back with the pot. As she poured, I said, "I don't even have to look at the menu. I can't remember when I had better hash browns."

"That's because you never eat them," Vicky mumbled into her coffee.

"I'll have the poached eggs, soft, with bacon, hash browns, and wheat toast."

Janice laboriously wrote all that down. She turned to Vicky, pencil poised. "You?"

Vicky suppressed a shudder. "The same. But hold the toast. Oh, and I'll have sausage instead of bacon. And fried eggs, not poached. Sunny-side up. I like my hash browns really well done."

"Otherwise," I said, "exactly the same." I swung around on my stool. In addition to the mayor, I recognized some of the other men at the big table. Janice's brother, John, a real estate agent, was watching us. I gave him a nod. He nodded back. The group included a tall African American and a younger white guy. I'd seen those two at the Yuletide Inn. Checking out the garden property with Gord. They were from Mega-Mart.

I swung my stool back around. I jerked my head at the table behind us and gave Vicky a slight nod. We'd gotten the information we came for.

"Will you look at the time," Vicky said. "Gotta run."

"I haven't eaten yet."

"No time." She slid off her stool.

"Sit down," I hissed. "I want my breakfast. You brought me all this way. This time you can pick up the check."

She harrumphed, but dropped back onto the stool. Janice placed two heaping platters in front of us. I sprayed ketchup all over my potatoes and dug in. I pretended not to notice as Vicky vacuumed up her food with as much enthusiasm as Mattie at Sandbanks's bowl.

"Would you like a piece of my toast?" I said sweetly.

"No," she grunted around a mouthful of sausage and eggs.

Janice topped up the coffee cups. "I hear you've had more trouble over in Rudolph," she said, barely able to control the glee in her voice.

"Comes with being so popular and prosperous, I guess," Vicky said.

Janice glanced at her brother and his companions. "Rudolph's misfortune might be Muddle Harbor's gain."

"What do you know," Vicky said. "I was thinking the exact same thing." She put cash on the counter to pay for the breakfasts. Janice reminded me to keep recommending the café to my customers.

"I hope you'll say something nice about me at my funeral," Vicky said once we were back on the sidewalk.

I carried a take-out bag with a rasher of bacon and a hunk of sausage I'd had to guilt Vicky into leaving for Mattie. "What do you mean?"

"I can feel my arteries clogging even as we speak. The things I do for you."

"You enjoyed it, didn't you?"

She sniffed and went to the van without saying a word.

Mattie appreciated his second breakfast.

Chapter 8

On the drive back to Rudolph, Vicky and I discussed what to do next. As I was in the clear for the murder of Gord Olsen (unless, Vicky pointed out, Simmonds decided my mom, Russ, Alan, and I were in on it together) I'd contact Simmonds to tell her what we learned.

Vicky dropped Mattie and me at home. I dashed around the side of the house and pretended not to hear the front door open and Mrs. D'Angelo shout, "Merry, shouldn't you be at the shop?"

Not for the first time, I thought it might be a good idea to cut a hole in the back fence so I could get in and out without being interrogated about my activities.

The second floor of Mrs. D'Angelo's stately Victorian mansion was divided into two apartments, and I ran into my neighbors, Steve and Wendy, coming down the stairs. Mattie greeted them with his usual excess of enthusiasm while Tina, their adorable baby, held her pudgy little arms out to me.

"How are the plans going for Saturday?" I asked.

Wendy's face creased into a frown. She worked at the town offices and had a big hand in planning the children's party weekend. "I won't pretend we're not worried, Merry. Temperatures are supposed to rise all week. If that happens, by Saturday the ice on the lake will be soft and the snow in the park nothing but slush and mud."

"Kids won't care," I said. "Not as long as Santa's there."

"Parents might care," Steve said, "if we get the freezing rain they're calling for."

"We can only hope it doesn't come to that," Wendy said.

"The weather forecast has been known to be wrong on occasion," I, ever the optimist, pointed out.

"Have a good day," Wendy said.

"You, too. Bye!" I waved to Tina, and she buried her head in her father's shoulder with a giggle.

My dad arrived at Mrs. Claus's Treasures shortly after opening. "Weather's not looking good," he said.

"We'll manage—we always do."

He gave me a smile. "That's true." He wandered through the shop, moving this, rearranging that.

"Did you hear anything more from the police?" I said.

"No."

"That's good, then."

"Jack was released from the hospital yesterday. Your mom and I went with Grace to get him and bring him home. He looked, I have to say, like death warmed over. Which, come to think of it, he is."

"How'd he take the death of Gord?"

"Hard. As could be expected. He wanted to be driven directly to the morgue, but Grace put her foot down and said he had to rest first."

"How'd he take that?"

"He didn't argue, if that's what you're asking. His brush with mortality has taken a lot out of him. He's listless, uninterested in everything. Perhaps he's the sort of man who can only fight one battle at a time."

The chimes above the door tinkled and I turned, plastering on my welcoming smile. I let the smile die when I saw who it was. Betty Thatcher.

"Noel. I thought that was your car outside. How's Jack? Do you have any word?"

"He's doing well, Betty," Dad said. "He was released from the hospital last night."

"Oh, that is good news." She smiled. I hadn't known she could do that. "He'll be up and about and back to running that hotel in no time."

"I'm sure of it," Dad said.

Betty continued smiling at him. Then she turned to me, and her smile died as quickly as mine had. "I'd better get back to my own business. I've been so busy all day, I can only take a second to stand and chat. Unlike some people."

"Clark not helping out today?" I said.

"He didn't want to take a day off, but I insisted. He's been working so hard, and we'll be so busy with the children's weekend coming up." She glanced around my shop. "I got some special toys in, Merry. Too bad you didn't think of doing that."

I ground my teeth as the chimes sounded her out. Dad laughed.

"Miserable bat," I said. "I'm surprised she cares about Jack."

"Don't be too hard on Betty, honeybunch. She hasn't always had an easy time of it. Natural enough that she's worried about Jack. We Rudolphers stick together, you know. Particularly us old-timers. You need more tree decorations on this table."

"No, I don't. The table looks fine. If you remember, we're pushing children's things this week." I'd arranged the big table in the center of the room, the one that caught people's attention the minute they came into the shop, with toys as well as whimsical decorations of the sort that would be featured on the children's table at Christmas dinner or in guest rooms for visiting families.

Dad gathered up the group of nine reindeer pulling a sleigh piled high with miniature gift-wrapped boxes and put them on a side counter. "Where are the boxes of tree ornaments?"

There was never any point in arguing with my dad. Santa knows best. Or he thinks he does. I pointed. "In the room on the right."

"They need to be front and center." He went to one of the alcoves and emerged weighted down with boxes of glass balls, strings of tiny lights, and brightly painted bells. He piled the boxes on the center table.

"Dad! That looks perfectly awful. I can't have a bunch of boxes as the main display."

"The pictures on the boxes show what's inside."

"That's not good enough. People want to pick things up, hold them. That helps them choose."

"They can hold the decorations to their heart's content once they've got them home," he said. "Now, I have to be going. We're meeting to discuss plans if it rains on Saturday, as is predicted."

"That'll cut down the number of attendees," I said. "Nothing like icy rain dripping down the back of your neck to put you off outdoor fun. What are you getting in that's special for Saturday?"

"Extra toys. I have some sets of reindeer pulling Santa's sleigh to decorate the children's dinner table. I hope my customers can find them wherever you put them."

"I mean, what are you planning to serve the shoppers?"

"Nothing. I don't hand out food and drink."

"I'd suggest hot cider," Dad said. "Maybe some cookies. Treats that smell of ginger and cinnamon. If the weather is bad you'll need something to lure customers in. I'll call Vicky now and put in an order for gingerbread cookies."

Dad left, talking into his phone. I shook my head. I contemplated putting the boxes of decorations back in the alcove. But if I did that, Dad would be offended next time he came in.

Sometimes I'm too nice for my own good.

A few customers wandered in and out of the shop. I sold one woman a wreath brooch to wear to a holiday party, and another picked up some table linens as hostess gifts, but that was pretty much it for the morning. Retail, particularly around Christmas and for Christmas goods, is highly dependent on the weather. I glanced out the window. Thick gray clouds hung overhead and the piles of once-lovely fluffy white snow were turning dark and gritty.

Nothing I could do about that.

At noon, I flipped the sign on the door to "Closed." I'd been wanting to talk to Detective Simmonds all morning, but I couldn't chance a customer coming into the shop when I was in the middle of a call with the police.

I told Siri, the personal assistant who lives in my phone and exists only to do what I command, to call Diane Simmonds. It still seems somewhat *Star Trek*kie to be giving orders into a little box, but it worked and the detective answered immediately.

"It's . . . uh . . . me. Merry Wilkinson," I said.

"Yes?"

Not one for small talk, our Detective Simmonds. "I learned something this morning that might be important in your investigation. I want to talk to you about it. I'm closed for lunch now, so I could come around to the station if you're in?"

"No need," she said. "I am, as it happens, just down

the street. I was going to pick up something to eat but I can come to your shop first. I'll be right there."

She wasn't kidding about being just down the street. She was rapping at the door in the time it took me to hop off the stool.

"What's up?" she said the minute she was inside.

"Have you ever been to Muddle Harbor?"

"The next town over? No. Should I?"

"Not if you're looking for a pleasant evening out, no. But you should pay a call on them. The Muddle Harbor folks don't like Rudolph. They lost no time in sitting down with the Mega-Mart people once Gord was dead and the inn property was no longer up for sale."

"How do you know this?"

"Vicky Casey and I went to Muddle Harbor this morning."

"Why?"

"To have breakfast. We like to get out of Rudolph sometimes. Away from places where we're constantly interrupted by people in search of the latest gossip."

Simmonds cocked her head to one side. I'd intended simply to tell her what we'd observed, but here I was already being questioned about my motives and lying in response. I heroically struggled on. "Anyway, we just happened to be at the Muddle Harbor Café for breakfast, and there they were, sitting around a table covered in blueprints and maps and papers. The Mega-Mart guys with the mayor and a real estate agent. The Muddites were looking mighty pleased with themselves, I might add."

"And . . ."

"And? Don't you think that's suspicious? I do. It's totally a motive for the murder of Gord Olsen. Grace and Jack will never sell the garden property, so the deal for a Mega-Mart is dead. The people of Muddle Harbor let no time pass before jumping in and attempting to lure Mega-Mart to their town. You need to ask yourself *cui bono*. Who benefits from the death of Gord Olsen? The town of Muddle Harbor, obviously."

"Believe it or not, Merry, I have been asking *cui bono*. I was taught to do that in detective school on day one."

"I didn't mean . . ."

"Why are you so quick to assume Jack won't sell the property? Is it only because you and your friends don't want him to? The man has been seriously ill. Perhaps he'll decide it's time to retire. As for the people from Mega-Mart, businessmen of my acquaintance check out a lot of options before deciding to locate their property in this town or that one."

"I know that but . . ."

"Merry, I appreciate that you're trying to help. Although I have to wonder if you're intent on helping the police or your friends. Please stop. Now, if you don't have any other information for me, I'll go and get my lunch."

"If you want those earrings, you should buy them today. That's the last pair I have in stock and they're popular." As long as I was lying, I might as well keep it up.

"Okay," she said. She headed for the jewelry display, but before she could reach it, her eye was caught by the arrangement on the center table. She studied the boxes of ornaments and picked one up. Then another. "I haven't even had time . . ." she said under her breath. Then, "I'll take all of these. One box of each."

"What?"

"A fresh start. A new home needs a new tree, don't you agree, Merry? You'd think it would be hard to forget that Christmas is coming in Christmas Town, but I seem to have been able to do that. My daughter's ten. If I can get home in time tonight, we should go out and get our tree. What's the best place for real trees?"

"The fire hall raises funds by selling them," I said. "As well as wreaths and greenery. They get everything fresh from Norman Casey's tree farm."

"A relative of Vicky Casey?"

"Her uncle. Pretty much everyone in Rudolph is related in some way or another to the Caseys."

"I'll remember that. I don't think one box of these will be enough. Not if we get a big tree. Do you have more?"

"Yes."

"Three boxes of each, then. And four of the lights."

I ran into the storage room and found the desired items. I carried them out and rang up the purchases. All the decorations, as well as the earrings, came to a tidy sum. Simmonds handed me her credit card. "Thanks, Merry. My ex-husband broke every single ornament in our house when I kicked him out."

"Oh," I said.

"I had some beautiful Christmas things. My grandmother's ornaments; the tea set her mother had brought from England."

"That's terrible," I said.

"They were lovely, but they were only things and can be replaced. As I'm doing right now. The only thing that matters is that I have Charlotte, my daughter. I can now start a collection for her to pass on to her children one day."

I put the boxes into paper bags marked with the Mrs. Claus's Treasures logo, and Simmonds gathered them in both hands. "As pleasant as it's been shopping here, I have to remind you once again, Merry, to keep your nose where it belongs." She gave me a long look. "This is a small town. Even people who aren't related know each other well. But that will not stop me from doing my job to the best of my ability."

I had absolutely no doubt about that.

After that hearty breakfast, I didn't need much for lunch, so I popped into the Cranberry Coffee Bar for a latte and a take-out salad, which I ate standing at the counter while waiting for more eager customers to knock down my doors. They did not, and I finished my lunch in peace. I then set about rearranging the displays.

Now that all the tree ornaments had been scooped off the main table, I put back the children's things. I *knew* my dad wasn't Santa Claus. But sometimes I did wonder.

I was stepping back to admire my handiwork when my phone buzzed. Mom.

"Merry! The most dreadful thing has happened."

I would guess people in most families upon hearing those words would immediately assume the worst: a tragedy involving their siblings, perhaps. But my mom could be almost as dramatic over an unraveling hem as a death in the family.

"What now?" I said, wondering if perhaps the porcelain Mr. and Mrs. Claus dolls would look better in the front window than the toy soldiers I had there now.

"Your father has been arrested!"

That got my attention, and all thought of painted dolls fled. "Are you sure? Calm down, Mom. Tell me what happened."

"I had a call from Tom Casey." Vicky's dad was a lawyer. "Noel used his one phone call to call Tom. He's gone down to the police station. Merry, what is happening?"

"I don't know, Mom. Detective Simmonds was in here a short while ago." Surely she couldn't be that cold, to buy my ornaments and tell me about vengeful ex-husbands and great-grandmother's tea sets while she was planning to arrest my own father as soon as she finished her lunch. "She didn't say anything about Dad."

"Go to the police station and find out what's happening. I have a class arriving in ten minutes. We have to prepare for Saturday's concert."

"Jackie's not working today. I can't just close the store."

"Of course you can. If this isn't a family emergency, I don't know what is."

"Okay, Mom. I'll do what I can."

By the time I hung up, my voice mailbox was already full.

Russ Durham telling me the police had arrived at the council chambers and ordered Noel to come with them.

A councillor with the same story as Russ.

A woman who worked at the library saying she was looking out the back window and had seen my dad being escorted out of the town offices and into the police station.

Even Mrs. D'Angelo chimed in, apparently unable to wait until I got home to start digging for dirt.

I locked the shop door behind me and galloped the short distance down the street to the complex containing the library, town offices, and police station.

I needn't have bothered hurrying as I wasn't allowed to talk to my dad or Mr. Casey. Sue-Anne Morrow and Ralph Dickerson, the town's budget chief, came running in, and they were also told to take a chair and wait.

"What on earth happened?" I said.

"We were finishing our planning meeting for Saturday," Sue-Anne said, "when two uniformed officers came into the room. They said Noel was to come with them. Now."

"Did they actually arrest him? Like read him his rights or something?"

"I don't know," Sue-Anne said. "I was so upset. It was quite dreadful."

"No," Ralph said. "They didn't."

"That's good, then," I said.

"Good!" Sue-Anne shrieked. "Our town's Santa Claus has been dragged off to the police station like a common criminal and you think that's *good*."

"Keep your voice down, Sue-Anne," Ralph said.

"Don't you tell me to keep my voice down, Ralph Dickerson," she snapped back. Although she did stop shrieking. "We do not need this publicity, not days before the children's party weekend."

"We don't need the publicity at any time," he said. "But we have it."

"The children's party makes it worse," Sue-Anne said. "Noel cannot be allowed to play Santa this weekend."

"Hey," I said. "That's not fair. What about innocent until proven guilty?"

She turned on me. "I am not talking legally, but morally. We can't ask visitors to our town to put their children on the knee of a man accused of murder!"

"My father has not been accused of murder or anything else." I wasn't sure who I was trying to convince more, myself or Sue-Anne. "They simply had a few more questions, and . . . well, as the police station is right next to town hall they didn't bother to phone and ask him to come on in for a little chat."

Even Ralph looked dubious at my logic. "Then why," he said, "is Tom Casey here?"

"Why indeed." Sue-Anne threw me a smirk before turning and heading for the door. The three-inch heels on her black leather boots rapped on the muddy linoleum floor. "You can stand around all day, Ralph, waiting for something to happen, but the voters of this town expect me to be proactive. I'm going back to the office to order them to begin the search for a new Santa."

"You can't . . ." I said.

The door slammed shut behind her. I looked at Ralph. He raised his bushy eyebrows and gave me a shrug. Ralph was a good money manager, my dad always said, but when it came to making a decision he'd go whichever way the wind blew. In a hurricane, such as the one that seemed to be descending on our town at this very moment, Ralph was totally useless. "Now that you're here, Merry," he said, scurrying for the door, "I have to get back to work. Let us know what . . . uh . . . happens."

I dropped into the plastic chair welded to the floor. Behind the Plexiglas wall the dispatcher pretended not to be watching me. In a nod to the season, a vase of red and white chrysanthemums, a few days past their prime, and seasonal greenery sat on her desk. I got up again and rapped on the window. She struggled to her feet, making sure I knew she was doing me an enormous favor, and came to the counter. "Yes?"

"Can you please tell my dad and Mr. Casey that I'm here?"

"Your name?" she said.

"What do you mean, my name? Nancy, you know my name as well as yours."

"Name?" she repeated.

I almost said "Mrs. Claus," but I bit my tongue. Nancy was not smiling. In fact, she was not looking at all like the woman who was a regular patron of my shop and whose daughter had been taking vocal lessons from my mom for ten years or more. Nancy used to be a receptionist at the hospital, and I knew she'd only been working here for a short while. She'd probably been told not to act friendly with her neighbors and had taken those instructions to heart.

"I am Merry—spelled M-e-r-r-y—Wilkinson—and my father is named Noel, and he will be with Detective Simmonds."

"When the detective's free," Nancy said, "I'll pass on your message." She scurried back to her console. I returned to my plastic chair. We pointedly avoided looking at each other from then on.

I pulled out my phone and, ignoring a once-again full voice mailbox, checked Twitter, searching for any mention of Rudolph. I found only the usual pre-Christmas excitement and our town's tourist information. That was good. The people over in Muddle Harbor had been known to spread bad news coming out of Rudolph far and wide, in the mistaken impression that bad news for us was good news for them. What the people of Muddle Harbor failed to understand was that Rudolph was popular because it was Christmas Town. If people didn't bring their kids to meet Santa and his elves, to shop in our themed stores, or stay in our B&Bs and inns, they weren't going to head ten miles down the road to a street of boarded-up shops and run-down motels, where the only decent restaurant served up oversized platters of eggs and bacon all day.

I debated how long I could sit here twiddling my

thumbs and tapping my toes. I did have a business to run. I tried to call Jackie to ask her to go into the shop, but got no answer. Mom's class would be over soon and she could come down, but I didn't want to ask her. She'd never learned when not to act as though she was projecting high drama to the farther reaches of the upper balcony.

I hadn't brought a book and there were no magazines laid out for my enjoyment. I assumed that was probably because they didn't exactly want people to make themselves comfortable at a police station.

My dilemma was resolved when I heard voices and footsteps coming down the hall. I leapt to my feet at the sight of my dad with John Casey. Detective Simmonds walked beside them. Simmonds and Mr. Casey's faces were set into professional giving-nothing-away expressions, but Dad smiled broadly when he saw me.

"Merry," he said as the door swung open to let them out. "You didn't need to come down and wait for me."

My eyes flicked to Simmonds. She remained in the inner room, standing beside the dispatch desk. She did not smile. She was dressed in a budget-priced gray trouser suit and white blouse. Her jacket was open and I could see the weapon at her hip and the badge pinned to her belt. Hard to believe this was the same woman who had recently gushed over Christmas tree ornaments and planned to take her daughter out to get their tree tonight.

"Let's go," Mr. Casey said.

Dad turned around. He waved to the watching

women. Nancy half lifted her arm to return the greeting, but realized she wasn't supposed to do that. She fluffed her hair instead. Simmonds stood still, her face empty of expression.

We walked outside into a sharp, biting wind. I wrapped my scarf around my neck and pulled on my gloves.

"Thanks for coming down, John," Dad said. "We'll talk later. I guess I've missed the end of the meeting, but I need to pop in and see what, if anything, has been decided in case the weather gets worse."

"The weather," Mr. Casey said, "will wait. Noel, we have to talk."

"About what?" Dad said.

"About what!" I yelled. A couple of cops crossing the parking lot glanced at us. Sometimes I do take after my mother, as much as I try to avoid it. "You've been arrested for murder, for goodness' sake."

"Not arrested," Mr. Casey said. "Brought in for questioning."

Dad waved his hand. "Nothing to worry about, honeybunch. They wanted my help with their inquiries."

I groaned.

Mr. Casey kept his voice low, but every word was crisp and concise. "Mr. Olsen was killed with a steak knife matching the ones used in the restaurant at the Yuletide Inn. The inn reports they are one short. It came to Detective Simmonds's attention that Noel ate a steak that night."

"I bet a lot of people had steak," I said. "That night

and many other nights. I also bet they don't lock the cutlery in a safe. They're trying to intimidate you, Dad. Don't let them."

"My point exactly." The edges of Mr. Casey's mouth turned up slightly. "You should consider going into law, Merry." It was no secret he had wanted Vicky to follow him into a legal career, and he'd been highly disappointed when she chose her mother's path instead and became a baker.

"I know it's your job, Tom," Dad said. "But I'm glad you came down. It was good of you. There's no need to get too worked up. I'm happy to help the police."

"Noel, we are going to my office to discuss this," Mr. Casey said. "Now. Simmonds isn't playing around. You were heard to threaten Gord Olsen."

Dad shrugged. "I was angry at him. People say things all the time they don't mean." He looked at me. "I should call Aline. She might have heard something about this and got concerned. You know your mother."

"I think," I said, "that qualifies as the understatement of the year. You go with Mr. Casey. I'll call Mom."

Dad glanced toward the town hall. People were standing at the windows watching us. Dad smiled and waved. I groaned, and Mr. Casey shook his head.

We walked down the passageway between the library and a row of shops to Jingle Bell Lane. Dad and Mr. Casey turned right and I went left, heading back to work. It might have been my imagination, but it seemed as if every group of people I passed stopped talking when I approached, and an inordinate number of shop owners had nothing better to do than peer out their windows to watch me go by.

I stood in the doorway of Mrs. Claus's for a moment, taking it all in. The lights on the Douglas fir glowed, the jewelry displays sparkled, the toys waited to be played with, and the linens and dishes were ready to be part of someone's holiday feast. The row of two-foot-tall wooden nutcrackers stood at attention behind the cash register and the cheeks of the porcelain Mr. and Mrs. Clauses were ruddy and welcoming.

My shop. I loved it and everything in it so much. All was as I'd left it, but while I'd been out the Christmas magic seemed to have faded. Some of the shine was gone.

If my dad couldn't be Santa, it would just about kill him.

Never mind if he was arrested for murder.

I called my mom, relieved when it went to voice mail. Easier to leave a message than to try to explain. I assured her that Dad had not been arrested, but simply brought in because the police had some further questions. Very routine. I said nothing about Sue-Anne's threat to find a new Santa Claus. I then went into the back to get rid of my coat and boots and splash some water on my face. The bells over the door chimed; I pasted on my professional smile and went out to greet customers.

I heard a hammering on the door as I was going through the shop's closing-up routine. I looked up to see Alan

Anderson balancing the weight of a large box. I hurried to let him in and help him put it on the counter.

"The trains you asked for," he said.

"Great, thanks. They're my most popular children's item, and I'm expecting them to do well over the weekend."

"If there is a kids' weekend," he said.

I was about to make some glib comment about rain not getting Rudolph down, when I read the look on his face. "What have you heard?"

"The town sent out an e-mail, asking someone to step into Noel's, and I quote, 'big shoes,' for the weekend."

"Did the message say why?"

"It didn't have to. Everyone heard your dad's being questioned about the death of Gord Olsen, Merry."

"Surely, they don't believe . . ."

He lifted one hand. "Not a single soul gives the idea of your dad as a brutal murderer a moment's serious thought. But, as we all know, impressions are everything. If word gets out that Rudolph's own Santa was arrested for murder and released for lack of evidence . . ."

"He was not arrested. He was simply questioned." I felt my blood beginning to boil.

"I know that, Merry. I'm not arguing with you."

"That means nothing. I was questioned," I said. "You were questioned, right?"

"Yes, I was. But I was not marched out of the council offices with two uniformed cops on either side of me. Noel was."

I put my elbows on the counter and my head into my hands. "This is such a mess."

He touched my back. I felt the delicious warmth of his fingers through my sweater. Then he abruptly pulled his hand away. He cleared his throat and his footsteps crossed the floor.

"Has anyone volunteered for this supposedly available Santa Claus gig?" I asked.

"Not that I heard." He picked up one of his nutcracker soldiers and turned it over. Alan's hands were those of a man who used them to make his living. He had calluses on his thumbs, the nails were short and torn, a deep scar marked the back of his right hand, and a fresh but healing cut crossed the pad of the left thumb. A small bit of the right index finger, so tiny it was almost unnoticeable unless you looked, was missing. The result, he told me, of an inattentive moment at the circular saw when he was first learning his trade. From then on, he made sure that when he was working, he never allowed himself to get distracted.

"I'd expect the council to show some support for Dad, after all he's done for this town over the years. Instead, they've been mighty quick to throw him under the bus."

"Sue-Anne's doing, I expect." Alan carefully placed the soldier back among his fellows. "If anyone does take over as Santa, I won't be acting as his toymaker. This town needs to stand behind Noel, even if we do lose a few visitors on the weekend." Alan left my shop without another word. My back still burned from his touch.

I locked up and went home, hoping for a nice, quiet evening.

But it was not to be. Mrs. D'Angelo was at her post

in her front window, and by the time I turned into our yard, she was waiting on the porch. I marched resolutely past her, refusing to make eye contact. "Merry!" she cried after me, her voice carrying in the chilly air. "I want you to know that I believe the police have arrested the wrong man. Noel Wilkinson is not a killer." At that precise moment it seemed as though half of Rudolph was walking past our house.

At least Mattie hadn't heard my dad was under suspicion for murder. He leapt joyfully out of his crate the moment I opened it and covered my face with kisses. Kisses, along with a healthy dose of slobber. I decided not to take him for a walk tonight—I was not in the mood for encountering curious but well-meaning townsfolk. Instead I found a tennis ball and we played catch in the backyard. Mattie bounded through the drifts, dug paths in the snow with his nose, and barked in delight as he tried to bite flakes shaken loose from the trees.

I was beginning to feel a great deal better by the time I called him to come in.

"That looks like fun," said a voice behind me. I turned and smiled at Wendy, my neighbor.

"A dog's life," I said, giving her a grin. She had Tina balanced on one hip. At least I think it was Tina. About all I could see was a yellow snowsuit, yellow boots, waving mittens, and the tip of a tiny pink nose sticking out of the hood. Mattie ran over to investigate, and Wendy leaned forward so the baby could greet him.

"I heard about your dad," she said.

I groaned. "Didn't everyone?"

"You know they're trying to find a new Santa for the weekend?"

"Are they having any luck?"

"The number they gave out for potential Santas to call to apply is mine. I haven't had one call. Not yet."

"That's good."

Wendy gave me an encouraging smile while her daughter struggled to be put down. "I'm sure it'll all work out fine."

"I'm disappointed in the council. They might as well have hung a sign on the front doors saying they think Dad's guilty. It's a betrayal. Pure and simple."

"Not the council, Merry. This is Sue-Anne's doing, and hers alone. I'm telling you this in strict confidence. There was a full-blown screaming match going on behind her office door this afternoon. Several of the councillors and some of the senior staff were telling her she was making a mistake. She wouldn't listen. Unfortunately, she'd gotten to Ralph first, and he had approved the expense to hire a new Santa—no one's likely to do it for free like your dad does—and she'd authorized the call for applications. The matter, according to her, was settled."

"Is anyone going to try to persuade Ralph to change his mind?"

"Conveniently, Ralph suddenly fell ill and had to rush home. His wife says he's in bed and not able to take calls." She chuckled. "You can probably forget about this being confidential information. Everyone in the building heard the argument, it was hard not to, and it'll be all over town soon." As we talked, Tina struggled mightily to get out of her mother's grip, encouraged by Mattie, barking at her to come down and play. "Time to get this one upstairs and supper on," Tina said. "I'll let you know what happens tomorrow, Merry."

"Thanks. I'd appreciate that."

They went inside, and Mattie and I followed. For once I didn't have to struggle to get the dog into the house. He had soon learned that where Tina went, little morsels of food sometimes dropped.

I put my phone on the kitchen counter and pulled off all my outerwear. Then I fed Mattie and dug through the fridge for something to make for myself. I pulled out a microwavable pizza. What can I say? I'm not famous for my culinary skills. The phone squatted on the counter like the Grinch in his lair the night before Christmas.

I did not want to call my parents.

I tore the wrapping off the pizza and put it in the microwave. I set the timer. I should probably have made something healthy, like a salad, to go with it, but I didn't have the energy.

I glanced at the phone.

I did not want to call my parents.

I called my parents.

"Hi, Mom. Just checking in to see if you and Dad are okay."

Mom let out a long sigh. I could sometimes tell the difference between when she was being theatrical and when she was genuinely upset. This sounded like an upset sigh. "Your father came home a while ago. He's in his study reading. He says he doesn't want to be disturbed."

"Has he . . . uh . . . heard what's going on at the council?"

"If you mean that they're looking for another Santa"—she bit off the words—"we have heard. I wanted to storm down there and give those ungrateful people a piece of my mind, but your father asked me not to."

"How's Dad taking it?"

"Let's say that in all the years of our marriage, I can count on the fingers of one hand the number of times he has told me he does not want to be disturbed."

"Not well, then. You can tell Dad reliable sources say this was Sue-Anne's idea and she went against the objections of most of the councillors."

"He knows that, dear. People have been calling with their support all afternoon."

Despite how I was feeling, I smiled inside. Good for the people of Rudolph. Most of them, anyway.

"Today's Tuesday," Mom said. "I'll have to decide soon if I'm going to cancel the concert in order to give my students and their parents sufficient notice."

"What concert?"

"Saturday afternoon, of course. My children's classes are scheduled to perform Christmas carols at the bandstand. My students have worked hard preparing for this, but I won't put in an appearance if the town continues to treat your father this way."

"You might lose some students, Mom."

"So be it."

"Why don't you and Dad go away for a few days? You haven't been to the city in December in years, not since Dad really got going with the whole Christmas Town thing. Remember how much you used to love Christmas in New York?"

"I suggested that, dear. Detective Simmonds told your father he was not to leave town."

"Oh," I said. That didn't sound good. "Give dad a kiss for me. Tell him if he needs anything, I'm here."

"Thank you, dear. I'm going around to the inn in the morning to meet Grace for breakfast. Why don't you join us?"

"I don't think . . ." I began.

"I'd like your support, Merry. I'm quite likely to haul off and punch someone in the face if they dare ask me about your father being arrested."

I pushed aside the image of my cape-clad Mom being clapped in handcuffs for assault and hauled off to jail and pulled up a mental image of the store calendar instead. Jackie was scheduled to open tomorrow. "Sure, Mom. I'll pick you up."

"Thank you, dear. Good night."

The microwave beeped to tell me dinner was ready. I pulled the unappetizing mess out. I plopped it onto a plate and tossed the plate onto the kitchen table. When

I'm having dinner at home alone I usually like to go online and catch up on the latest news while I eat. Today I simply didn't want to know what was going on in the world. At least not in the small corner of the world that was Rudolph, New York.

Mattie's ears stood up; he jumped to his feet and barked.

A second later the doorbell rang.

I pushed aside my meal and trudged downstairs to answer the door. Russ Durham stood there, his head and shoulders dotted with freshly fallen snow. Before he could offer greetings, Mattie hit him full in the chest. Russ staggered backward with an *oooofff* as a rush of air exited his lungs. My arm shot out and I grabbed him. When I was sure my visitor wasn't going to end up flat on his back with a dog on top of him, I turned to Mattie and reminded him that we didn't jump on our friends. To my considerable surprise he stopped jumping, although every muscle in his body quivered with barely controlled excitement.

"I'm glad someone's happy to see me," Russ said, dusting himself off.

"Sorry about that. He's young."

Russ gave Mattie a hearty pat on the head. Thinking all was now okay, Mattie leapt, but this time Russ was ready for him and kept his footing. I chastised the dog again.

"I hope you don't mind my dropping in," Russ said, "but I have some news I thought you'd be interested in."

For a brief moment, my hopes soared. If I was really lucky the police would have made an arrest.

A look at Russ's face told me I was not likely to be really lucky.

"Come on in," I said. I led the way upstairs, as Mattie did his best to twist Russ's legs into knots. Russ glanced around the apartment. My place looked like a playground. Chew toys and the remains of stuffed animals littered the floor. Colorful bungee cords dangled from the ceiling with balls attached. The rugs were rolled up and anything resembling a fragile item had been stuffed onto a high shelf. I'd been so concerned about puppy-proofing the house and so busy at the shop I hadn't even decorated my own home for Christmas. My beloved things were still packed away in moving boxes.

Russ saw the pizza laid out on the kitchen table. "I'm sorry, looks like I've interrupted your dinner."

"Not a problem," I said. "It's scarcely worth eating. Would you like a drink?"

"A beer would be nice, if you have one," he said.

"Be right back." I went to the fridge, got a beer for Russ, and poured myself a glass of white wine. When I turned, he was standing at the kitchen counter, opening my iPad. "Might as well show you."

"Should I be worried?" I asked. I was worried. Russ was not smiling his usual friendly, borderline flirty smile.

He sighed. "Our friends over in Muddle Harbor didn't wait long to get the word out. Have a look at the online paper."

We took the drinks and the iPad into the living room

and took seats around the coffee table. I typed in the URL for the *Muddle Harbor Chronicle*. The web page had been updated with the banner "Breaking News" and more exclamation marks than belonged in a respectable newspaper. Then again, the *Chronicle* was not a respectable newspaper. I read with increasing horror. A photograph of my dad, dressed in full Santa gear, was front and center. The headline read "Rudolph's Wilkinson Questioned Second Time in Brutal Murder."

"Oh dear," I said.

"Oh dear, indeed," Russ said.

"I suppose this will be on the front page of tomorrow's paper?"

"No doubt about it."

"This is a stock photo," I said. "Easy to come by. But the one in Monday's paper had been taken the night before, of Mom and Dad leaving the police station. How would the *Chronicle* have known to come to Rudolph?"

"They might have someone listening to a police scanner," Russ said. "Simmonds did call for a car to go and pick up your dad."

"I was there. She used her cell phone, not the radio."

"Might have been someone already in Rudolph, then, who heard what was going on at the inn and headed down to the police station. Everyone has phones these days, Merry."

"I guess," I said. "But if I ever get my hands on any Rudolphite who would try to make Dad look bad, I'll . . . I'll do something."

Russ gave me a smile. "I'm sure you will, Merry."

I read the rest of the piece. It said nothing more about the death of Gord Olsen than was already common knowledge. It said nothing more about my dad. It didn't have to.

"What about the *Gazette*?" I asked. "What are you going to say about this?"

"Lots of people are being questioned," Russ said. "You and me, for example. I see no reason to single out Noel in particular."

I exhaled a breath I hadn't realized I'd been holding. "Thanks." I reached for my glass.

"But"—his tone was so ominous my hand froze in the air—"if Noel is arrested, I can't bury it, Merry."

"That will not happen," I said.

While we talked, Mattie'd been attempting to lure Russ into a game of fetch. He finally had enough of being ignored and let out a single sharp bark of annoyance. Russ picked up a pink bunny with only one ear. "May I?" he asked me.

"Sure. But don't throw it. I'm trying to discourage flying objects in the house."

Man and dog set to an intense game of tug-of-war. Mattie crouched low. His butt wiggled with excitement, and his bushy tail itself was turned into a flying object. I could tell by the ripple of muscles in Russ's arm and the clench of his jaw that he was putting his all into it. I sipped my wine and watched them, feeling a smile creep across my face.

Finally, Mattie won. He wrenched the poor tattered

rabbit from Russ's hands and did a series of victory laps around the kitchen and living room. Russ leaned back and picked up his bottle. He raised it in a salute. "To the victor go the spoils."

I laughed. "You don't think that's the end of it, do you?"

Mattie dropped the toy at Russ's feet with an expectant look in his caramel-colored eyes.

"No more," I said in a very stern voice. The dog paid me his usual amount of attention. Meaning, none. "What do you think?" I asked Russ. "About who killed Gord, I mean?"

"Hard to say. I've never seen anyone make so many enemies so fast. People who work at the inn have a strong motive. Gord threatened their livelihoods. Same for the business owners in town if the Mega-Mart project went ahead. Some people are saying it was Grace."

"I've heard that too, but I don't buy it. She might not have liked Gord or been in favor of what he wanted to do, but Grace loves Jack above all else. She would never cause him pain."

"All I'm telling you is what I'm hearing, Merry. The people who are suggesting she killed Gord are also saying, 'Good for her.'"

I harrumphed.

"How well do you know Mark Grosse?" he asked around a mouthful of beer. He was trying to appear nonchalant, but I sensed it was not an idle question.

"Not well at all. I've met him a couple of times. He seems very nice."

Russ put down his beer bottle. "You might suggest that Vicky not get too involved with him."

"What are you saying, Russ?"

"I'm not entirely sure, but Mark had a lot to lose if Gord got his way. I have some feelers out with friends in the city, and let's just say Mark might not have left his last job voluntarily."

"What does that mean?"

He shrugged.

"You can't leave something like that hanging. If you do, you're as bad as those people whispering Grace's name."

"I'm sorry I mentioned it. I was thinking about Vicky, and I'm only giving you a heads-up because I know how close you two are. I won't repeat it to anyone else without positive confirmation. And"—he lifted one hand to stop my outburst of protest—"I won't repeat it at all unless I consider it relevant." He nodded toward my untouched pizza, now looking about as unappetizing as the picture on the box. "Seeing as to how I interrupted your dinner, can I take you out?"

I felt blood rushing into my face. The idea was tempting, but I wasn't sure how Russ would take an acceptance. I wasn't sure how I'd take it. An image of Alan Anderson popped unbidden into my mind: His unkempt blond curls, his warm blue eyes, his shy smile, his strong, competent hands. "Not tonight, thanks. It's been a hard day."

He pushed himself to his feet. "Another time, then."

"Sure, another time." I stood up also. Russ looked almost as disappointed as Mattie when he realized the game was over.

I walked Russ to the door.

"I'll let you know if I hear anything," he said.

"Thanks. I appreciate that."

Chapter 9

If anything, the print edition of the *Chronicle* was worse than the online "Breaking News."

"Wilkinson OUT!" screamed the headline in the same size font they'd use if intelligent life were found elsewhere in the universe. Where they'd located that picture of Dad-as-Santa looking as though he were auditioning for a role in a Christmas horror flick, I had no idea. I suspected they'd been hoarding it in their basement for years, gloating over it, and waiting for exactly the right moment to bring it out.

You can be sure I don't subscribe to the *Chronicle*, but first thing in the morning one of Mrs. D'Angelo's vast network of gossips personally delivered the poisonous rag to her door. My landlady didn't even wait for me to try to sneak past her porch. (I sometimes wondered if she had a motion-activated alarm in her house that sounded whenever I stuck my head out.) She hammered on my door when I was going through a yoga routine, trying to work out some of the various kinks that had taken up residence in my joints. Since coming home to Rudolph, I'd been so busy setting up the business I hadn't had time to look for a gym, and my regular Central Park jogging regimen had crumbled to well-intentioned dust. I'd asked Vicky, as she popped a mouthful of cookie dough into her mouth, if she could recommend a gym. She'd given me a startled look. Vicky, I then remembered, was one of *those* people, the fortunate few who could eat what they liked, when they liked, and never put on an ounce. Her metabolism was set so high she didn't need exercise to burn off excess calories. In that she was like my mom. I take more after Dad, whose cheerful round belly and pudgy cheeks were not props beneath his Santa Claus costume.

Mrs. D'Angelo caught me mid–downward dog. The protests of the real dog, confined to the bedroom so I could lie on the floor without being licked to death, were escalating, and I feared she'd come to tell me to keep him quiet.

No such luck. When I opened the door, she waved the paper in my face. "Have you seen this outrage, Merry?"

"No," I said, "I haven't even seen the sun yet. Oh, look, it's morning." A weak sun was trying, but failing, to get its head over the horizon and out from under the bank of thick storm clouds to the east.

My sarcasm was lost on Mrs. D'Angelo. She'd thrown

a wrap over her shoulders and stuffed her feet into boots without tying the laces. She wore a sleek satin lilac nightgown with a lace-trimmed, plunging décolletage that left less to my imagination than I wanted. I wondered if she always wore sexy lingerie to bed. As far as I knew there was no Mr. D'Angelo, and I'd never seen strange cars parked in her driveway overnight.

"You should consider suing," she said.

Against my better judgment, I plucked the paper from her fingers and skimmed the article quickly. It was short on facts and long on insinuation, but one fact they did have absolutely right: Dad had been fired as the town's Santa Claus after "two uniformed officers escorted him from a meeting of the Rudolph town council to question him about the brutal murder of . . ." I glanced at the article's byline. Dawn Galloway. Never heard of her.

Mrs. D'Angelo reached for the paper. I thanked her and shut the door in her face. She didn't think I was going to give it back for her to share with everyone else in town, did she?

I never did finish my yoga routine. Instead I let Mattie out of his prison cell, otherwise known as my bedroom, and got ready for the day. I was supposed to be having breakfast with Mom and Grace at the inn. I couldn't think of anything I'd rather do less. I sent Jackie a text telling her where I was in case of an emergency (almost hoping there would be one), stuffed Mattie into his real prison cell, his crate, and left.

Punctual as ever, Mom was waiting by the front door

when I pulled into the driveway of my parents' lovely Victorian house. She climbed into my car and leaned over to give me a peck on the cheek.

"How's Dad?" I asked, pulling into the street.

"Not good. I've never seen him so downcast."

I decided not to mention the contents of this morning's *Chronicle*. They might not ever see it—surely no one would be brave enough to show it to my parents. "He's going to protest, isn't he? He's more popular on the council than Sue-Anne is. She acted way out of line by searching for a new Santa without council approval."

Mom sighed. "He's too proud. He says if they want him to resume his duties as Rudolph's official Santa Claus they will have to come, and I quote, 'crawling on their hands and knees.'"

"What a mess."

The sun had managed to put in an appearance after all, and by the time we drove down the long road to the Yuletide Inn it was shining on last night's freshly fallen snow. We passed a young couple with skates thrown over their shoulders and families pulling well-wrapped kids on wooden toboggans heading for the bump in the garden the inn grandiosely called a hill. Snowmen of varying quality were dotted across the lawns.

The police tape, I was glad to see, had been taken down.

"The forecast for the weekend is still looking bad," Mom said. "Not that it matters anymore. Let it rain all it wants. Wash this whole miserable town away."

"Mom!" I said, shocked to my Christmas-loving core. "You don't mean that."

"No, I don't suppose I do. But this year I am not feeling the goodwill, Merry."

Grace waited for us in the hotel lobby. Logs crackled in the fireplace, the tree glowed, the decorations shone, and happy families headed out for a day of winter fun. I scarcely noticed. I was also not in the Christmas spirit. And, judging by her face, neither was Grace. Shadows the color of clouds heralding a winter storm were under her eyes, and new lines radiated out from the corners of her mouth. She was usually perfectly groomed. Today, I wondered when she'd last washed her hair and if she had ever before worn that tatty sweater outside of her house.

She got to her feet when she saw us and put on a smile that seemed genuine. "You brought Merry, how nice." She greeted us with hugs and a light kiss.

"How's Jack?" I asked.

"He's doing well." Her smile faded. "Physically, at any rate, but he's showing not the slightest amount of interest in anything. I've been trying to bring some decisions regarding the hotel to him, to get him involved, but he simply shrugs and tells me to handle it. He was listless before, but since hearing about Gord it's as though he's lost the will to live." She choked back a sob.

Mom put her arm around her friend's shoulders. I remembered what Russ had told me last night. Impossible. How could anyone even consider that this fragile woman had stabbed her own stepson?

Grace pulled herself away and wiped at her eyes. "We'll have our breakfast in the restaurant. Jack's not wanting company. One of the chambermaids is with him now. I've hired a private nurse to spend the afternoons with him so I can get some work done at the hotel."

"The restaurant's fine," I said.

Grace led the way through, and the hostess showed us to a table in a quiet corner overlooking the snow-covered gardens.

"Nice to see people out enjoying the day," Mom said.

"Yes," Grace said, with little enthusiasm. "Just coffee for me, please," she told the waitress, "but you two help yourselves."

An assortment of fresh fruit, cheeses, and breakfast pastries was laid out on the long table. I, at least, was hungry. It had been a long time since the microwave pizza I never did eat. "Can I get you something, Mom?"

"Orange juice and a bran muffin would be nice, dear. Thank you."

I went to the buffet and studied the offerings. The long baguettes looked very much like they'd come from Vicky's bakery, and the sliced bread beside the toaster was dotted with seeds or thick with raisins. Mark had lost no time getting back to his regular suppliers. *Mark. Was it possible?*

No. I pushed Russ's cryptic comments aside and loaded up plates for Mom and me.

I was tucking into a slice of baguette topped with butter and soft, runny cheese when a shadow fell over our table. Mom and Grace stopped chatting.

Irene's hands were on her hips, and you could almost see the hostility radiating from her. She was glaring, not at Grace as I might have expected, but at my mom. "You. You dare to show your face here."

Mom threw me a glance, the expression on her face one of total bewilderment. "I'm afraid I don't . . ."

"The police arrested your husband for the murder of my husband, but they let him go. They can't have *Santa Claus* in the pokey."

All around us conversation ground to a halt. Diners froze with coffee cups halfway to their lips and toast was put down unbitten.

"I assure you . . ." Mom began.

I wasn't in the mood to be polite. I jumped to my feet. "That's a baseless accusation. My dad was here the night your husband died, so he was questioned in the course of a normal police investigation, as were you, I believe. He has no influence over the police."

"That's not what I heard," Irene sneered. "Noel Wilkinson owns this town—everyone says so."

"That's preposterous."

The hostess hurried up to our table. "Is everything all right, Mrs. Olsen?"

"No," Irene said. "Everything is not all right. You"—she pointed a red-tipped finger at Mom—"need to ask yourself why your husband would want to get rid of Gord. Because it seems to me"—she swung the finger at Grace—"only one person benefited from my Gordy's death. Her."

A deep quiet had settled over the dining room. The staff stopped clearing dishes or bringing in fresh trays. Breakfast eaters were listening either in rapt interest or shocked silence.

Mom's face matched the color of her red blouse and glass earrings. She pushed back her chair and rose slowly to her feet. She took a deep breath and her chest expanded. She was a highly trained, professional opera singer, and I feared for Irene's eardrums. Not that she didn't deserve to have them shattered, but the rest of us were also in range.

"You better leave, Irene," I said.

"Not until I've had my say. I know what's going on here. They left the dinner together that night, didn't they? Your father and *her*. Her husband was in the hospital fighting for his life, and she couldn't wait to get another man into his bed. What did you tell Noel, Grace? That you'd be *ever so grateful* if he killed Gord for you?"

Mom slapped Irene across the face. The sound was like a gunshot. The onlookers let out a collective gasp.

Grace leapt to her feet. "Let's go, Aline. We don't have to listen to her nasty insinuations."

Irene's face was a picture of shock as a red blotch slowly spread across her cheek. "How dare you."

"I can't say it wasn't deserved." Mark joined our little group. "Get out of here, Irene." He kept his voice low.

"You can't order me around."

"I certainly can. This is private property, and I am evicting you from my restaurant. Leave or I'll call the police."

"You do that and I'll tell them she hit me."

"You want to wash your dirty laundry in front of the police, go ahead. Everyone here's heard enough of it."

Irene bristled. Mark stared at her, unblinking.

"I was wrong," Irene said, "in one thing only. She isn't the only person who wanted Gordy dead. Suited you to have a free hand with the spending, didn't it, Mr. New York Chef?"

Mark grabbed her arm, but she shook him off. "I'm leaving. For now. But I'm not going far. I will see that you people are put in jail where you belong." She marched out of the restaurant, her head high. Everyone watched her go. And then, as if at a hidden signal, the patrons started eating and chatting (although perhaps somewhat loudly) and the staff began banging dishes and cutlery.

Mom dropped into her chair. Her eyes were round and her face white. "I can't believe I did that," she said.

Mark beckoned to the hostess. "Can you please go to the lobby and ensure that Mrs. Irene Olsen has left?" He turned to us with a grimace. "Don't want her lying in wait to start another confrontation."

"Thank you, Mark," Grace said. "You handled that well."

"I put in my time in some less-than-respectable eateries. Even the top-ranked places can get rowdy if enough wine flows." He turned to me with a smile. "Say hi to Vicky for me. Tell her the breads are as good as ever."

"I will."

He went back to the kitchen, and the hostess reported that Irene had left. None of us felt like finishing our breakfast, but Grace suggested we wait for a few minutes before making our exit, to let the guests' attention return to their own business.

"I don't suppose," I said, "you have any idea of what Irene and Gord's marriage was like?"

Grace raised one eyebrow. "Not in the slightest. Why do you ask?"

"Don't they say the spouse is the first person the cops suspect? What better way to deflect suspicion from oneself than to turn it on someone else. Dad, you, even Mark. Irene's casting a wide net."

Grace thought for a moment. "I can't say they seemed at all close. No secret glances or little touches here and there."

"Many couples don't act like that after years of marriage," Mom said, "but they don't turn around and kill each other."

"True," I said. "But it's a possibility. If you're planning to murder your spouse, or even just thinking of it, wouldn't it be better to do it someplace far from home? Where the police can't easily question your friends and neighbors? Even better to be in a place where everyone and their dog is mad at the spouse."

"You might be right," Mom said. "But what can we do about it?"

"I'll talk to Detective Simmonds. I'm sure she's thought of Irene herself, but if not, it's time she did."

Grace pushed her chair back. "I need to go home and check on Jack. I think it's safe to leave now."

Chapter 10

When I dropped Mom at home, she turned to me with a sparkle in her eyes and a big grin on her face.

"What are you looking so pleased about?" I asked.

"I can't wait until I tell your father what I did." Her sleek, fur-trimmed leather gloves made a punching gesture. "Pow! You know I am opposed to violence at all times, but that sure felt good." Another air punch. "All those years I bit my tongue against tyrannical directors and spoiled-rotten divas. I should have just belted them in the chops. Pow!"

Now, that was a truly terrifying thought. "Don't get too carried away, Mom. Irene could have you charged with assault, you know. There were plenty of witnesses. Wilkinsons are spending enough time down at the police station these days."

She sighed. "You're right, dear. I'll have to relive my moment of glory only in my head. Pow!"

She almost danced up the path, ducking and diving, her fists punching the air. If someone ever decided to mount an operatic version of *Rocky*, Mom was a shoo-in for the main role.

When I arrived at the shop, I was pleased to see that the place was humming with activity. Jackie was ringing up purchases and chatting happily with the customer in front of her. I was even more pleased as Jackie continued punching in numbers on the cash register. This woman had bought a full set of table linens: two runners, one oatmeal and one red; twelve place mats that said "Ho, ho, ho"; and a matching number of red napkins embroidered with white snowflakes. The linens were accompanied by red and white serving dishes and a giant white turkey platter.

"Why don't you help these ladies take their purchases to their car?" I said to Jackie. "I'll take over here."

Jackie did a poor job of hiding a grimace. She didn't like doing heavy lifting. Neither did I, which was why I hadn't volunteered to do it. And I'm the boss.

I recognized the big spender as the shorter of the Fine Budget Inn wives. Her thin friend was behind her in line with one of Alan's necklaces, circles of highly polished wood linked by a long leather chain, draped through her fingers.

"Nice to see you," I said with a smile. "I hope you're enjoying Rudolph."

"We love it! It's adorable," the thin one exclaimed. "I'm so disappointed that my husband's deal fell through. I want to come to Rudolph every year."

"Kathy!" her friend said. "You know we're not supposed to talk about the business."

"Oh pooh, Arlene. It's no secret anymore." She turned to me. "Our husbands were interested in helping the owner of the Yuletide Inn convert it to a Fine Budget. But, well, he up and died and it looks like the deal's off."

"Oh," I said. I wasn't going to say I was sorry. Even if her friend was dropping five hundred bucks in my store. "Why are you still here, then?" A mite blunt, but Kathy didn't seem like one who noticed that sort of thing.

"Fred says he's not ready to give up yet. He says the owner's wife is still . . ."

"Kathy! I swear your mouth is going to get you in real trouble one day. Now, pay for that necklace while I show this young lady where our car is." Arlene picked up the smallest and lightest of the shopping bags and sailed outside while Jackie followed, staggering under the weight of the goods.

Leaving me with the chatty Kathy and her necklace. "Would you like a gift box for that?" I asked.

"No thanks. It's for me." She pulled out her credit card, and I completed the transaction. I wrapped the necklace carefully in tissue and folded it into a small bag with the store's logo. "The owner's wife's still interested in the deal?" I said casually. "Do you mean the wife of the owner or of the man who died? He wasn't the owner but his only child."

Kathy shrugged. "I don't know. Fred gave me his wink that means he has something up his sleeve and said he wasn't ready to head for home quite yet." She beamed at me. "Which means more shopping time for me. I can't wait until I wear this necklace at our bridge club holiday luncheon. Of course, we're not supposed to try to one-up each other, but after Norma brought out that . . ."

Jackie and Arlene came back into the store. Rats, she must have been parked right outside. Kathy picked up her bag and said, "Thanks." The women left.

"What was all that about?" Jackie said. "The inn's still for sale?"

"A franchise opportunity, not a sale. Irene, Gord's widow, is just making trouble." I said it, but I wasn't so sure. Irene had no power to do anything. Executives from a big corporation like Fine Budget Inns weren't fools. They wouldn't waste their time talking to someone who had nothing to offer.

Could Kathy possibly have meant Grace was talking business with the men? Surely not. Grace loved the inn exactly the way it was.

"I have great news," Jackie said.

"I could use some about now. But first, can you run to Cranberries and get me a latte? You can buy one for yourself, too." I dug in the cash register and came up with the money. I was in dire need of a caffeine fix; I'd barely had one sip of my coffee at breakfast before the whole Irene incident exploded.

A few more customers came in, and I told them to let me know if they needed help. I try to be friendly without being pushy. I myself have been known to leave a store when faced with an overly enthusiastic "greeter."

Jackie was soon back, with a medium latte for me and an extra-large concoction topped by a mountain of whipped cream for her. I eyed her slim figure, wondering when all the calories she consumed would start taking their toll. "What's the big news?" I lifted the lid off my latte, breathed in the scent of hot milk, and took that first welcome, delicious sip.

"Kyle has a new job."

While we talked, we kept our voices down and our eyes on browsing customers, ready to leap into action the moment anyone seemed in need of attention.

"That is good news," I said. "Glad to hear it." Kyle was Jackie's boyfriend. What she saw in that grumbling, lazy, chronically underemployed guy, I never did know. Jackie was young and pretty with a cheerful, bouncy personality. She went through boyfriends at an amazing rate but lately she seemed to be sticking with Kyle. She could do so much better. But, who am I to judge anyone else in matters of the heart? I sure could have done a lot better than wasting years on the miserable slug who dumped me the moment the granddaughter of the owner of the magazine empire where we were employed waved her inheritance-expecting finger in his direction.

I took a deep drink of my coffee.

"Kyle's going to be Santa for the rest of the season!"

I sprayed coffee all over Jackie's shirt.

"Hey!" She leapt out of the way.

"What!"

"Jeez, don't get your knickers in a knot, Merry. Kyle'll be a great Santa. He'll need a lot of padding to fit into your dad's costume, but he can do that. Kyle really loves kids." Her voice trailed off on the last sentence, as though she was not entirely sure of her facts.

"For one thing," I said through clenched teeth, "my dad's costume belongs to him, not to the town. I don't suppose anyone told Kyle that. And second . . ."

"Merry," Jackie said, for once being the more sensible one. She jerked her head toward the customers, all of whom had stopped browsing to watch us.

"Oops," I said. "Coffee was too hot. You'd better go into the back and wipe your shirt down."

"Okay," she said. I followed her. She tried to shut the door to our tiny restroom, but I stuck my foot in it. "Kyle cannot be Santa. My father is Santa."

"He's not now, Merry. The job was advertised. Kyle was the most qualified applicant." She smiled at herself in the mirror and tilted her head to one side. I figured Kyle was the only applicant. No one else would dare.

Jackie finished admiring herself, wet a paper towel, and began swiping at the stain. It was a cotton shirt in a deep shade of beige. Shouldn't be too hard to remove the coffee spatter. "If I can't get this stain out, Merry, you're going to have to buy me a new blouse."

"Ask Kyle what he's going to do for a costume. He'll end up paying more than he'll earn. If he can get one in time."

"Shouldn't be a problem," she said. "He made two hundred and fifty bucks the other day selling a picture he took with his phone. He's thinking he might become a photographer and get himself a real camera, but I don't know. They can be expensive. As for the costume, not a problem. The Nook has some cheap Santa costumes in stock."

"The Nook! Those 'suits' have plastic pants in one-size-fits-all! The beard ties around the ears with string!"

"Hello?" called a voice from the shop. "Can I get some help here?"

I gave Jackie one last growl and went out front.

"Do you have those plates in blue?" a woman asked me, pointing to a display of white china cocktail plates decorated with lightly sketched sprigs of green and red holly.

"No," I said. I might have added, "They're Christmas plates, of course they don't come in blue, you fool," but I did not.

She left without buying anything.

Jackie came out of the back. Her shirtfront was sodden. "I have to go home and change," she said.

I grumbled. She could have just dabbed at the coffee marks with her damp paper towel, she didn't have to wash the darn thing while still wearing it. I suspected she was off to tell Kyle that others might not receive the news of his job opportunity with as much joy as she had. My suspicions were confirmed when she pulled her phone out of her purse the moment the door swung behind her and threw me a guilty sideways look before ducking her head down and scurrying away.

A drop of rain fell on her head. Then another. Cars kicked up slush as they drove down Jingle Bell Lane. It was raining. Oh joy.

If Sue-Anne wasn't careful, she'd ruin Rudolph's reputation as the place to bring your kids to meet Santa. I couldn't blame her for the rain, but I sure could blame her for replacing Dad with a slacker twenty-something with a tie-on beard and a plastic costume.

Sue-Anne. Never mind the town's reputation—what about Dad's? How far would Sue-Anne go to ruin the person she saw as her only rival for mayor? Not that Dad wanted to be mayor again, but when one was blinded by ambition it could be hard to realize that not everyone was equally obsessed. I'd considered Sue-Anne as a suspect in a murder once before. Just because she hadn't done it that time, didn't mean she didn't do it this time.

A handful of customers came into the shop. A few people bought some small items, but I wasn't busy enough to get my mind off the matter at hand.

Jackie eventually came back, having changed into a short, tight skirt and a sparkly blue T-shirt under a cropped jacket. I glanced out the window and saw Kyle hurry past, heading for Rudolph's Gift Nook.

"You'll be pleased to hear, Merry," she said, "that I took my blouse to Mom's and she said she should be able to get the stain out. I sure hope so. It's one of my favorites and it cost a lot more than I normally spend on clothes." She let out a martyred sigh.

Thinking about Sue-Anne had reminded me I had another suspect in mind. Now that Jackie was back to mind the shop, I called Detective Simmonds. She answered on the first ring. I told her I had something to discuss with her about the death of Gord Olsen, and she told me to come on down to the police station.

"I'm going out for a while," I said.

"Where?" Jackie asked.

"None of your business," I replied.

Outside, the rain was falling steadily. The snow was melting into slimy puddles on the road and sidewalks and dripping from the eaves of the buildings. People hurried by, heads buried in coat collars, feet sloshing through puddles. Cars kicked up icy mud.

I ran across the street, but before going to the police station, I swung into Victoria's Bake Shoppe. I wasn't exactly planning to bribe an officer of the law, but I'd never finished my latte and it would be rude not to take one to Detective Simmonds.

The lunch rush was over and only a handful of people were sipping soup and munching on sandwiches when I came into the bakery. Marjorie was behind the counter, rearranging the display to fill in the numerous gaps. I hadn't intended to get anything to eat, but the moment the scent of baking bread and hot soup hit me, I was starving. No dinner last night and a rudely interrupted breakfast at the inn this morning. I needed to be alert and on my toes if I was talking to the sharp Detective Simmonds, not on the verge of collapsing from hunger.

I studied what was left. Exactly two mince tarts, my favorites. I pointed to them. "Can you pack those to go, Marjorie? And two coffees, please. One with cream and the other black." I put packets of sugar and creamer into the bag for Simmonds, as I didn't know how she took her coffee.

Vicky came out of the back, wiping floury hands on her apron. "Thought I heard your voice," she said. Her entire face was lit up and she had a spring in her step. I raised one eyebrow in question.

"I just got off the phone this very minute," she said.

"Did you win the lottery?"

"Even better."

"And . . ."

"And," she said, laughing, "Mark asked me for a date. A real date. Tonight." She lifted her arms in the air, stood on her tippy-toes, and twirled in circles. We'd been in ballet class together as kids. Only one of us had any talent. It hadn't been me.

I wasn't as thrilled for my best friend as I should have been. I remembered last night, Russ's warning about Mark. "What are you doing on this date?"

"He has the night off, so we're going to meet for an early dinner and then go to a movie." Her smile stretched from one side of her face to the other. "Now, to decide what to wear. It's only a casual dinner, so I don't want to look like I've dressed up or anything. Do you think jeans are okay, Merry?"

"I think an ankle-length skirt and a high neckline would be appropriate," Marjorie said.

"Don't you have work to do, Aunt Marjorie?"

"I am working," she said, tucking the mince tarts into a take-out box. "I'm serving this customer right here."

"Gotta run." I handed over my money. "Catch you later. Call me in the morning and tell me how it went."

"She'll call you when she gets home," Marjorie said. "Which will be ten minutes after the movie gets out."

"You're no fun," Vicky said as the door swung shut behind me.

At the police station, I told Nancy that Detective Simmonds was waiting for me. "Name?" she barked.

"Merry, that's M-e-r-r . . . Never mind, here she is now. Good afternoon, Detective."

Simmonds nodded to Nancy, and the receptionist buzzed me through to the inner sanctum.

"I brought coffee," I said, holding up the evidence.

"Thanks, I could use one about now." Simmonds led me down the hallway to her office. It wasn't much of an office, more a desk piled high with papers in the corner of a room full of equally disheveled desks. The decor was fading, chipped industrial beige and the art the very latest in wanted posters. I took the offered seat and glanced around the room. "You could do with some holiday cheer in here."

The corners of her mouth turned up. "I'll check for that line in the budget." I handed her the coffee and opened the box of tarts. We each took one. "I've put on about ten pounds since moving to Rudolph," she said.

"We are situated way too close to that bakery." She bit into the mince tart. "Marvelous."

And it was. The pastry was light and flaky, the filling rich and sweet, packed full of dried fruits. The tarts had been crowned with a Christmas tree cut out of pastry and sprinkled with sugar.

A photo featured prominently on Simmonds's desk. A standard school picture of a young girl, all freckles and a big toothy grin.

Simmonds glanced at the picture, and her face melted into soft lines. She looked almost human. "Charlotte. My daughter."

"She's lovely."

"She is." The detective shook off the sentiment and her hard, professional shell fell back in place. "What do you want to tell me?"

"Irene Olsen. Gord's wife. She's still at the inn and she's in the mood to stir up trouble. I know the police always suspect the spouse first, so I thought you should be aware of that."

"You know how the police operate, do you? What, from your extensive watching of *CSI: Miami*?"

I refused to be intimidated. "You can't tell me that's not true."

"Go on," she said.

"So, I thought . . . well, that I'd ask what you know about Irene."

Simmonds leaned back in her chair and made a steeple of her fingers. "You're tenacious, Merry, I'll give you that."

"I know for a fact my father did not kill Gord Olsen. Whether in cahoots with Grace or anyone else."

"Who said anything about Grace?"

"Uh . . . I'm simply making a point," I said, intimidated.

She studied me for a long time. I tried not to fidget. "The marriage between Irene and Gord Olsen had its difficulties," she said at last. "There have been incidents of domestic disturbances at their home. No physical assaults, as far as the police are aware, but pots and crockery thrown, and one occurrence in which Mr. Olsen charged at Mrs. Olsen with the lawn mower, and she ran screaming through the neighbor's hedge. The neighbor called the police, but by the time officers arrived, Mrs. Olsen had returned to her own home. The homeowner threatened to sue the Olsens for the cost of repairing a valuable hedge. To be honest, Merry, I hadn't been aware there was such a thing as a valuable hedge. Must be a California thing."

"So Irene's definitely in the frame then," I said.

"It's not unknown for couples with a history of fighting to end up killing one another," she said, "but I have to point out that when it happens, it's more often than not loud and messy, and the survivor is immediately overcome by guilt and regret. As far as we can determine, Mr. Olsen was killed by a person who followed him into the garden quietly, struck quickly, and left. Making no fuss."

"What do you suppose Gord was doing in the garden at night, anyway?" I said. "He didn't strike me as the type to be contemplative."

She studied my face. I sat quietly, hoping I wasn't about to be tossed out of the police station. Instead, to my surprise, Simmonds smiled slightly and said, "Mr. and Mrs. Olsen had dinner at A Touch of Holly, here in Rudolph. According to the restaurant staff, the couple didn't behave at all out of the ordinary. They didn't speak to anyone there, other than the hostess and their waiter. They ate their meal, largely in silence, and drank one bottle of wine between the two of them. The only memorable thing about the Olsens was the insultingly small tip they left, after consuming an expensive wine and dishes from the top of the price range. If you ever want your visit to be remembered by restaurant staff, Merry, a miserly tip is more memorable than a large one."

"I'll keep that in mind," I said.

"According to Mrs. Olsen, they came straight back to the inn after dinner. Irene Olsen retired to her room, and we've determined that Gord made the rounds of the hotel. He told the receptionist to fasten the top buttons of her blouse; popped into the kitchen, where he got into an argument with the chef. Basically, he was sticking his nose into anything and everything and upsetting more than a few of the staff. People were busy and can't say precisely what time he was around. Whether Gord Olsen went into the gardens by himself to check out something, or if someone accompanied him, I don't know. Perhaps someone asked him for a quiet word. No one has come forward to say they saw Gord going into the garden. Our investigation continues. Now, I've told you more than I probably should have, Merry. Thanks for coming in."

I didn't take the hint. "What's Gord and Irene's financial situation? Maybe she didn't kill him in a moment of passion, but she thought it all out ahead of time. Premeditated."

"I'm not going to reveal the details of the Olsen bank account to you, Merry. Suffice it to say, I've known people to kill over what would seem to us like ridiculously small amounts, but I don't believe that's a factor in this case. Now, I've work to do."

"Mark Grosse."

She raised one eyebrow. "What about him?"

"He's new to town. You say you suspect my dad because he had an argument with Gord. Well, so did Mark, and more than once, it would seem. What have you found out about him?" I wasn't trying to throw Mark under the bus. But the way I looked at it, there were a lot of suspects. The problem was that many of them were people I cared about: Dad. Vicky. Grace. I had to make Simmonds understand that she needed to be looking at everyone. If Gord had tried interfering in Mark's kitchen the night he died, was it conceivable for Mark to have grabbed a ready-to-hand knife and followed his boss's son outside?

"The way I normally conduct an investigation, Merry," Simmonds said, "is that I ask the questions. Now, I appreciate the coffee and the treat, but I suspect we both have work to get back to. Thank you for your time." She tossed her coffee cup into the trash. The basket was about four feet from her chair, and the cup sailed in a graceful arc to land directly in the middle.

"Good shot," I said.

"High school state basketball champion."

"Being Santa Claus is important not only to my dad," I said, "but even more to the town. The children's weekend's coming up, and the guy they've found to replace Dad is going to be a major disaster. Rudolph lives by its reputation as Christmas Town. If we lose that, we'll be nothing more than another decaying postindustrial town."

"I understand, Merry, and I admire your passion. But that's not my concern. Finding a killer is the only thing on my mind."

"You didn't have to make such a big thing of it," I said. "My dad would have been happy to answer your questions. You didn't have to march him out of the council office like he was a crooked politician on some sort of perp walk. Right after you'd been in my shop, too. That wasn't fair."

"You're right."

"I am?"

"In my defense, I didn't ask anyone to go around and get him. I had questions about that knife, and I told a junior officer to phone Mr. Wilkinson and ask him to drop in when he had a moment. My instructions were misunderstood. It won't happen again."

An image of Candice Campbell popped into my head.

I had no doubt the officer in question was that sneaky little rat. "In that case, can't you tell the town council Dad's not under suspicion? Then they'll take him back." I smiled at her, willing her to realize how sensible I was being.

She did not smile back. "The thing is, Merry, your father *is* under suspicion. He *is*, despite your attempts to deflect my attention, my prime suspect."

Chapter 11

That had not gone as I had intended. Sure, I learned a few things, but I seemed to have refocused Simmonds's steely-eyed gaze even more intently on my father.

Simmonds escorted me to the inner door. Nancy smirked. When I was in the vestibule, pulling on my gloves and zipping up my coat, Simmonds returned to her office. I opened the door, and a woman pushed past me into the police station, without sparing me a glance. She was about my age, with brown hair cropped short, dressed in a long, puffy black coat and a tattered blue scarf.

"I'm here to see Detective Simmonds," she announced to the Plexiglas partition.

"Name?" Nancy asked.

"Dawn Galloway. *Muddle Harbor Chronicle*."

That caught my attention, all right. I let the outer door close slowly and fished in my bag, searching for something. Anything.

"The detective is not speaking to the press," Nancy said.

"I want to introduce myself," Dawn Galloway said. "Give her my card."

Nancy struggled mightily to get to her feet. She approached the partition as if it were at the end of a very long, rough road. "Leave your card with me. I'll see she gets it."

"I won't take but a moment of her time," Dawn said.

Nancy thrust her hand into the little slot at the bottom of the partition. Dawn slapped a card into it. "If she's busy, I can wait."

Nancy's eyes flicked to me. "Are you wanting anything further, Merry?" *Now* she remembered my name.

"Nope," I said.

Dawn whirled around. "Merry. You must be Merry Wilkinson. Pleased to meet you." She thrust out her hand. "Dawn Galloway, *Muddle Harbor Chronicle*." Instinctively, I put out my own hand. I tried not to wince in pain. Her grip was strong enough to break bones. I suspected she'd been taught to be forceful in journalism school.

"I read your article this morning," I said. "You have a nerve coming here after printing that."

"Just trying to get the facts, Merry. The people need to know—isn't that right? What brings you here? Has your father been arrested again?"

"He wasn't arrested the first time."

She pushed the door open and almost shoved me outside. "Why don't we go for a coffee? My treat. You can tell me your side of the story."

"I don't have a side," I said, "but I can tell you the truth standing right here." The precipitation in the air hadn't been able to decide if it wanted to be rain or snow. So it compromised and was now both. My face stung under the barrage of icy pellets. "My dad didn't kill Gord Olsen."

"*Brr*, but it's cold. A nice hot coffee will take the chill off. Can you recommend a good place, Merry?"

"No," I said and walked away.

"Perhaps I'll go to Victoria's Bake Shoppe," she called after me. "People say Vicky Casey's business was in danger of being ruined by Gord Olsen. I've heard you and she are friends. Is she the sort to fly off the handle and act violently?"

I stopped walking.

"Just asking," Dawn said.

"Are you allowed to print out-and-out lies?" I asked.

"I report on what I hear. Is it true Gord Olsen stopped sourcing his baked goods from Vicky Casey?"

"Yes, but . . ."

"See? Just the truth. It's not difficult. Tell me about Mark Grosse."

"I don't know anything about Mark Grosse." Why was I talking to this horrid woman? I should be marching resolutely down Jingle Bell Lane with a firm "No comment" trailing behind me in the icy air.

"Being a top chef's a cutthroat business these days," Dawn said. "Oops, bad choice of words there. Anyway, I heard there was some trouble back in the city. The golden boy had to pack up his pans and tall hat and escape to the boonies, where no one knew him."

"I know nothing about that. And I care even less," I lied.

"While I'm waiting to see Detective Simmonds, I'm going to pop into town hall. Is that it over there?"

"Yes."

"Nice and close. They can keep an eye on all the comings and goings in the police station. I'm going to get a comment from Acting Mayor Morrow on Mayor Baumgartner's statement this morning about Santa Claus." She paused, waiting for me to ask.

I bit my tongue. Hard. I didn't know what the mayor of Muddle Harbor had had to say about Santa Claus, but I was determined not to give Dawn Galloway the satisfaction of my begging for scraps of information. This time I did walk away.

"Maybe it was your father after all, then," Dawn called after me. "Santa Claus himself. Imagine what a scandal that would be."

I put my head down against the freezing rain and hurried away from the police station. I almost collided with Betty Thatcher, coming in the other direction. "Can't you watch where you're going?" she snapped.

"Sorry," I muttered. I made to dodge around Betty and stepped on a patch of slushy ice. My left foot slid out from under me and my arms windmilled. I would have fallen flat on my face had Betty not grabbed me. She acted purely on instinct, and her expression said she wished she'd left me to my fate. I muttered my thanks and ran off, watching where I put my feet.

I didn't go back to the shop, but headed in the opposite direction for the offices of the *Rudolph Gazette*. Everyone was implying things about Mark, but no one was coming out and saying what had happened. If he had done something awful, I needed to warn Vicky before she got too deeply involved with him.

Russ was in his office, reading his computer screen and frowning mightily. He looked up when I came in and gave me a smile. Like small-town papers everywhere, the *Gazette* was a shadow of its former self. The paper used to fill an entire building in the center of what was then Main Street. Now Russ didn't even have an office, just a battered and battle-scarred wooden desk in one corner of a crowded, stuffy, overheated room. He was called the editor in chief, but that was nothing but a grandiose title. Other than the receptionist, who doubled as a copy editor, two women who sold advertising, a part-time entertainment section editor, and one junior reporter, more interested in finding a job on a big paper than investigating the goings-on in Rudolph, Russ was it.

"Please don't tell me something bad has happened," I said. "I don't think I can take any more."

"Randy Baumgartner, mayor of Muddle Harbor, released a statement this morning."

"I heard something about that. How bad is it?"

"He says that in light of the events in Rudolph that

required the town's Santa Claus to be removed from his post, Muddle Harbor will provide a safe holiday environment where families can bring their children. Santa will be greeting guests at the Muddle Harbor rec center Saturday and Sunday."

I groaned. "You know what people are going to think being 'removed from his post' means."

"I do. No one ever said the Muddites play fair, and Sue-Anne is playing right into their hands."

"There's a *Chronicle* reporter in town. I ran into her at the police station. Simmonds wouldn't see her, so she's gone to try to get a statement out of Sue-Anne."

Russ pushed himself out of his chair and reached for his jacket. "Is that so? I'd better get in on that."

"Wait," I said. "Mark Grosse. I have to know what you learned about him."

"Walk with me, Merry." He headed for the door at a fast clip. I ran after him.

Russ's fast clip ended abruptly when he hit the fresh ice forming on the sidewalk. "Mark Grosse," he said as we penguin-walked toward the town hall. "I still have plenty of contacts in the city, including the restaurant reviewer for the *Times*. Mark Grosse was making a name for himself in the farm-to-fork movement. Local foods, sustainably raised, with prices to match. He was hired as executive chef at a hot new Manhattan restaurant, the Crooked Fork."

"I've heard of it. Everyone was talking about it when I was living in the city. It was huge. That was Mark?"

"Yup. The owner was aiming to make it one of the top

restaurants in New York. The first reviews were stellar, the place was an immediate hit. Politicians and Broadway stars ate there. The common folk had to make reservations months ahead of time. Common, meaning those who could afford seventy-five-dollar steaks and twenty-dollar purple Russian fingerling potatoes served with butter from a cow the waiter could tell you the name and ancestry of. And then . . ."

We arrived at the town hall. Russ stopped talking.

"And then . . ." I prompted.

"I'll tell you later."

"You can't leave me hanging like that."

A babel of excited voices was coming from inside the building. Russ ran up the steps. I followed, still mindful of my footing.

In the reception area a crowd had gathered around Sue-Anne Morrow and Dawn Galloway. Sue-Anne's face was an unattractive shade of puce and her breathing heavy. Dawn was writing in a notebook. Everyone else was shouting. My neighbor Wendy was the only person to notice Russ and me come in. She gave me a grim-faced nod.

"You can't do that," Sue-Anne shouted.

Various people hollered words such as "outrage" and "disgrace." Someone threatened to sue.

Russ pushed his way through. "What's going on here?"

The intruder thrust out her hand. "Dawn Galloway. *Muddle Harbor Chronicle*."

"Jeez," Russ said. "When did they hire you?"

"Yesterday. But that doesn't matter. I . . ."

"You can tell Mayor Baumgartner . . ." Sue-Anne said.

"Sue-Anne," a man yelled, "you are so out of your depth here." I recognized one of my dad's oldest friends and a staunch ally of his on the council.

"We have to present a united front," a woman said. No one paid any attention to her.

"I'd suggest," Russ said, trying to be heard above the din, "that you people stop arguing in front of a reporter. Two reporters, actually." He turned to Dawn. "Russell Durham. *Rudolph Gazette.* What's going on?"

"I came to ask Acting Mayor Morrow for a comment. She flew into a hissy fit."

"I did not . . ." Sue-Anne said.

Russ ignored her. "Comment about what?"

"About those blasted Muddites putting on a children's Christmas party, that's what," someone shouted from the back.

"I didn't realize," Dawn sniffed, "Rudolph is the only town around here allowed to have holiday celebrations."

"Not at all," Russ said. "Everyone's welcome to celebrate the season as they see fit. It's just that some folks are being a mite underhanded in attacking other towns."

"That's not the Christmas spirit," I said. Everyone ignored me.

"Would you agree with Mr. Durham, Mrs. Morrow?" Dawn asked, pencil poised.

Sue-Anne gaped.

"I'm sure we all have work to get back to," Russ said. "Good-bye, Dawn."

"I'm not finished here."

"Yes, you are."

Her shoulders were set, and for a moment she looked as though she were going to argue, but then she relaxed. She gave Russ a smug grin that seemed to say, *Just between us newspaper people*, then held up her phone. "First, a quick picture."

Sue-Anne lifted her chin and sucked in her stomach. Russ stepped between them. "I'll get someone to send you an official photo. How's that?"

"It'll do," Dawn said.

Wendy stepped forward. "Let me show you to the door," she said. The door was about two feet away.

"If there are any new developments," Dawn said, "feel free to contact me, Mrs. Morrow." She walked out.

Once the door shut behind her, the room exploded. The anger, as far as I could tell, was aimed at Randy Baumgartner in particular and the entire population of Muddle Harbor in general.

"We ought to head over there and burn the whole place to the ground," one of the councillors said.

I pushed aside an image of torches and pitchforks.

"That sort of talk isn't helping," Russ said.

"What we have to do," I said, "is issue a statement of support for my dad and ask him to come back as Santa Claus."

Sue-Anne turned on me. "We can't have a Santa who's under police investigation!"

"By removing him from his job, you might as well come out and say you think he's guilty."

Sue-Anne threw up her hands. "We're damned if we do and damned if we don't. Ralph, what's your take?"

"Me?" Ralph Dickerson said. "I, uh . . . I think that . . ."

"What's done is done," someone said. "No matter what we do now, the Muddites will twist it to suit them."

The door crashed open and Alan Anderson flew in, propelled by a gust of cold, wet air. His head and shoulders were soaked and his coat dotted with rain. He shook off water like a dog coming out of the lake. He spotted me and gave me a soft, shy smile, before turning to the group and asking, "What's going on?"

No one bothered to enlighten him. "We're ruined anyway!" the ever-cheerful Ralph said. "I hope you business folks aren't relying on a big weekend." He walked away, muttering. The crowd began to break up. Sue-Anne glared at me before turning on her stiletto heels and tapping her furious way back to her office.

Soon only Wendy, Russ, Alan, and I remained in the reception area.

"That went well," Wendy said.

"What happened?" Alan asked.

"Some new reporter from the *Chronicle* came in asking to speak to Sue-Anne. I buzzed her office and she came down. When the reporter told her what Randy Baumgartner had said, you could hear Sue-Anne's screech in every corner of the building. Naturally, everyone came out to see what was going on." Wendy dropped her voice. "Sue-Anne's a drama queen. Never happy if she isn't in the center of the crowd. She has yet to understand that some crowds are not worth being in the center of."

"They really hired Kyle Lambert to be Santa?" I said. Wendy nodded. "Yup."

Alan groaned. "Kyle. I can't imagine a worse choice."

"No one else applied," Wendy said.

"They should cancel the weekend's festivities," Russ said. "Easy enough to blame it on the weather."

"You can suggest that to Sue-Anne," Wendy said. "Tell her she's going to miss her first chance to officially open the weekend as the acting mayor. Tell her she's not going to have her picture in the paper looking suitably mayoral. I've heard she went to Rochester to shop for a new coat and hat to wear."

"I get your point," Russ said. He headed for the door, and Alan and I exchanged glances before following him out.

The three of us stood on the steps, watching the cold rain fall and people running for cover.

"Wasn't supposed to start raining until Friday," Russ said.

"Maybe that means it will end soon and we'll get more snow for the weekend," I said, ever the optimist.

"Better if it keeps raining." Alan spoke to Russ. "I've told Merry I won't be putting in an appearance as the toymaker if Noel isn't Santa."

"My mom won't bring her classes to sing in the bandstand," I added. I glanced toward the lake. The park between the town offices and the bay was a vast expanse of white, with the occasional snowman looking wet and miserable. "Weren't they going to make a rink for skating in case the bay's too soft? They'd better get to work if they want it to be ready Friday night."

"Your dad offered to take care of that," Alan said.

Russ laughed. "This whole town would fall apart without Noel Wilkinson. I can guarantee Sue-Anne and Ralph will look out the window Saturday morning, notice there's no place for skating, and tear strips off the staff."

"The only way we can save this town," I said, "is by proving my dad's innocence. Russ, finish your story." I shivered as a raindrop found its way through my scarf and slid down the back of my neck. "But first, let's get someplace warm."

"Bakery's still open," Russ said.

"Definitely not a good idea to go there," I said, thinking of how happy Vicky had been. "Not if we're talking about Mark."

"What about Mark?" Alan asked.

"Come on. We can use my office. It's closest," I said. We hurried down the sidewalk to Mrs. Claus's Treasures. Night had come early, heralded by rapidly moving black clouds, and the lights of my shop glowed warm and enticing against the gloom. Jackie was trying on earrings and necklaces for a pudgy older man, obviously shopping for his wife's Christmas present. Two women studied stuffed Santas, another had her arms piled high with boxes of tree decorations and rooted through our stock searching for more.

"Oh good. You're here," Jackie called as I came in. "I could use some help."

"Be right out," I said, leading the way to my office.

The men stuffed themselves in, and I shut the door firmly behind us. I hung my coat, scarf, and gloves on the hook. Russ and Alan didn't take off their coats. The small, enclosed room soon filled with the unpleasant scent of wet wool drying.

"What about Mark?" Alan asked again as he leaned up against the wall.

Russ repeated what he'd told me so far. Then he took a deep breath. "And it was all a scam."

"What was?" I asked.

"The escarole and mustard greens grown by hand. The chicken and pork enjoying happy chicken and pig lives until a quick, easy death. The heirloom tomatoes and carrots. Yeah, there was some of that, but mixed in with stuff that came from the same suppliers as your local fast-food emporium."

"Oh dear," I said.

"Couldn't people tell they were being served inferior food?" Alan asked.

"The restaurant started off serving the real stuff," Russ said. "And once it was the hot place to be seen, no one wanted to criticize it."

"Like the emperor's new clothes," I said.

"A seventy-five-buck steak marked up from three-fifty in the food aisle at Mega-Mart."

"This was Mark's doing?" Alan asked.

"He was the executive chef," Russ said. "That means

he was the person in charge of the kitchen. He was fired, and the restaurant closed. It would have been a big story, in the New York restaurant world anyway, but the news didn't get the press it might have. The very day Mark was fired was the same day those people were served poisonous mushrooms on the Lower East Side."

"I heard about that," I said. "It was a big deal. The restaurant switched suppliers, and the new guy they got to hunt for woodland mushrooms made a mistake. People were really sick, some spent weeks in the hospital. Didn't someone die?"

"An elderly man, yes. So when it comes down to it, between mushrooms that kill you versus lettuce not grown in properly aerated soil, no one cared much about Mark's place. He quietly disappeared."

"We know where he ended up," Alan said. "At the Yuletide Inn. You think that has something to do with the death of Gord Olsen?"

"It might," I said. "Mark's come here, to Rudolph, to make a new start. Jack might or might not have known about his past, but that doesn't matter. Not many people would give Mark a job. He needs to stay at the inn, at least until he can build his reputation again."

"And Gord was going to fire him," Alan said.

"There is something I'm not sure of," I said. "I was there when Mark had a fight with Gord. Gord was going to make him cut costs, buy factory bread, that sort of thing. If Mark was the sort to cheat customers, why would he care if they weren't getting local produce for the restaurant at the inn?"

I fell forward with a yelp as the office door just about sent me flying.

"For heaven's sake, Merry, do you work here or not?" Jackie yelled. "I'm swamped out there, everyone's coming in out of the rain, and you're having a private party. Must be nice to be a *boss*."

"We'll let you get back to it," Russ said. He and Alan retied scarves and pulled on gloves and headed out.

Chapter 12

A rainy day is good for business. Sometimes. People who are already in town hit the shops if they can't go skating or tobogganing or walking in the snowy woods. Today we had a very good day at Mrs. Claus's Treasures, but I worried about the upcoming weekend. People who weren't already in town and seeking winter activities wouldn't come if the day looked threatening. In Christmas Town at Christmas, we needed crisp, snowy days to put everyone in the holiday mood.

Less than one week remained until December 25th. I could do nothing about the weather, even my dad couldn't do anything about that, so I decided to think about what a successful day we'd had today.

Jackie hadn't been kidding when she burst into my office to say she was swamped. I'd emerged to find a virtual madhouse as customers desperately sought that perfect tree ornament or place mat. Cash registers don't ring *cha-ching* anymore, which is a pity, but the sound of folding tissue paper and the hum of the credit and debit machine was music to my ears.

All of which is to say, I managed to forget about the troubles facing Vicky, Dad, and Rudolph, and I was in a good mood when we closed the shop, tidied up, and headed home. I'd ordered Chinese takeout from a place on the outskirts of town and enjoyed simply having some quiet time to myself.

Now, I was curled up in bed with a mug of hot chocolate (topped with two melting marshmallows), a dreaming dog, and a good book. I was about to switch out the light when the phone beeped. Incoming.

A text from Vicky: *Too late to talk?*

Me: *Nope. Call.*

The phone rang. "You still up?" Vicky asked.

"Just reading. How was it?" I didn't really have to ask. Her voice sounded light and dreamy.

"Dreadful movie," she said.

"Waste of an evening, then," I teased.

"We didn't stay until the end of the movie." She giggled. "We went for a coffee at Cranberries and walked in the park down by the lake for ages. He just left."

"I know walking in the rain is supposed to be romantic, although I've never seen the appeal myself, but in the freezing rain?"

"The rain stopped a while ago. The temperature's dropped below freezing again. Some of the snow might even stay."

"Did you make another date?"

"Promises only," she said. "It's going to be busy at the restaurant up until New Year's. But he wants to see me again. I want to see him again. Oh, Merry, this is it! This is the real thing!"

"You've said that before," I reminded her.

"Yes, but this time it's really real."

"Slowly, slowly," I said.

"That's why I have you," she said, laughing. "To keep me from getting ahead of myself."

That had always been our relationship. Wild, impulsive Vicky and no-nonsense, practical Merry. Vicky pushed me into doing things I wouldn't even consider on my own; I held her back, or at least I tried to, from letting impulse get the better of common sense. This time, I was worried about a lot more than her impulsive nature. I was worried about her delicate heart.

"Has Mark told you anything about his past?" I asked.

"We talked for hours, Merry."

"Did he say why he left the city?"

"Why are you asking that?" A note of suspicion crept into her voice.

"Did he?"

"He landed his dream job as executive chef at a major Manhattan restaurant. The owner turned out to be not entirely ethical, and the restaurant closed less than a year later. He decided he was fed up with the big city and wanted to try something new. I'm so glad he did!"

"That's nice."

"Merry, do you know something you're not telling me?"

"I want you to take care, that's all. I don't want to see you get hurt."

"Goes without saying. So why are you saying it this time?" she asked.

"He is under suspicion for the murder of Gord Olsen, remember?"

"Yeah, but he didn't do it."

I took a deep breath. "You don't know that, sweetie."

"Yes," she said. "I do know that. I know it the same way you know your dad didn't kill Gord. Good night, Merry."

"Vicky, I . . ." She'd hung up.

I threw my book across the room. It hit the framed photograph that stands on my night table, and the picture crashed to the floor. Mattie woke with a start and let out a sharp bark. "Oh, be quiet," I said. He whined at the tone of my voice and cocked his head. I cursed myself and crawled across the bed to pick up the picture of my family. Fortunately, the glass hadn't shattered. I studied the photo. It had been taken the last time we'd all been at home for Christmas, before we children headed out to make our own way in the world. Dad wore one of his vast collection of tasteless Christmas sweaters and a red hat with a white pom-pom dangling on the end. Mom was dressed in a glimmering silver floor-length gown and draped with pearls, and my sisters and my brother and I were in our best clothes. I remembered the taking of this photo. The prime rib and roast potatoes had gone cold while Dad fussed with the delayed setting on his camera and agonized over the best placement of everyone. Chris elbowed Eve in the ribs, she kicked him in return, Carole stuck out her tongue, and Mom had said to Dad, "For heaven's sake, take the blasted picture while I still have my youth."

Good times. My family.

I threw off the covers, climbed out of bed, and stomped into the kitchen. I switched the kettle on to make tea and dropped into a chair at the table. My lovely, peaceful mood was completely shattered, and I was now wide awake. I pulled a pad of paper and a broken pencil over. I wrote a single word at the top in big block letters. *Suspects.*

The only way I could get this mess out of my head and have any hope of being able to sleep was to write it all down. Feeling somewhat like Nancy Drew, I started filling in names. And there were a lot of them. I wrote *Noel Wilkinson* at the top and put a line through it. Then *Vicky Casey* and another line. They were followed by *Mark Grosse, Grace Olsen, Irene Olsen, Sue-Anne Morrow, Randy Baumgartner* (or other Muddites). At the bottom I wrote *Persons Unknown*. I studied the names and thought about means, motive, and opportunity. That was no help, because everyone on my list had all three of those things.

The tea had gone cold, Mattie had been let out for another pee, and my head was still a jumble when I finally gave up and went back to bed. I decided I had to trust Detective Simmonds. She seemed like a smart woman, and she had access to far more information than I did.

I woke with a crick in my neck and in a thoroughly bad mood. I opened one eye. The room was still pitch-dark and Mattie was murmuring in his sleep. I lay on my back and looked at the ceiling. No insights into either the Olsen murder or the sad state of my love life were to be found there, so I got up. Before showering and dressing for a day at the shop, I took Mattie for a particularly long morning walk. It was so early, all the lights were off downstairs, and Mrs. D'Angelo wasn't lying in wait for me. The happy dog bounded on ahead and the not-so-happy woman trudged along behind. Yesterday's rain had frozen overnight, making the walk highly treacherous. The sun was struggling to make an appearance in a dark, cloudy sky when we turned toward home. As I put my key in the lock, a drop fell onto my head. I glanced up to see a big icicle melting. Not good: the temperatures were rising again and those dark clouds were fat with rain.

Even after the long walk, I was one of the first people on Jingle Bell Lane that morning. Of the few people I passed, no one looked any happier than I felt. I tried to cheer myself up by humming Christmas songs under my breath. All my best singing is humming, much to my talented mother's dismay. Still, she couldn't be too disappointed in how her children turned out. My sister Carole was currently touring Europe in the chorus of a production of *Carmen*, my other sister, Eve, was trying to get her foot in the door in Hollywood, and my baby brother, Chris, was studying stage design in New York City. Of the four Wilkinson siblings, only Chris and I could make it home for Christmas this year. The irony of the Christmas-loving Wilkinsons having children with the sorts of jobs that meant they spent the holidays far from home was not lost on me or my parents.

I had my head down and my eyes focused on the slushy sidewalk, looking out for icy traps. I arrived at the shop and fumbled in my pocket for my keys. I put my key in the lock, turned it, and pushed at the door. Only then did I lift my head.

My breathing stopped and my heart rate sped up.

A stuffed toy Santa Claus about a foot tall with black button eyes, woolly beard, and a red suit made out of felt dangled right at my eye level, from a nail hammered into the door. A rope had been tied around the doll's neck. Santa hung there, his head lolling to one side.

I grabbed the hideous thing and pulled as hard as I could. The nail came out easily, and I was clutching the doll. I ran into the shop and slammed the door behind me. I threw the doll onto the floor and bent over, resting shaking hands on my knees, my breath coming in short, hard gasps. I was drenched in sweat.

When I'd regained some control over my limbs and my breathing, I straightened and glanced around my shop. My nerves tingled, but all was quiet. The few lights left on overnight, on the tree and in the window, glowed peacefully. Nothing seemed to have been disturbed. The last thing we do before locking up is run the vacuum cleaner: the floor gets filthy with the on-slaught of snow or mud-covered boots all day. I could see no fresh footprints or tracks on the floor. In the back, all the lights were off. I grabbed a heavy glass candle-stick out of a display. My heart pounded so hard I could almost feel it pushing against my ribs. The floorboards of the old building creaked beneath my weight. I took a deep breath, threw open the door to my office so hard it hit the wall, and slapped the light switch. Nothing other than the usual chaos, and there was nowhere for anyone to hide. I didn't think someone would be in the shop—why leave a warning on the front door?—but I was still careful. I checked the restroom. The window was too small for anyone but a child to get through, and the bolt was in place and undisturbed. In the storage room boxes were piled high, but the room wasn't very big, and one glance told me no one was attempting to conceal themselves. Only when every light in the place had been switched on and I was sure no one, or no other surprises, waited for me did I return to my office and drop into the chair.

I sat there for a few moments, trying to collect my thoughts. Then I pushed myself to my feet and ventured back to the main room. I stood in the entrance, eyeing the thing lying on the floor. I approached it hesitantly and gave it a nudge with my foot. I almost expected the doll to leap into the air, brandishing a knife pulled from his pocket, but it simply lay there, limp and unthreat-ening. Nothing more than a cheap toy Santa. The rope around its neck only a cord used to keep a decoration in place, not the hangman's noose it had appeared to be on my front door.

But I had no doubt that someone had deliberately left me a little gift.

This had to be a warning. Plain and simple. But a warning about what? I was nothing more than a shop owner in a small town in Upstate New York. I wasn't interfering with a terrorist cell or butting into the domain of the mob.

Was I?

I bent over and carefully picked up the doll. I studied it, looking for some sort of message. Nothing. The label said "Made in China." I didn't sell this particular type of Santa Claus toy in my shop, but it was the sort of thing available just about anywhere at this time of year.

I put the doll on the counter and pulled out my phone. My initial thought was to call my dad. My dad would know what to do, but I hesitated, my fingers hovering over the digits. Dad had enough to worry about these days. I punched in another number.

"Mornin', Merry," Alan Anderson said.

"Uh . . . good morning."

"Is something wrong?"

"Yes! I mean, yes. Do you have time to come into town?"

"Are you at the shop?"

"Yes."

"I'm leaving now. Be there in fifteen."

"Okay," I said.

Alan hadn't asked if I was okay, if I needed anything, if I was sure. He just said he'd come. Because I asked him to.

I snapped a few pictures of the doll, and then took it behind the counter, wrapped it in a clear plastic bag, and shoved it into a drawer. I then slammed the drawer shut. It was nothing but a harmless doll, but I didn't want to look at it anymore. I knew I should call Detective Simmonds, but I feared she'd arrive with lights and sirens, maybe a full CSI team, and spend the day fingerprinting my front door, looking for clues among the toy trains and wooden soldiers, the dishes and linens, the tree ornaments and mantel decorations. That would certainly attract a crowd to my shop. A crowd of the ghoulish and the curious. Serious shoppers would run a mile in the opposite direction.

I glanced around for things to keep me busy while waiting for Alan. The jewelry display had been thoroughly gone through yesterday. I was arranging winter-themed earrings on a jewelry tree when a hammering sounded on the door. I opened it a crack, and Alan slipped in.

"You look like you've seen a ghost. What's happened?" His handsome face was full of concern, and he put his strong, scarred hands on my shoulders.

I could feel the warmth of him spreading all the way through to my heart. I smiled, momentarily forgetting what I'd called him about. Unfortunately, I remembered all too quickly. "I want to show you something." I reluctantly moved out of his grip and went behind the counter to take the doll out of the drawer. I held it up, still in the bag.

Alan's face was a question mark.

"When I arrived this morning to open up, I found a surprise. I can't help but think it's intended as a message. It was hanging from a nail, like this." I used my own hands to illustrate a body hanging from a noose. I even stuck out my tongue for emphasis. "This rope was tied around its neck."

Alan reached for it but pulled his hand back as though it had come too close to a flame. "Has anyone else seen this?"

I shook my head.

"Call the police."

"I don't want them here, making a big fuss. They'll close down the shop, and who knows how much business I'll lose."

"This isn't a joke, Merry. It's a threat."

"I know."

"Next time they might not stop at a warning."

I wrapped my arms around myself. "What does it mean?"

I was standing behind the counter, facing the shop. Alan stretched out his hands. I'd probably caught him eating breakfast. He'd stuffed his feet into boots but hadn't taken the time to tie the laces. He smelled of woodsmoke and sawdust. He hadn't shaved yet, his stubble was thick and dark, and his mop of curly blond hair mussed. His cheekbones were sharply outlined in his thin face, and the look in his blue eyes was . . . more than I could interpret. "It means, Merry," he said, in a deep, low voice, "that if anything happened to you, I'd . . ." he left the sentence unfinished.

"Alan," I said.

He coughed and took a step backward, color high in his cheeks. "Do you have any idea who might have done this? Anyone you've argued with lately, or annoyed for some reason?"

Other than my best friend? I buried that thought quickly. "No more than usual."

He gave me a tight smile. "Whatever 'usual' means."

"It has to have something to do with the Gord Olsen murder," I said.

"That's what I'm thinking. You've been poking around, haven't you, asking questions, trying to get to the bottom of what happened?"

"I have. But so's Detective Simmonds, and I bet no one has placed a noose on her front door."

"And that," Alan said, "tells me you're getting closer to the truth than she is."

Chapter 13

"Mornin' y'all. Looks like it's going to be another miserable day."

I let out a screech, and Alan whirled around.

"Gee, sorry if I interrupted something," Russ Durham said.

"Come in and shut the door," I said.

"What's going on?"

"Nothing!"

"Yeah, looks like nothing to me. Alan?"

Alan glanced at me. I shook my head. Russ was a friend, and I trusted him. But he was above all a newspaper reporter. About the last thing I needed was to have this story spread across the front page of the *Gazette*.

"Okay," Russ said, "keep your secrets. I was going to call you later, Alan, then I saw your truck outside. Making deliveries?"

"What?"

"Yes," I said. "Alan dropped off a box of . . . of . . . toys. For the weekend."

Russ glanced around the room, empty of delivery boxes. "If you say so. You said yesterday you wouldn't accompany Santa as his toymaker if the town didn't reinstate Noel. Is that still the case?"

"Unless something's changed," Alan said. "Has it?"

"Not as far as I know. Care to make an official statement about that?"

"No." Alan was a man of few words when it suited him.

"Aline Wilkinson has withdrawn her children's vocal classes from their scheduled performances. She gave me a statement. Although I'll have to do a comprehensive editing job to make it suitable to print in a community newspaper."

"Speaking to the press is her right." Alan turned to me. "Merry, I think you should do as we discussed, and I'll stay with you if you'd like me to. I have deliveries to make this morning, but the way things are looking, it might not matter if the stores restock their toys."

"At least the rain's holding off," Russ said.

"What's the forecast for the weekend?" I asked.

"Temperatures still rising, and the chance of freezing rain," Russ said.

I groaned. "Might as well shut the whole town down. Rename it Grinchville. Are people canceling?"

"I made a few calls last night to the hotels and restaurants. You know how optimistic people can be about the weather, so they're not canceling yet. But if they wake up Saturday morning and it's raining, they won't come out. Those few brave folks who don't mind the weather and want their kids to meet Santa might not come to Rudolph anyway. Muddle Harbor has placed ads in the Rochester and Syracuse papers. Santa has, apparently, set up his castle in the Muddle Harbor rec center, where families can be warm and dry, not to mention safe, meeting Santa and his helpers."

"Castle?" I said. "Since when does Santa have a castle?"

"It must be left over from that summer when they tried to put on a Renaissance fair," Alan said.

"Oh yeah, that."

Alan and I paused for a moment, remembering the string of bad ideas that had come out of the town of Muddle Harbor.

"So," Russ said, "you going to tell me what's going on?"

"No," I said. "Alan, you go and make your deliveries. Russ, will you do something for me?"

"Sure."

"Is there any way you can find out the whereabouts of Randy Baumgartner and John"—I struggled to remember the last name of Janice's brother—"John someone-or-other, the night Gord was killed?"

Russ lifted one eyebrow. "You want me to track down the whereabouts of a man named John?"

"He's a real estate agent. Can't be many of those in Muddle Harbor. He's bound to have ads all over the place, particularly in the *Chronicle*."

"That'll help. I can at least try to eliminate the mayor and this John fellow."

"Thanks. Simmonds might have asked them for alibis. I mentioned them to her the other day."

"Merry," Alan said, "are you forgetting the warning?"

Russ's reporter's eyebrows twitched at the word. He studied my face. I tried to look strong and resolute. It wasn't easy. "Not at all, but I'm not going to be cowed into walking away from this. The longer this drags on, the worse it's going to be for Dad and everyone else under suspicion." Now that I'd had time to get over my fright, my blood was rising. The only possible reason anyone would have to threaten me had to do with the Olsen murder and me poking around asking questions. If I was, as Alan had suggested, closer to the truth than the police, I couldn't stop now.

"You might want to wait a while before talking to Simmonds, Russ," I said. "I'm going to take Alan's advice, call her now, and ask her to come over."

"I'll wait with you," Alan said.

"No. I'm good. You guys have things to do." I glanced at the clock. "It's almost opening time, and I'm safe here in my shop."

"Safe?" Russ said. "Safe from what? Will someone tell me what's going on here?"

"When I know," I said, "I'll let you know."

Russ and Alan were reluctant to leave, but I eventually managed to convince both of them that I didn't want them around. That wasn't entirely true. I did want them around. I wanted to feel safe with them. But Alan had his business to see to, and I didn't want Russ writing about what had happened in the paper. He'd tell me he wouldn't, but I thought it better not to tempt him.

The minute they left, I called Simmonds. She told me she was picking up a coffee at Cranberries and arrived at my door less than five minutes later. This time she was the one bringing the coffee and muffins.

I pulled out the plastic bag with the doll and told her where I'd found it. "Please, you can't make a public display of investigating this. I can't afford to frighten my customers."

She smiled at me as she took the bag. "Don't worry, Merry. We can be discreet. You say there was no sign of a break-in?"

"I checked thoroughly. Nothing has been disturbed. I'm almost positive they didn't come inside."

"I'll take the doll as well as the nail and the rope and check them for fingerprints. There's probably no point in fingerprinting the door, you must have hundreds of people pushing your door open. I'll run this against our databases and see if anything similar has been reported previously."

"Thanks." Simply handing the doll over to Detective Simmonds made me feel a lot better. "This has to have something to do with the Olsen murder," I said.

"What makes you say that?"

"It's a warning. Someone thinks I'm getting close to finding out what happened and is telling me to back off."

"That's possible. But there could be other reasons."

"There aren't," I said firmly. "This proves one thing beyond a doubt."

"And that is?"

"That my dad didn't do it. My father would never do anything to frighten me."

"I'm inclined to agree," she said.

"You are?"

"I'll let you know what we find out," she said. "In the meanwhile, stay out of this, Merry. And look out for yourself."

The moment Simmonds was out the door, Betty Thatcher was in. "What did she want?"

"To wish me the compliments of the season," I said.

"Don't give me that, Merry Wilkinson. Something's up here. I know it. Simmonds left with a plastic bag. You don't wrap your goods in plastic bags. Although why you waste money on those fancy paper bags with your store logo on it, I never can figure out."

"People like customized bags," I said, wondering why I was defending my business practices. "It's worth the extra cost."

She sniffed. "Must be nice to have a hobby business. Not like folks like me who have to make my living from my shop. But I don't complain," she complained, "when fancy-dancy stores like this one muscle in on my business. Clark and me manage fine."

"How nice for you," I said. "Sorry to chase you off, but I have a lot of work to get to."

Betty jerked her head toward the street. "Did she have anything to say about the Gord Olsen business?"

"No."

She shifted her feet and studied the details of my carpet. "I want you to know, Merry, that I don't believe what they're all saying."

"What who's all saying?"

"That your dad killed Gord."

"No one's saying that!"

"Then why is Noel not going to be Santa this year? That young Kyle Lambert was in my shop buying himself a costume. He told Clark he'd been hired as the official Santa Claus for the children's weekend. Anyway, I read it in the *Chronicle*."

I ground my teeth. I tried to remember that Betty had started this conversation by saying she didn't think Dad was guilty. "I'm surprised you read the *Chronicle*, Betty. It never has anything positive to say about Rudolph."

"A customer brought it into my shop. She asked me if it was true."

"And what did you tell her?"

"I said it was a pack of lies."

"Oh. Thank you for that."

"If you hear anything from that lady detective," Betty said, "you'll let me know, won't you?"

"Sure," I said.

Betty crept back to her lair. I didn't like her one tiny bit, but I did grudgingly appreciate her support for Dad. She might hate me and my shop but she was a lifetime Rudolphite, after all. And we Rudolphites stuck together.

Or did we?

Something about a photograph had been niggling at

the back of my mind. A photograph and the *Muddle Harbor Chronicle*.

Jackie told me Kyle had earned two hundred and fifty bucks from the sale of a picture he took with his phone. I'd been preoccupied with everything that was going on around here and had dismissed her comment without a thought. Now that I was thinking about it, I realized that only one photo taken in Rudolph lately would be worth selling.

Kyle had been the one who snapped Dad and Mom leaving the police station the night of Gord's death. He'd sold the photo to the *Chronicle* for two hundred and fifty dollars. And now he was putting some of his ill-gotten proceeds toward the cost of a Santa Claus suit. The traitorous rat.

I filed that tidbit of information in the back of my mind to pull out when I needed it, and flipped the sign on the door to "Open."

The rain held off, but it was a dismal day, punctuated by the steady drip of water falling from the roof as the snow melted. A few people came into the shop in the morning, their expressions a match to the day and to my mood. What shoppers there were, were listless and their hearts weren't in it.

"We've come from Toronto for the children's weekend," a woman told me as she idly pawed through the table linens. Her silver hair was expensively cut and colored, her makeup discreet. A diamond tennis bracelet sparkled in the lights from the tree. "I've been wanting to bring my grandchildren here for a long time, and this year I convinced my daughter that her kids are old enough to enjoy all the children's activities. Her husband didn't want to come in the first place, and now he's trying to talk her into leaving and heading up to Quebec for some skiing. They've had snow at Mont-Tremblant, he says." She looked at me hopefully. "The weather won't spoil everything, will it?"

"We'll move the events indoors, if we have to."

She grimaced. "Hard to have the snowman-making competition indoors, isn't it? That's all my grandson and my husband have been talking about for months. They've drawn up a series of sketches on how to approach the build and everything." The edges of her mouth turned up in a fond smile. "My husband's a retired architect. He misses it sometimes. What about this Santa Claus business?"

My heart sank. "What Santa Claus business?" *As if I didn't know.*

"They say the man who plays Santa has been charged with murder. Doesn't sound very wholesome, does it?"

"He wasn't charged. He was questioned because he might have been a witness." I was getting very tired of repeating that.

"If that's the case," the woman said, "there's a murderer on the loose in this town." She put down the napkins. "Perhaps we'd be better off going to Quebec. You've some nice things here, but not today, thanks."

She left.

I cursed.

Jackie arrived at one to begin her shift, and I told her I'd be out for most of the day.

"Not again! Merry, you can't leave me alone here. Suppose we get busy?"

"Look, Jackie, if this shop's going to survive, we have to find out who killed Gord Olsen. I've had a customer tell me they're leaving because there's a killer in town."

"He's long gone," Jackie said.

"How do you know that?"

"Kyle said so. He says it's a mob thing. We all know the mob's heavily involved in construction, right? Gord wanted to build a Mega-Mart, right? Someone in the mob probably didn't want the contract to go to their enemy."

For the first time ever, I wanted to believe something Kyle had to say. But no arrest for Gord's death wasn't good, either. We didn't need the shadow of an unsolved homicide hanging over Rudolph. Not if it made people think they were in danger of being murdered in their hotel beds.

I went home and got my car. I didn't even go upstairs to check on Mattie; I didn't want the complications of dealing with the excited puppy when I was trying to do something about solving a murder. Guilt at leaving him followed me down the street.

I drove through town. As I passed Victoria's Bake Shoppe I tried to peer inside, but couldn't see anything. I knew I should pop in to see Vicky and try to get over the way we'd left things last night after her phone call. But what I was about to do wouldn't earn me any thanks from her, and so I didn't stop. More guilt piled on.

The snow on the lawns surrounding the Yuletide Inn was still in fairly good condition, and the long driveway and meandering paths had been scraped of snow and ice and well salted. The temperatures were slightly above freezing, but a sharp, icy wind was blowing in from the lake, so I was pleased to see some families out, the kids well wrapped against the cold. A big red old-fashioned sleigh sat at the far end of the parking lot, and it warmed the cockles of my heart (whatever cockles might be) to see it. A local farmer would be bringing Dancer and Prancer, his two gorgeous Clydesdales, on Saturday to ferry families between the inn and town in the sleigh.

I could only hope there would be activities in Rudolph for the families to enjoy.

I drove around the back and parked beside the delivery bay at the rear of the kitchen. It was almost two o'clock, and I hoped I wasn't too early. I stuck my head in the door. "Hello?"

The kitchen wasn't quite a hive of activity, but it was still busy. Giant pots emitted clouds of steam, knives flashed over rows of brilliantly colored produce, and in a far corner dirty dishes were stacked high while a young, long-haired man up to his elbows in soapy water tried to control the onslaught.

"Merry!" Mark called. "Nice to see you. Come on in." He waved a razor-sharp knife with a ten-inch blade at me. I swallowed. A chicken lay on the counter in front of him.

"I don't want to interrupt your work," I lied.

"Not a problem. I took yesterday off, so I came in early to get started on dinner prep."

"Are you going to be full tonight?" I said.

He grimaced. "Not as full as I'd like to be." He lowered his voice. "We've had cancellations, at the inn as well as the restaurant. Grace was counting on being fully booked every night until New Year's, but right now it doesn't look like that's going to happen. People don't want to vacation at a hotel where someone was recently murdered."

The chicken on the butcher's block was plump and healthy looking. Other than the being-dead part, that is. I glanced around the big, busy room. The vegetables looked good. The tomatoes ranged from the usual round red to small and yellow or deep purple and misshaped, meaning they weren't mass-produced; the carrots were purple and yellow as well as the standard orange. A mountain of kale waited to be washed.

Mark followed my gaze. "Wondering where your food comes from, Merry? It's not always easy at this time of year to get fresh produce in New York State, but small-scale farmers are doing great things with greenhouses and cold frames these days. The tomatoes are from California, nothing I can do about that, but I managed to find a good heirloom supplier. What brings you here?"

I cleared my throat. "Do you have a minute to talk, Mark? Privately, I mean."

"Sure." He called to the woman who was standing at a giant sink and washing vegetables under a steady spray of water. "Anna, I'm taking a short break."

"Okay, Chef," she called without looking up.

Mark put down the knife. I was glad of it, and felt guilty for being glad. He led the way into a small, cramped room that served as his office. As well as the usual computer paraphernalia and piles of invoices and bills, stacks of cooking magazines and catalogues from restaurant suppliers filled the room. Two posters hung on the wall. Both were typical tourist stuff: one of the French Quarter of New Orleans at night, the other Manhattan taken from a plane.

He caught me looking at the posters. "My two major influences. I cook modern urban American with a Cajun accent." He grinned. "Although not at Christmas. At Christmas, Grace wants traditional all the way." He rubbed at his short hair. "What's up?"

"Look, Mark, there's no nice way to say this, so I'll just come out and say it. I know it's not really any of my business, but you're seeing my best friend and her well-being matters a great deal to me. I've heard about what happened to you in the city. And, well, I have to wonder how important this job is to you?"

"I'd ask if Vicky put you up to this, but I know she didn't. Last night I told her the whole sordid story."

"Oh," I said.

"You're right, it is none of your business." His brown eyes were dark with anger. "But, to stop you from going around making insinuations . . ."

"I'm not . . ."

"I'll tell you that this job is important to me. Very important. The cooking world is surprisingly small at my level, and reputation is everything. Mine's pretty much shot, through no fault of my own, so I need to rebuild it. This place is perfect for that."

"You say no fault of your own . . ."

"The restaurant owner convinced me to work for him

because he said his place would be all about fresh, quality local products from small farms. That's the sort of cooking I believe in. Things went well for a while, the restaurant was a big success, and I was establishing good relationships with farmers. Then he brought his brother in to help." Mark made quotation marks in the air with his fingers. "Some help. The brother started cutting corners, so slowly at first, I wasn't quite aware of what was happening."

I glanced around the office, the desk piled high with papers. "Don't you receive the products, pay the bills?"

"Yeah, I do. My only crime, if you want to call it that, was slacking off. The restaurant was a hit, successful beyond my wildest dreams. I wanted my hand in every pot of soup and every drop of salad dressing. I was overwhelmed, glad to hand off some of the business affairs to the brother. Turns out the brother was buying inferior goods, billing the restaurant for the best stuff, and keeping the difference. When I finally found out what was going on, I went to the owner. He refused to believe me, wouldn't even talk to his brother, so I quit on the spot. Unfortunately, the night before an influential restaurant critic had eaten a substandard meal at our place, and his article hit the papers. The owner publicly blamed me, because that's the kind of man he is, and said he'd fired me."

"I'm sorry," I said.

"Yeah, you and me both. But Karma comes around. He had more money than brains and not the slightest idea how the restaurant business works. He figured if he fired me publicly everything would get back to normal. Except, as I could have told him, the night after word got out, the dining room was almost completely empty. And it never got better. They soon closed." Mark shrugged. "Restaurants don't recover from bad press. Ever."

I believed him. Maybe because I wanted to, and maybe only because I liked him, but I believed him. I could imagine how furious he'd been when he found out that Gord Olsen wanted to source inferior food. That would have been the final nail in the coffin of Mark's reputation.

I realized that by convincing me he was not a con artist, Mark had just given me a very good reason for him to kill Gord Olsen.

He read the expression on my face. "If your next question is 'Did I murder Gord?' the answer to that is no, I did not. The police asked me if I had an alibi, and the only one I could give them is this place. Gord had come in at some point in the evening and stuck his nose where it didn't belong. I ordered him to leave, and he wisely did so. I didn't see him again. Things were winding down at the time the cops say Gord was killed, but we were still on the hop. I could have slipped out for five, ten minutes, but if there was a problem, and there often is, I would have been missed. No one missed me." He spread out his hands. "Now, if you'll excuse me, Merry, I have work to do." His tone was cool, his eyes flat.

"Other than my parents, Vicky's the dearest thing in the world to me," I said. "I know you guys went out last night. I have to make sure you're not . . ."

"A vicious killer." To my surprise, he laughed. "We should all be so lucky to have friends like you, Merry.

I like Vicky. I like her a lot. Don't you dare tell her I said so." The green sparks were back in his eyes.

"Mum's the word," I said.

I left Mark to do magic with a dead chicken and a mountain of kale and headed for my car. Was I absolutely positive he had not killed Gord? No, but I was pretty darn sure. When I got home I'd put a line through his name on my list of suspects.

I drove slowly around the corner of the building, taking care as snow was piled high on either side of the lane, making it even narrower than normal. A dark shape broke from the shoveled path at the employees' entrance and dashed into the road. As carefully as I was going, when I hit the brakes my wheels spun and my car skidded to a halt. It was Grace, and I'd missed her by inches. Heedless of the weather she wore an open sweater and pumps. She turned as if to say something rude, but she recognized me and hurried over. I rolled down the window. "What is it? Is something wrong?"

"Jack," she said.

"I'll follow you." Mom had told me Grace hired a private nurse to stay with Jack a few hours a day so Grace could look after things at the inn. Jack had been out of the hospital for only a few days. I hoped it wasn't another heart attack. Surely a second attack so shortly after such a serious one would prove fatal.

I parked in front of the cottage, and by the time I was out of my car, Grace had thrown open her front door. I didn't bother to take off my coat or boots, but ran after Grace into the living room. The moment I saw Jack, I felt overwhelming relief. He was sitting in a reclining chair with an afghan in shades of green and red covering his thin legs. His face was pasty white, and his sparse, graying hair was standing on end, but he was alive and conscious. A woman, short and chubby, dressed in faded pink hospital scrubs, leaned over him. "There, there," she said, using the same tone Dad employed to comfort a fractious child who didn't really want to sit on a scary-looking stranger's knee. "Nothing's out there." She turned as she heard us come in. "Oh, Mrs. Olsen. I'm sorry to bother you, but he's so upset."

"What happened?" Grace knelt on the floor beside her husband's chair and took his hand. He looked at her through watery red eyes. I was shocked at the change in his appearance. Less than two weeks had passed since his heart attack. He'd been a laughing, robust, storytelling man then. Now he was just old. His strong, square jaw seemed to have shrunk, the color in his once-twinkling blue eyes was flat and dull, and the eyes themselves were red rimmed.

"I don't know." The nurse wrung her hands together. "I was in the kitchen getting him a cup of tea when I heard him yelling to beat the band. When I came in, he was pointing at the window."

"Jack, darling?" Grace said.

He turned to her. His rheumy red eyes were wide and frightened. "Someone's out there. Watching me."

"Don't be silly." The nurse sounded like she was admonishing a three-year-old for being afraid of monsters under the bed.

"It was a guest, Jack," Grace said. "They cut through the back sometimes, heading for the woods. You know that, darling." She looked up at the nurse and me. "Even though we have a fence around the cottage property, a gate with a latch, and a sign that says 'Private,' you'd be surprised at how many people don't think that applies to them if they want to cut thirty seconds off their walk."

Jack shook his head. "He was there, looking in the window. I saw him."

"Why don't you get that tea, Harriet?" Grace said, her voice soft and calm. "I'll stay with Jack for a bit. I'm sorry if I frightened you, Merry."

"I think you should call the police," I said.

Harriet gasped.

"It was nothing," Grace said.

"In most cases I'd agree," I said. "But in light of . . . what happened here recently, can we be so sure?"

Grace pushed herself to her feet. She took my elbow and led me to a corner of the room. We stood next to the large balsam, its cheerful lights turned off. The gas fireplace, however, was on, and the room was stiflingly hot and stuffy, filled with the cloying smell of medicine and illness. Grace's voice was a whisper. "What are you saying, Merry?"

"I'm saying someone killed Jack's son. Can we be so sure it stops there? Maybe they have reason to be after Jack, too."

"You can't be serious!"

"I am perfectly serious. It won't do any harm to give

Detective Simmonds a call. She can check for footprints or something."

"It can do a lot of harm, Merry. I'm working night and day to reassure everyone that this inn is safe and respectable. I can't have the police tromping around again."

"Simmonds can be discreet," I said.

"No. You're making something out of nothing, Merry."

"Are you planning to do a deal with Fine Budget?" I asked bluntly.

She blinked. "What?"

"The Fine Budget people are still here. They say the deal's still on."

Grace's eyes shifted. I stood my ground. I felt horrible just thinking it, but was it possible Grace wanted total control of the business for herself? She seemed to be devoted to her husband, but could it all be an act?

She lifted her chin and faced me. "Not that it's any of your business, Merry Wilkinson, but I am prepared to listen to what they have to say. I have to think about the future, for Jack as well as me. If he doesn't get back on his feet soon, I'll have trouble caring for him as well as managing this place. At best we earn a small profit every year. We've had a number of cancellations today, for rooms as well as the restaurant. I can't afford that, not at this time of year. Maybe it is time to sell." She turned her face toward her husband. Jack was staring at the window, his expression wary. Tea things clattered in the kitchen. "I need my Jack back." Grace wiped at her eyes.

"What do the doctors say?"

"That he needs time. His body had a major shock with the heart attack, and now he's grieving the death of Gord. It's a lot to handle."

"Grace," Jack called.

"Just a minute, dear."

"Don't minute me," he said with a trace of his old voice. "I can't abide people whispering in corners. Never up to any good, whisperers."

A smile lit up Grace's face. She hurried to Jack's side and called to me over her shoulder. "Merry, can I ask you to have a look outside? Then we'll decide about making that phone call."

"What phone call?" Jack asked.

I slipped out of the front of the house. I kept to the shoveled sidewalk leading to the lane. A driveway curved around the cottage, heading to the detached garage tucked away at the rear of the property. I walked carefully, watching where I put my feet. The lane had been plowed down to bare concrete and I could see no footprints. Jack and Grace's cottage backed onto the woods and had a small private garden surrounded by a chain link fence. The gate stood open, held in place by drifts of snow. The sign saying "Private" was covered in sticky snow that obscured most of the letters. It wasn't coming down now, but strong winds were tossing flakes through the cold air. Two sets of boot prints were clear in the otherwise untouched expanse of snow. A line of prints pointing in each direction left the cottage driveway, went through the open gate, and crossed the lawn. I followed, being very careful not to step on the prints. Drifting snow had not filled in any of the depressions caused by the boots' treads, so they had to have been laid down only moments ago. I pulled out my cell phone and snapped a couple of pictures. I thought back to the snow-covered garden after Gord's death. There had been footprints, for sure, but if I'd noticed any details I didn't remember. These ones had a deep zigzag pattern. The prints went in a straight line, directly from the gate to the back of the house. I followed them across the lawn, up the stairs of the deck, across the deck to the French doors. I peered inside. Jack sat scowling in his chair, Harriet fussed with tea things, and Grace stood by the windows, watching me.

I pointed to the prints, which were directly up against the doors. Someone had stood here, all right, shifting their feet, peering in. Watching Jack. Grace had been at the inn. Had they not known Jack had a caregiver? Did they expect to find him alone in the house?

What would they have done if he had been alone?

I lifted my phone to show it to Grace. She nodded.

I had Diane Simmonds's personal number in my contacts list so I phoned her rather than 911. I agreed with Grace. Cruisers screeching into the inn under lights and sirens—again!—would not be good for business.

Simmonds answered immediately and said she was on her way. I walked to the end of the driveway to wait. While waiting, I called the shop to check in.

"Jackie O'Reilly's Christmas Treasures," Jackie announced when she answered the phone. "The sole employee speaking."

"Ha. Ha. How are things?"

"So-so. I could be robbing you blind, Merry, you do know that, don't you?"

"Jackie, I'm not in the mood at the moment. I should be back in about an hour, and Crystal comes in at five so you can have your dinner break then."

"I'll try to live that long," she said.

I hung up without further comment.

Now I had two names to cross off my list: Mark and Grace. Okay, I'm a lousy judge of character, but I'd seen how concerned Grace had been at her husband's agitated condition. I was positive there was no way she'd do anything to harm Jack. Considering the perilous state of his health, even a shock could kill him.

I didn't have to wait long before I saw someone pulling into the private lane. I'd told Simmonds to meet me at the cottage. She'd come alone, driving an unmarked car. I told her what had happened and took her around the back to see for herself. Drifting snow was beginning to fill in the prints, smudging the edges. Simmonds squatted beside them and snapped pictures. She pulled a pen out of her coat pocket, laid it beside the prints, and took more pictures. "For measurement," she said. "These'll be gone soon."

She straightened and followed the line of boot prints as I had done. I pointed out my own, and she kept close to them. She took more pictures at the French doors, where the prints were churned up. Obviously someone had stood in place for a while, shifting their feet while they peered inside.

"Is Mr. Olsen fit to answer a few questions?" she asked me when we were back on the pavement of the lane.

"I think so. He was frightened, but it might have given him a spark of interest. Be warned, though. Grace won't allow you to upset him."

Simmonds gave me a grin. "In that case, I'll put away the bright lights and truncheon."

Back in the house, I gave Grace what I hoped was a reassuring smile. Simmonds spoke to Harriet, the nurse, first. Harriet had seen nothing, she said, and heard nothing. She'd been in the kitchen, which is at the front of the house, overlooking the inn, not the backyard, when she heard Jack yell. She found him highly agitated, struggling to get out of his chair. He said someone had been at the window, watching him, but by the time Harriet checked, she saw nothing. Jack wouldn't be calmed, so she called Grace.

"I know what I saw," Jack said. "I'm not totally helpless yet, you know."

"We don't think . . ." Grace began.

But all Jack could tell us was that he'd seen a person standing at the French doors, staring in. He didn't know if it was a man or a woman, and couldn't guess at their height, other than to say it was around average. The window faced west and the winter sun was low in the sky behind this person. He, or she, wore a bulky, shapeless coat with a hood. Jack looked up, saw someone staring at him, and yelled. The person disappeared when Harriet came into the room.

Simmonds closed her notebook, thanked Jack for his time, and told Harriet and Grace to call her if anything else happened. She headed out. I hurried to follow.

We stood on the steps of the cottage. A few cars drove by as employees arrived to start their shift or headed home at the end of it.

"I can stay," I said, "until the guard arrives."

"What guard?" Simmonds said.

"You are stationing someone here to protect Jack, aren't you? It's obvious the person who killed Gord is now after Jack." As I'd been watching Simmonds question the Olsens and Harriet, I kept thinking of Irene Olsen. With Gord dead, it would be unlikely his widow would get anything upon Jack's death, but I didn't know the contents of his will. Gord's children would inherit, but I'd been told Irene and Gord didn't have kids. Was it possible she was pregnant? That would surely change everything.

"Merry," Simmonds said, "I don't have those kinds of resources. And even if I did, I don't come to the same conclusion you do."

"It's obvious. Someone's after Jack. He's hardly in any condition to defend himself in case of an attack."

Simmonds rubbed at her face. "You're letting your imagination run away with you."

"That's ridiculous. I didn't imagine that hanging doll nailed to my door this morning."

"No, you didn't. I believe you when you said you found it there."

"You believe me?" It never occurred to me, not for a

moment, that anyone wouldn't believe me. Was Simmonds saying she'd considered it possible I'd placed the doll there myself? Why would I do that? "This isn't about me. It's about Jack."

"Mrs. Olsen admits that hotel guests sometimes come into the yard out of curiosity or thinking there's a shortcut."

"Yes, but . . . There's a gate. And a sign."

"Judging by the amount of snow blocking it, the gate has been open for some time. Signs don't always stop people, Merry. Not to mention, that particular one is covered with so much snow it's difficult to make out what it says."

"Okay, okay." I waved my arms for emphasis. "I admit it's possible some curious hotel guest wanted to have a peek. Maybe they thought the cottage was available for rent. But to come right up on the deck and peer in the windows? That's creepy."

"It's creepy, all right, but not uncommon. Folks sometimes think if they're paying money at a hotel they have the right to stick their nose into everything. And I do mean everything."

"What about the boot prints?" I said. "They're still clear enough to make out details of the tread. Do they match the ones at the scene of Gord's death?"

"No."

"No? Are you sure?"

"Yes, Merry, I am sure. The tread on those formed a hash pattern. These are completely different. I'll grant the size is similar, but with winter boots it can be hard to tell. Some people buy big boots to leave room for thick socks, some do not. Men's and women's snow boots are very similar, unlike most shoes."

"If the killer has any brains at all, he'll know you're looking for his—or her—boots, so he would have gotten rid of them. Were these ones new, did you notice? You can tell by the tracks if the treads are worn down, can't you?

"Merry, stay out of my investigation."

"But . . ."

"No buts." She pulled her keys out of her coat pocket. "I'm going back to town, and I'll file a report on this."

"Aren't you at least going to fingerprint the glass doors?"

"Merry, there's no point. In this weather it would be unusual for anyone to be outside *without* gloves." She held up her own hands as evidence. "I'll ask for a patrol car to swing by the hotel regularly."

She climbed into her own vehicle and drove away.

Chapter 14

I wanted to stop at the bakery and try to make up with Vicky, but by the time I got back to town, the "Closed" sign was in place and the lights were switched off. Instead, I went home and let Mattie out. We played with a toy made of thick, twisted rope in the backyard for a long time. Unlike the pristine expanse of untouched snow at Grace and Jack's, my yard was so churned up not a single foot—or paw—print could be distinguished from another. As I alternately threw the toy, chased a happy Mattie for it, and attempted to wrestle it from his slobbering jaws, I started to feel a bit better. I was furious at Detective Simmonds. She'd almost come right out and said I was overreacting, if not actually causing trouble in an attempt to focus attention on myself.

Mattie grabbed the rope and galloped in joyous

circles around the yard, swinging the colorful toy from side to side.

I knew I should just let it all go. Someone, after all, had warned me to do exactly that. What could the hanging Santa doll have been but a warning?

Time to let the police take care of it. It was their job, after all. It was what Diane Simmonds wanted me to do.

That would be the sensible thing. But I didn't know if I could be sensible. I cared too much about this town. About the people in it. My dad. Vicky. From what I'd observed, Simmonds was a good cop. Smart, dedicated, committed. But she was still a newcomer, an outsider, and from a big city, to boot. What would she know about the small-town ties and complicated rivalries that were the lifeblood of Rudolph?

Mattie gave a single decisive bark. I blinked and refocused my attention. The rope was at my feet, and Mattie's head was cocked in what I was beginning to recognize as his exasperated look when I failed to concentrate on an important matter at hand. "Okay, okay." I bent over to pick the toy up. He lunged for it; we grabbed it at the same time and wrestled for it.

I ended up face-first in the snow, legs and arms kicking, laughing. I rolled onto my back. It was getting late and the sun was a weak, white ball low in a pewter sky. At this latitude, this close to the solstice, it's dark before five o'clock. Mattie's face appeared above me. His warm brown eyes danced with the sheer joy of being alive. He licked my nose. I reached up and pulled him to me and wrapped him in a giant hug.

"Am I interrupting a tender moment?" Wendy said.

Mattie ran to greet her, and I struggled to my feet. "Playtime that went horribly wrong." I shook snow off.

The snowsuited bundle in Wendy's arms squirmed. My neighbor held her baby out so she could greet Mattie. The young dog was amazing around the little girl. His nose twitched, but he didn't try to lick her face, and he let her run her pudgy hands through his fur.

"Couple more months," Wendy said, "and they'll be able to play together."

"I can't wait. I'm going to feel the results of that fall tomorrow." I called for the dog, and we walked upstairs with Wendy and Tina. "How are plans for the weekend going?" I asked.

Wendy pulled a face. "A couple of the councillors paid a call on your dad. Asked him to come and be Santa."

"That's great."

"He said he wouldn't go against the decision of the acting mayor. Sue-Anne herself has to ask him to."

More like crawl on her hands and knees over shards of broken ice, I thought. My dad could be stubborn sometimes.

"Plans, such as they are, are under way to move Santa and the games into the community center. The shop and restaurant owners who were going to have treats for sale on the sidewalk are still intending to, unless the rain is bad enough to drive everyone inside."

"No change in the weather forecast?"

"According to Sue-Anne's assistant, who checks it about every five minutes, it's not looking good."

"Speaking of shops, I need to get back to mine. My employees are on the verge of mutiny."

"I'll be dreaming of a winter wonderland tonight," Wendy said.

I fed Mattie and made myself a cheese sandwich to take to the shop. Jackie might grumble and complain, but I paid her well over minimum wage just so she'd put up with me. And because she was an excellent salesperson. She had a way of delighting the men with her pretty looks and flirtatious charm that somehow didn't turn their wives off.

I called my dad before going to the shop. Simmonds might not think someone creeping around Jack's house important, but I did. I hadn't wanted to worry Dad about the warning on my door, and I still didn't plan to tell him or Mom, but Jack was his friend. He'd be furious if he found out I'd kept this from him.

"Hi, Mom," I said. "How are you?"

"Dreadful. I was about to take the phone off the hook. Every one of my parents has called, sometimes more than once, about my canceling the weekend concerts."

"Are they mad at you?"

"Sentiment seems to be running around eighty percent in my favor. Some understand that I have to side with my husband, some simply think the town is making a mistake. Unfortunately, it's the other twenty percent who make the loudest noise. 'Suzie and Johnny have practiced so hard . . .' and on and on they go. You'd think a talent scout from *American Idol* was coming to Rudolph with the sole intention of hearing them. They are not at all mollified when I inform them that their child's class will be included in an extended version of my Epiphany concert at St. Jude's. One parent informed me that they are Baptist so they do not want their child singing in a Catholic church. I informed her that I am not a warrior goddess but I have sung the role of a Valkyrie."

Sometimes I wasn't so sure my mother *wasn't* a warrior goddess. "You tell 'em, Mom. I'm calling to speak to Dad. Is he there?"

"He is still ensconced in his study. I'm starting to worry, dear. A delegation came earlier from the town council and he practically threw them out of the house."

She passed the phone to my father, and I told him about what had happened at the Olsens'. He didn't waste time saying "are you sure" and "perhaps you imagined it." "As far as I know," I said, "Irene's still staying at the inn. I suppose there's nothing suspicious about that—the police have yet to release Gord's body and Jack is her father-in-law—but I would have thought that after that scene over breakfast at the restaurant yesterday, she'd find more welcoming accommodations."

"I doubt she's paying at the Yuletide," Dad said.

"I didn't consider that."

"Do you know if the caregiver they've hired is with him around the clock?"

"No. Grace told me they've only taken on an afternoon shift so she can get some work done at the inn without leaving Jack alone."

"I'm going there now. I'll spend the night and stay with Jack tomorrow until the nurse comes."

"That's nice of you, Dad, but you can't move in permanently."

"It's not as if," he said, "I have anything else to do this weekend."

"Oh right. You have to consider that they might never catch the person who killed Gord."

"I'll take it one day at a time, honeybunch."

We hung up, and I went back to work.

I might as well not have bothered, business was so slow that evening.

Chapter 15

I expect every single person in Rudolph, New York, checked the weather report the moment they got out of bed on Friday morning. I did, and it was still saying thirty-three degrees and a chance of freezing rain for Saturday and Sunday.

The children's weekend didn't kick off until Saturday morning, but all the shops on Jingle Bell Lane were putting on a welcoming party atmosphere tonight with treats like cookies, hot cider, and candy canes available for shoppers and their kids. I hadn't spoken to Vicky yesterday, and I felt bad about that. She was supposed to be dropping trays of gingerbread cookies off at Mrs. Claus's Treasures in the afternoon. I was looking forward to apologizing and giving her a hug.

I had no reason to get to work early, so I took Mattie for a long walk and lingered over a leisurely breakfast of granola and yogurt until I couldn't justify lingering anymore. It would be a long day at the store, as we were open until ten tonight. Saturday and Sunday, I was planning to wear my Mrs. Claus costume of ankle-length red skirt, white blouse, red and white checked cap with a mop of white curls attached, and plain glass spectacles. The outfit made me look thirty pounds heavier and twenty years older. Or was it twenty pounds heavier and thirty years older? Today, I decided to dress a bit nicer for the shop than I usually did. I chose a black dress over opaque black tights, with a red leather jacket and red jewelry. I couldn't go for heels as I'd be on my feet for twelve hours, but black ballet flats would be okay.

When I came around the corner of the house, Mrs. D'Angelo's front door flew open and she marched onto the porch.

"Morning, Merry. I'd say good day, but I don't think it's going to be, is it?"

"You never know," I said. "Weather reports have been wrong before."

"Even if the weather does improve, the death of poor Jack's son is still hanging over our town." She wore her dressing gown and her ever-present phone was fastened to her hip, but the expression on her face was so sad I stopped in my tracks. She'd said "poor Jack's son," not "Jack's poor son." "Do you know Jack Olsen well, Mrs. D'Angelo?"

"Not so much these days, dear. We're of an age, though. I knew him quite well back in the day. My Howard and I were friends with Jack and Karen." I had no idea if Howard was Mr. D'Angelo, but that didn't matter now. Karen was Jack's first wife. Gord's mother.

"Did you?" I said. "I suppose that made things difficult when Jack and Karen divorced."

"You'd have thought so, but none of us were surprised. Every woman in town felt dreadfully sorry for Karen. Jack was quite the cad in those days, I can tell you."

"In what way?"

She tapped the side of her nose. I smiled expectantly. "One for the ladies, I mean. In high school he was a heartbreaker, and being married didn't slow him down much. He had affairs constantly. Jack Olsen was always the talk of the town. Everyone knew, except for Karen, of course. The wives are always the last to know." Her face twisted in disapproval, and I took a guess as to what had happened to Mr. Howard D'Angelo. "I finally decided I couldn't bear to stand by and watch poor, dear Karen being the butt of jokes all around town. She needed to know, and it was my duty as her friend not to let her hear about it from people spouting mean-spirited gossip."

I kept my face impassive. I had no doubt my landlady had enjoyed every minute of her "duty."

"They divorced and Karen moved away with the boy. I thought we were friends, but she cut off all contact with everyone in Rudolph. We never heard so much as a word from Karen again. When Jack up and married Grace, we were surprised at how suddenly he changed his ways. He seemed devoted to Grace. Still does. Of course, a leopard rarely changes its spots, so perhaps

Jack learned how to be discreet." She sniffed in disapproval at the very idea of discretion.

I didn't agree. If Mrs. D'Angelo didn't know about
it, it didn't happen.

"You're saying some people had reason not to like
Jack. That was a long time ago, but people can have long
memories." I was thinking of discarded girlfriends, enraged husbands or fathers. Had someone waited all these
years to get revenge on Jack? It seemed unlikely, but
Jack's heart attack did put him in a perilous position,
and perhaps his enemy saw his chance for revenge, or
they felt driven to do what they believed they had to do
while Jack was still alive.

Then again, carrying a grudge for more than thirty
years and murdering a man's son for no reason but cold
revenge seemed beyond all reason to me.

"Long memories, yes. And there are reminders, of
course." Mrs. D'Angelo fluffed her helmet of steel gray
hair. Today the peignoir beneath the tatty dressing gown
was a pale peach concoction.

"What sort of reminders?"

"Where there are affairs, the men sometimes leave
little traces of themselves behind."

"Huh?" Then I got it. "You mean babies?"

"There were rumors, of course." Her face fell. "But
nothing more than that." Her phone rang and Mrs. D'Angelo had it out in a flash. "I have to take this, dear. Marie!
You will not believe what Merry Wilkinson told me."

I walked away. As far as I could remember I hadn't
told Mrs. D'Angelo anything, but that never stopped her

from leaping to her own conclusions or making up rumors out of whole cloth. I pushed the gossip about Jack out of my mind. If someone had been waiting for years to get revenge on Jack, I could see no reason why they'd kill Gord.

I trudged into town. Cars passed, kicking up slush. I was wearing my heavy winter boots to deflect most of the muck. The snowbanks were full of mud and axel grease, which is never a good look. It might not be a good look, but it was a good match to my mood. I cut through the park, and as I was rounding the bandstand my phone rang. "Please tell me they've made an arrest in the Olsen murder and it's starting to snow."

"Sorry, Merry," Russ Durham said. "No can do. I have an update from the police on that matter we talked about yesterday. Are you still at home?"

"No, I'm on my way to work. What did you learn?"

"The police don't know anything about the whereabouts of your real estate agent, whose name, by the way, is John Benedict. You were right, and he was easy to find. The real estate section is the biggest in the *Chronicle*. He wasn't on their radar so they didn't ask him for an alibi. I put a bug in Simmonds's ear about that."

"Good. What about Mayor Baumgartner?"

"Cast-iron alibi."

"No such thing," I said. "People can be persuaded to lie to the police if they think there's something in it for them. Let me guess, his alibi is a town councillor. Maybe someone with a nice piece of undeveloped country property perfect for a big-box store."

Russ chuckled. "They don't get any more cast-iron than this. He was in the Rudolph jail at the time in question."

"You can't be serious."

"Perfectly. Looks like His Honor can't hold his liquor. He was arrested in a brawl in the Red Bull at eight o'clock the night Gord Olsen died."

"Good heavens."

"He was held overnight and released the next morning. Not the first time, either, I was given to understand. Seems that Mayor Baumgartner prefers to do his drinking outside the Muddle Harbor town limits. And, as he has a shockingly low tolerance for alcohol, he's usually locked up before the rest of us have finished dinner."

"He was at the Red Bull?" Unlike every other business in or near the town limits of Rudolph, the Red Bull Tavern made no attempt to maintain the year-round Christmas spirit. Although I had been told that in December some of the strippers wore red hats and . . . other seasonal accessories.

Russ chuckled again. "Yup."

"Thanks, Russ. That doesn't help us any, but at least it eliminates one suspect."

"Merry"—Russ's voice turned serious—"don't get involved. Let the police handle it. I don't know what warning you and Alan were talking about yesterday, but I can guess. This isn't a game, and whoever murdered Gord Olsen isn't playing around."

"I know that," I said. And I did. *What could I achieve that the cops with their manpower, forensic labs, phone records, bank account warrants, and all their other resources couldn't?*

I knew these people. I also knew that wasn't likely to be enough.

"Thanks, Russ," I said.

"You take care, Merry. Call me if you need anything."

"I will," I said. We hung up.

For the rest of the way to work I wasn't thinking about the people of Rudolph or the children's Christmas weekend, or even about who killed Gord Olsen. I was thinking of Russ Durham, of the way his deep Southern accent had caressed my name, of the concern in his voice. It was nice, I thought as I walked, nice to know he cared. Nice to have a friend.

But a friend, I realized as I put my key into the lock of my shop, was all I wanted him to be.

Not long after opening, Clark Thatcher came into Mrs. Claus's Treasures. He was a twenty-something man, but he dressed like a juvenile delinquent, in pants slung so low he had trouble walking, and when he bent over he left far too little to the imagination. He wore a sports team T-shirt that may have been clean a long time ago, and sneakers the size of Santa Claus's float, dragging filthy laces behind them. My storage room shares a wall with the Nook, and on several occasions I'd heard Betty yelling at him to go home and change. But he never did, and one time she told me, without looking into my face, that Clark gave the shop a hip urban vibe young people liked. I don't think Betty knows what a hip urban vibe means.

"Got any change, Merry?" he asked.

I had plenty of change. The day was only beginning. "Some. How much do you need?"

He dug in his pocket and came up with a tattered bill. He waved Benjamin Franklin at me.

"I don't have a hundred dollars' worth to spare. Sorry."

"Guy paid with this and took all my change. What am I gonna do?"

"Go to the bank like anyone else?"

He looked confused at the concept.

"The bank? You know, the place a couple of doors down, next to Candy Cane Sweets, the one with a big blue sign out front."

"I know where the bank is, Merry, but Mom told me not to leave the store."

"You're going to have to," I said. "None of the other stores will be able to help you, either."

The right side of his lip twisted in a grimace. "Okay. Guess I can lock up for a few minutes."

Something was very familiar about that grimace. I'd never looked closely at Clark before, but I did now. His eyes were small and dark brown like his mother's, but whereas her face was round and came to a sharp little point, his chin was almost perfectly square.

Was it possible?

"Hold on a minute," I said. "I want to ask you something, Clark."

He hitched up his pants. They fell down again. "Whatever."

I pulled out my phone and flicked quickly through my pictures. "My sister bought her son a toy Santa. But . . . uh . . . the dog got it and destroyed it. She asked me to get her another one just like it. Do you stock these in the Nook?" I held out the phone.

Clark stepped closer to have a look. He smelled of unwashed clothes, tobacco smoke, and far too many male hormones. I watched him carefully. He shrugged, not caring much. "Yeah, it's one of ours. But we're outa stock now, sorry."

I put my phone away. "I'll look around town, then. Do you know if any of the other stores carry the same one?"

Another shrug. "Don't know."

"Where's your mom, anyway?" I asked. "She's always at the store in the morning, isn't she?" Betty was at the Nook whenever it was open, every day of the week and all hours of the day. Clark was her only employee, and she didn't trust him on his own. I didn't know if the reason she didn't have staff was that she couldn't afford them, or if she simply didn't mind doing it all herself. (I had also considered that she was such a mean old dragon, she couldn't keep anyone on.) As far as I knew, Clark was her only child. There had never been any mention of a husband, and I never cared enough to ask about her life away from Jingle Bell Lane.

I was beginning to care now. "Did she say where she was going or how long she'd be away?"

If Clark thought it was none of my business, he didn't show it. "Just out. Back in an hour. Like yesterday."

"Oh, she went out yesterday?"

"Yeah. In the afternoon. I guess she's starting to trust me around her precious junk." Another twist of the lip. I'd seen that gesture before, and I knew where.

Jack Olsen used the exact same mannerism. The square shape of Clark's face, particularly the strong chin, was identical to Jack's.

Jack Olsen was Clark Thatcher's father.

"What time did your mom go out yesterday?" I asked.

Clark's eyes narrowed. "What do you care what she does?"

"Uh . . . a car was driving down Jingle Bell Lane yesterday, looked very suspicious. The police asked me to keep an eye out. I was going to ask Betty if she'd noticed it."

He stuffed the hundred-dollar bill in his pocket and headed for the door, bored with my company. "Around two or two thirty, I guess. She was real upset when she got back. She's been acting pretty strange lately. I told one of my buddies about it, and he said it's the change. Whatever that is."

Clark sauntered out. *Was it possible?* Yes it was. Clark Thatcher bore a strong resemblance to Jack Olsen. I'd never noticed it before, but there was no reason I should have: I'd never seen the two of them together. According to the font of all knowledge, Mrs. D'Angelo, Jack had numerous affairs during his first marriage, and some people suspected he'd fathered children by his lovers.

Betty Thatcher had, against all habit and custom, left Rudolph's Gift Nook in the care of her son yesterday afternoon around the time I was at the Yuletide Inn talking to Mark Grosse. She'd left her shop again this morning.

I ran toward my office to grab my bag before I remembered that I had, as usual, left my car at home. No time to get it. I punched buttons on my phone and headed for the front door. "This is an emergency. I need a ride."

"What kind of emergency?" Vicky Casey said. "I'm up to my elbows in pastry."

"The kind that can't wait." I ran out of my shop, not bothering to get my coat or boots or to lock the door behind me. "I'm heading your way. I'll be there in one minute. I am not kidding, Vicky, this is important."

"The van's out back. You can borrow it."

"I can't drive a shift. You'll have to take me. Please, Vicky."

She didn't hesitate. "One minute. I'll meet you at the van."

The town maintenance crew had been out in force. The sidewalks were scraped clean and enough salt had been laid down to turn Lake Ontario into an inland sea. I flew down the street, passing startled browsers and curious townspeople. The walkway leading to the road at the back of the bakery joins up with the police parking lot. I debated running into the station and demanding to see Detective Simmonds. She'd dismissed my concerns yesterday, and I feared she'd accuse me of overreacting at best and deliberately trying to attract attention to myself at worst. Still, I hesitated. At that very moment, Officer Candy Campbell appeared, keys swinging in her hand, heading for the building. She saw me and stopped short. "Where are you off to in such a hurry, Merry? Let me guess. You're going to solve a murder, aren't you?" She laughed. "Better not. I overheard Simmonds yesterday complaining about civilians with overactive imaginations. That wouldn't be you she was talking about, would it?"

I turned left, toward the bakery, instead of right to the police station.

Vicky was waiting for me in the van, the engine running. I leapt in. "What's up?" she asked.

"Get to the Yuletide, fast as you can." I turned in my seat. "Better wait until Candy's out of sight. Wouldn't she just love to give us a speeding ticket."

Asking Vicky to step on it was kinda like asking Mattie to eat. No persuasion necessary. We tore out of town.

"You going to tell me what's going on?" she asked, as the snow-laden trees streaked past.

"I might be off my rocker, but I have a very bad feeling. Let me talk to Dad." I told Siri to call Dad. The phone rang for a long time before it was picked up.

"Hello?" my mother said.

"Mom! I'm glad you're there. Let me speak to Dad."

"He's not here."

"Where are you?"

"I'm at home. Where else would I be? My regular ten o'clock student arrives in fifteen minutes."

"Where's Dad?"

"Still at the inn, I would imagine. He spent last night with Jack and Grace, remember?"

"Yes, yes. But why are you on his phone?"

"He forgot it. It was ringing, so I picked it up. Now that I'm talking to you, dear, I have to say I'm worried about Eve. She . . ."

I hung up.

Vicky turned her head and looked at me. "Spill, Merry."

The car swerved and I yelped.

"I am on it," Vicky said, calmly returning to our lane. "What's happening?"

Words tumbled all over themselves as I tried to explain my thought process. "Sounds pretty far-fetched," she said when I'd finished.

"Maybe, but I need to warn Dad to be on his guard."

Vicky took the turn into the Yuletide Inn on two wheels. "Mark told me you came around to talk to him yesterday."

"We can discuss that later. Park over there. In front of Jack and Grace's house."

"I just wanna say he thinks I'm lucky to have such a good friend."

I looked at her. "He does?"

"Yeah, he does. And," she said softly, "I think so, too."

"Gee, thanks." Back to the matter at hand. "Drop me off and go and get Mark."

"He might not be in this early."

"If not, find Grace and come to the house. Let me out here." I didn't even wait for the bakery van to come to a full stop before I leapt out. I stumbled as my flat-soled shoes hit the ground, but managed to keep my footing and sprinted up the front path.

I leaned on the bell. I tried the handle. Locked. "Dad! It's me, Merry. Open up." I hammered on the door. No answer. I put my ear to the door. I might have heard voices from inside, but I couldn't make out any words. I'd have to go around the back to see what, if anything, was happening.

For once the normally busy hotel grounds were quiet. No staff were arriving for work or taking a smoke break. No happy families heading out to enjoy the day. Vicky was not coming to the rescue with a knife-wielding Chef Mark Grosse.

I jumped off the front step and ran to the side of the house. The driveway was wet with slush and cold water leaked through my shoes. My dad's car was parked in front of the garage. I hesitated and glanced back at the front door. No one had opened it to stand there looking out, wondering what was going on. I didn't know what to do. Why had I sent Vicky away? I'd have to chance someone answering the front door while I was on my way to the back.

I saw them the moment I reached the path to the gate. Footprints. Fresh ones. The imprint of zigzag treads perfectly clear in the slushy snow. The same marks I'd seen yesterday. The older ones were fading into indeterminate depressions as the snow softened with the rising temperatures. Not worrying about where I placed my feet I ran across the snowy lawn and up the slippery steps to the deck. I had enough presence of mind to keep a firm grip on the banister. I wore thin leather ballet flats with no tread. It wouldn't help anyone if I slipped and broke a leg.

Something was very much out of place, but for a moment I couldn't think what it was. Slowly recognition dawned. The drapes were fluttering gently in the breeze. *Outside the house.* No one would leave their French doors open in this weather, certainly not with an invalid in the house. I crept forward. The snow on the deck seemed particularly bright and sparkly. When my eyes focused I realized that shards of glass covered the snow and ice.

One panel of the French doors was shattered.

Chapter 16

This time I did call the police. Good thing I had Simmonds in my contacts list. I didn't even have to punch in my password and find her name. I held down the big round button, trying to keep my voice steady and said, "Call Diane Simmonds." Good old Siri, the Apple electronic assistant, understood and in seconds that seemed like hours, I heard the strong voice of the detective saying, "What is it now, Merry?"

I did not bother to exchange the usual courtesies. "Someone's broken into the Olsen house. There's glass everywhere at the back and no one's answering the door."

"Do not go into the house, Merry. Go to the road and wait for us to arrive. I'm sending officers now."

"Sorry," I said, "but my dad's in there." I cut off her protest and stuffed the phone into my jacket pocket.

Heart pounding, I reached the French doors. I pressed my back against the wall and tried to stretch my neck to peer inside.

Legs. I saw legs, stretched out on the carpet. Long legs dressed in baggy brown trousers. The right sock was worn almost through at the heel.

Dad. He never did take care of his clothes, and my mom said she wasn't his housekeeper.

"What do I want!" a woman screamed. "You know what I want. What I've always wanted."

I stepped forward. Glass crunched under my shoes. My dad was on the floor, not moving. I couldn't tell if he was dead or alive. One of the sturdy iron candlesticks lay beside him. I crossed the threshold and slipped into the house, taking care not to touch the jagged shards of glass protruding from the edges of the doors, thankful I wore winter clothes. Jack Olsen sat in the same chair he'd been in when I was last here, the same blanket tossed over his legs. But he'd lost the slightly vacant expression he had yesterday. His eyes flashed with anger, and his fists were clenched so tightly the knuckles had turned white.

Betty Thatcher faced him. She held a knife out in front of her. It was a kitchen knife, an ordinary kitchen knife you can find just about anywhere, but the blade was long and deadly sharp.

"Betty," I said.

She half turned. "You! Why can't you stop interfering in other people's affairs? I saw you leaving the police station the other day. I should have left you to fall and crack your nosy head open. I tried to warn you off, but would you listen? No, not you. You're not wanted here. This has nothing to do with you. Leave now."

"You hurt my dad," I said.

"He's okay. Little tap on the head is all."

At that moment I heard the most wonderful sound in the world. My father groaned and tried to roll over.

"Told ya," Betty said. "Now you can go. Take that silly man who thinks he's Santa Claus with you."

"I can't do that, Betty. You're scaring Jack. He's recovering from a heart attack—this is bound to be very upsetting to him. Why don't you put the knife down and we can talk about it?"

"I'm done talking," she said. "All I've ever heard are promises. Promises that come to nothing." She reached into her coat pocket with her free hand and pulled out a piece of paper. She waved it in Jack's face. "I want your signature on this. Now."

"A signature given under duress has no legal standing," Jack said. "You're wasting your time, you stupid woman."

"Don't you call me that," she screamed.

"I know about Clark," I said. "I know he's Jack's son. You only want what's best for Clark, don't you, Betty?"

"Darn straight," she said. "All these years, Jack's been promising to do right by my boy. Someday, it's always going to be someday."

A knock on the front door. Vicky called out, "Merry!

Open the door." In the depths of my pocket, my phone rang.

I didn't dare turn around, but I heard Dad groaning as he struggled to his feet. I couldn't go to him and help. I kept my eyes fixed on Betty. If she lunged for Jack, I had to be able to reach her in time. He was angry now, and that was good, but he was in no physical condition to dodge her or the business end of that knife. "I've called the police," I said.

"We don't need the cops," Betty said. "This is a private matter."

"What's the paper say?" I asked.

My phone stopped ringing. The hammering on the door continued.

"A new will," Betty said. "Jack promising to leave the inn to Clark. Now that Clark's Jack's only living son, I figure it's time he acknowledged my boy publicly."

I couldn't help it. My eyes flicked to Jack. His face was deathly pale. His lip twisted in the way that had been my first clue as to what was going on. "You killed my son," he said in a voice as icy cold as the wind blowing through the living room drapes. "You killed Gordon."

I felt the air change as someone stepped through the shattered French doors. I glanced aside quickly to see Mark Grosse. The blade in his hand was longer and sharper than the one Betty clutched.

"The police are on their way." I tried to signal to Mark to stay back.

Betty didn't seem to have noticed the new arrival.

"You said you'd give my Clark a job at the hotel. Train him to be in a position to take it over one day. But you went and fired him!"

"I fired him," Jack said, "because he was a waste of space. All he had to do was replace a lightbulb in a guest room, and he walked in without knocking when the guests were enjoying a private moment. I'm lucky we weren't sued. I had to give them the entire weekend for free and comp all their meals on top of it. I gave Clark a chance, Betty. He messed it up."

I doubt Betty even heard him. "You promised me you'd share the property with both your sons. Then *he* arrived and started talking about selling it all off. You said you'd give Clark another chance for a job in the hotel. But there wasn't going to be a hotel, not if that Gord had his way. So he had to go. What else could I do?"

"Put the knife down, lady," Mark said. "I have a bigger one."

"We're good here, Mark," I said. "Aren't we, Betty? Jack, why don't you sign the paper and we can all go home."

In the distance, I heard the welcome sound of sirens approaching.

"I'm not signing anything," Jack said. *Oh great,* now *he was getting back to his spirited self.* "I told you Clark will be provided for, and he will. More than he deserves. But he isn't getting any part of my business."

Betty threw the paper in his face and took a step forward. I felt as much as saw Mark tense as his grip tightened on the knife. Vicky continued hammering on the door. The sirens were getting closer. My father stood silently beside me.

"Clark can't make change," I shouted. "He was given a hundred-dollar bill to pay for a five-dollar item and he has no change left. He . . . he told me he was going to close the Nook for the day and take the hundred around to the Red Bull. Treat some of his buddies."

"What!" Betty screeched. She turned and took a step toward me, her eyes round and wild. "I knew he couldn't be left alone for more than ten minutes." She shook her hand. The knife wavered. Without stopping to think, I took a single step forward, grabbed her wrist, and held on as tightly as I could. I looked into her eyes and tried very hard to keep my voice calm and steady. "That knife looks sharp, Betty. We wouldn't want any accidents."

The knife clattered to the floor. Mark rushed in and scooped it up as Betty began to cry.

With an almighty crash the front door fell in and at the same time uniformed men and women poured through the shattered French doors.

"Whoa! Wasn't me," Mark said in the face of an officer's drawn gun. He dropped both knives as if they were on fire.

"He's one of the good guys," I said to Detective Simmonds. She nodded to the cop and he put his weapon away. Vicky threw herself into Mark's arms and my father gathered me into his.

"Are you okay?" I said.

"I'm going to have one heck of a headache later," Dad

said. "I don't even know what happened. I heard a noise, came out of the bedroom, and wham. When I came to, I was on the floor and you were in the house."

"What's happening? This is my home. Where's my husband? Let me through!" Grace burst into the room. With an anguished cry she dropped to her knees in front of Jack's chair.

"Close one," Jack said.

An officer hustled a handcuffed and weeping Betty Thatcher out the door.

"You people go up to the hotel," Simmonds said to us. "Wait for me there. Mr. Olsen, do you need to go to the hospital?"

"Nope."

Candy Campbell attempted to gather me, Dad, Mark, Vicky, and Grace and herd us to the hotel. She would have had as much success herding cats.

I glanced around the room. Vicky and Mark clung to each other murmuring sweet nothings, and Grace wept while Jack patted her back and said, "There, there. All's well that ends well."

We should, I thought, leave the happy couples alone. Alone as much as they could be in a room full of cops securing a crime scene. I took my dad's arm and said, "Let's go."

Dad and I passed more officers coming in. Outside, people were lined up at the hotel windows and a crowd had gathered on the lane, watching an officer stringing yellow tape around the cottage property.

Dad and I stepped out of the house. "Hey!" someone called. "It's Santa."

Dad waved. For a moment I wondered why everything in the distance seemed blurry. I glanced at Dad. He was grinning from ear to ear, holding his hands out.

He was catching snowflakes. Light, fat, fluffy flakes of snow were falling steadily from a cloud-filled sky.

Chapter 17

"Ho, ho, ho," said the deep voice from the shop doorway.

"Look who's here," a woman said to the restless six-year-old tugging on her coat. "It's Santa!"

The kid, who'd moments before been whining and stomping his feet with such vigor I feared for the more delicate of my ornaments, stood stock-still, wide-eyed and openmouthed.

"Have you been a good boy?" Santa asked him.

The child nodded, struck dumb.

"Santa's going to the park," the head toymaker said. "For games."

"We'll be right there, Santa," the mother said.

My dad nodded to the music box resting in her hand. "Your great-grandmother will get a lot of pleasure out of that." With a wink and another wave to the child, he left.

The woman's eyes were as wide and delighted as her son's. "How did he know my great-grandmother's still alive? This will be her one hundred and seventh Christmas, and she looks forward to it as much as she did when she was a child."

"He's Santa," the toymaker said.

"Are you Santa's wife?" the child asked me.

"Yup," I said. Normally I might be offended if someone suggested I was old enough to be married to my own father. But I was in my Mrs. Claus getup and today everyone would believe what they wanted to believe. The air over Rudolph was chock-full of that special Christmas magic.

"Shall I wrap that for you?" an elf said. The woman nodded, and Jackie took the music box behind the counter. Jackie and Crystal were dressed in the elf costumes they'd made for the Santa Claus parade. I'd decided not to notice that Jackie had made some adjustments to her costume since the parade; her elf was now more the type to be found in the adult section of the DVD store. The customer paid for the music box and, after helping themselves to another gingerbread cookie from the table by the door, she and her child left.

"Busy?" Santa's head toymaker, aka Alan Anderson, asked. About the only recognizable part of Alan were the clear blue eyes and the calm voice. He'd glued a full gray mustache to his upper lip and bushy sideburns to his cheeks, his nose was filled out with putty, and he peered at me through rimless spectacles. He wore a woolen jacket, knee-length breeches, and shoes with bright brass buckles.

"Run off our feet," I said. "And it's only noon."

"You should have a break for a while. Santa's about to have his first session of the day."

"That reminds me," I said. "Jackie, have you heard from Kyle? How's it going?"

"He's totally complaining about being demoted to second subassistant apprentice toymaker or something," she said. "But seeing as to how your dad made the town honor their agreement with him so he's still getting paid, he's okay with it."

I would hope so. I'd made a discreet phone call last night to Kyle to inform him that I'd see him run out of town if he ever again tried a stunt like betraying Rudolph to the *Muddle Harbor Chronicle*. He'd blustered and stammered something incomprehensible about "free speech" but backed off once he realized I wasn't asking him to give up the money he'd earned by selling the photograph. I hadn't told Dad about it, or anyone else.

"The second subassistant apprentice toymaker is making more than the master toymaker," Alan said, pretending to grumble. "Who's charging his usual rate of nothing."

"Only fair," I said. "They did call Kyle yesterday afternoon to tell him the job was off."

"He paid for his Santa costume out of his own pocket," Jackie said. "When he went to take it back the Nook was closed. Who knows if he'll ever get a refund? Whoever would have thought it? Betty Thatcher a killer. I wonder what'll happen to the Nook now."

"Got a minute?" Alan said to me.

"Sure." We stepped out onto the sidewalk to talk with some degree of privacy. It had snowed all day yesterday and into the night, and this morning a brilliant yellow sun shone in a pure blue sky, and the temperature was a perfect thirty degrees. The town had decided not to chance letting people skate on the bay, and it was too late to make a rink, but at Dad's suggestion, the ice hockey games had been turned into field hockey in the snow. Enough fresh snow had fallen for the snow sculpture competitions and the toboggan races on the hill. Over the sound of sleigh bells and laughter, I could hear faint strains of "We Wish You a Merry Christmas" as my mom's junior class began their concert.

It was Christmas in Rudolph and all was right with the world.

All, that is, except for the locked door and unlit storefront next to mine.

"Did you sleep okay?" Alan asked.

"No trouble," I said. "Honestly, Alan, I felt better knowing it was over and we were all safe again." I shook my head. "Poor Betty. She must have been driven crazy all these years, waiting for Jack to acknowledge his son."

"Don't feel too sorry for Betty," he said. "Gord didn't deserve to die to make a place for Clark."

"I know that. I wonder what Clark's going to do now. He can't manage the Nook on his own."

"I'd better be going," Alan said. "Someone has to write down all those kids' wishes."

I smiled at him. He made no move to leave. Instead he lifted his hand and touched my cheek. He ran his finger lightly down the side of my face. "I'd kiss you, Merry Wilkinson, if you weren't in that costume."

"Why not?" I teased. "This is a glimpse of what I'm going to look like when I'm old."

"And I'll be old along with you. We don't want rumors running around saying Mrs. Claus is having an affair with the head toymaker."

I smiled at him. I'd been smiling so much for the last twenty-four hours my face hurt.

Yesterday, Simmonds had kept my group of witnesses confined to the inn's meeting rooms until she had a chance to interview us. Dad couldn't tell her much, as he hadn't seen who'd broken into the Olsens' house and hit him, but Simmonds made me go over and over everything that had happened since I'd arrived at Grace and Jack's home. When Dad and I were finally allowed to leave the inn, Alan Anderson had been sitting by the fireplace in the lobby, waiting for us. He leapt to his feet and stuffed a paperback book into one of his big coat pockets.

I'd had a text from Russ saying he had to head back to town to write his story. Did I have a comment for the press? I passed the phone to Dad, who called Russ and chatted about the community spirit of Rudolph and a safe, welcoming atmosphere, blah, blah, blah.

"Thanks for waiting," I said to Alan.

He studied my face for a long time. I felt like a fool, standing there, smiling up at him while he smiled back at me. I didn't mind feeling like a fool at all.

Dad gave me back my phone. "I need a ride," I said. "I came with Vicky, but she had to get back to work."

"I'll take you," Alan said.

Dad cut him off. "No need. Your place is in the wrong direction. Russ tells me the weekend is back on and Sue-Anne is practicing being contrite even as we speak. That means you have work to do, Alan. I assume you'll be my toymaker again."

"Wouldn't miss it."

"Good. Good. Come along, Merry, don't dawdle. They didn't get that skating rink made, did they? I'll check the temperature and see if it's going to be cold enough overnight to freeze the bay solid. Probably not, but it doesn't hurt to find out."

Dad headed for the door, still talking.

"Alan," I said.

"Go with your dad, Merry. I'll see you tomorrow. I have . . . we have . . . things to talk about."

"We sure do," I said.

He gathered me into his arms and kissed me. I kissed him back, and we held each other for a few long, lovely, precious seconds.

"Merry!" Dad called over his shoulder. "Phone your mother. Tell her to contact her students. The game's afoot!" He could always find a suitable Sherlock Holmes quote for every occasion.

"Can't keep Santa waiting," Alan said, giving me his soft, gentle smile.

I had Dad swing past my house so I could let Mattie out for a quick pee and find a pair of shoes to replace the brown Birkenstocks that were the only thing in my size in the hotel's lost and found (another pair of shoes ruined!), before dropping me at the store. I was totally exhausted, mentally as well as physically, and facing one of the busiest weekends of the year, but it was the Friday before Christmas, and I couldn't ask Jackie and Crystal to handle the store alone. By the time we got back to town, snow was falling steadily and the sidewalks of Rudolph were crowded with eager customers. That evening had been the busiest since I'd taken ownership of Mrs. Claus's Treasures. Everyone in town, residents and tourists, wanted the inside scoop on what had happened at the inn, and most of them (the visitors, anyway) were polite enough to pretend they'd come to shop. Other than a whispered word to Jackie, I spent the rest of the day repeating, "The Rudolph police department will be releasing a statement shortly." Fortunately, I'd been looking out the window to gauge the amount of snow we were getting when I saw Russell Durham heading our way. I escaped to my office and told Jackie to tell him I wasn't in.

"Hiding in the back" was the phrase she actually used, and Russ didn't push it.

Now Alan and I stopped grinning foolishly at each other as we heard the sound of bells approaching. Dancer and Prancer were coming our way, heads held high, tails flicking, huge hooves shaking the ground. They pulled a sleigh full of excited children and happy parents, heading for the park.

"Hey," Alan said, his arm resting lightly on my shoulder. "Look who's in front."

I jumped up and down and waved. Jack Olsen sat on the bench next to the driver. He was bundled up in a heavy coat, a plaid blanket arranged over his knees, and a scarlet and green scarf wrapped many times around his neck. His sunken cheeks glowed red and his eyes shone. He saw Alan and me watching and lifted his hand. Grace sat behind him, and she also waved at us. Her smile was radiant.

"It is so nice to see Jack enjoying himself," I said. "We were all afraid he was about to give up on life after the death of Gord, but the confrontation with Betty put the spark back in him."

"Once relit," Alan said, "hard to extinguish."

"I'm not going to judge," I said. "And I don't know the whole story, but it seems to me Jack has to bear some of the blame for what happened. He never acknowledged paternity and was sneeringly dismissive of Clark when he came to work at the inn. Poor Betty, still hoping that after almost thirty years Jack would do the decent thing by her and her son."

"I'm just glad it's over and your dad's good name is cleared."

"The first customers through my door this morning were Arlene and Kathy," I said.

"Who the heck are Arlene and Kathy?"

"The Fine Budget wives. They checked out of the inn this morning and left their husbands having breakfast and making calls while they came into town for one last shop. They have flights home later today. Kathy told me she hopes to get back here for a vacation next year. But, she said, the deal to turn the Yuletide into a Fine Budget franchise is off."

"That's good to hear."

News of police activity at the Yuletide Inn had, of course, been all over town in minutes. The moment it was revealed that Noel Wilkinson, far from being a suspect, had himself been attacked by the crazed killer of Gord Olsen, Sue-Anne called to ask Dad to resume his role of Santa. Which, being the sort never to hold a grudge, he happily agreed to do. When they realized temperatures were dropping and snow was going to fall all through the night, the town swung into action to get the children's weekend back on track.

"Gotta run," Alan said.

"Why don't you come over for dinner tonight?" I said. "It won't be much, but I have some soup in the freezer." This weekend was all about children and families; the shops wouldn't be too busy after the supper hour, so I could take the evening off.

"I'd like that," he said.

"If you don't have plans for Christmas dinner," I said without thinking, "I'd love to have you join us. My brother, Chris, will be home, and Mom and Dad and some of their friends are coming to my place." Christmas was now three days away. Not only did I not have enough plates for twelve guests—now thirteen—I had forgotten to order a turkey or a roast; I had not thought about chairs or dishes in which to serve the sides. I would be working until three on Christmas Eve, the same time as all the other shops closed.

"I think I'm already invited," Alan said. "When your mom heard that my parents are visiting my aunt in

Phoenix this year, so my brothers aren't coming home, she said I would be joining them. It wasn't a question. She didn't tell me we were going to your place."

"I'm thinking pizza," I said, "or Chinese. On paper plates on laps. While Mattie tries to climb into said laps."

"Sounds absolutely perfect."

"My dad won't think so."

Alan grinned. He touched my face one more time, then turned and walked away. I watched him hurrying down Jingle Bell Lane, heading for the park, where Santa held court in the bandstand. A line of giggling children fell in behind the head toymaker.

Diane Simmonds came into my shop in the early afternoon. She wore jeans and a puffy blue coat, and a young girl was with her. The resemblance between the two was remarkable: the emerald eyes, the untamed mop of red curls. I said, "Hi, Charlotte."

She blinked. "How'd you know my name?"

I tapped my nose. "I'm Mrs. Claus. My husband tells me things."

She edged closer to me, and I leaned in. "I know there's no Santa," she said in a whisper. "My mom told me because we're living in Christmas Town we have to pretend there is."

"Wait until you meet Santa," I said. "You might change your mind."

"Do you have a moment?" Simmonds asked me.

"A quick one," I said. Jackie and Crystal were busy with customers, but no one seemed to need my attention just then.

"Honey, you go and pick out your gift for Grandma. And then you can choose a few pretty things to decorate the house."

Charlotte headed straight for the dolls. I took her mother into my office. Simmonds did not take a seat. "This is a day I intend to devote strictly to my daughter, but I figured you deserved to know some of what we found out."

I nodded.

"Betty Thatcher has made a full confession. As she told you, she was enraged when Gord Olsen began making plans for the future of the inn, cutting her son, Clark, completely out. Jack Olsen had made vague promises to her over the years that he'd leave Clark one half of his business. That turned out to be a lie. Olsen told me his will leaves money to Clark in trust, knowing he has no business sense whatsoever and would likely just squander any inheritance he does get."

"He's probably right about that," I said.

"Betty had heard talk that the inn was going to be sold, and she was furious because Clark wasn't consulted. She tried to get into the hospital to see Jack, but was turned away as only family was allowed to visit. That enraged her even more. On the day Gord Olsen died, she'd been at the inn earlier, dropping off some items Grace ordered for decorations."

I remembered the cheap ornaments in the ladies' room.

"When Betty was leaving, she ran into Gord. She told him Clark was his half brother and demanded he involve Clark in plans for the inn. Gord essentially laughed in her face."

"I can see him doing that. He wasn't a nice man."

"Gord walked away, leaving her steaming. She saw a room service tray left unattended and pocketed a steak knife."

I shivered.

"She says she didn't plan to kill Gord. She liked the knife and figured she deserved something nice from the hotel. That may or may not be true. It will be up to the prosecutor to prove premeditation. She returned to the inn later that evening, intending to tell Grace about Clark and demand Grace get Jack to do something. Instead, she saw Gord heading into the gardens, parked her car, and followed him. He mocked her and she stabbed him with the knife that just happened to still be in her pocket."

"What about the holly?"

"The holly on Gord's chest? She says she had some scraps of decorations in her pocket, and the holly came out when she pulled out the knife. She left it there, thinking it was a nice touch."

I shook my head. "I don't buy that. That holly was fresh, not plastic, and you told me it had been cut from a display in the hotel. Betty doesn't use real greenery in any of her decorations, and doesn't sell it. Betty doesn't care much about the Christmas Town spirit."

"Why do you think she used it?"

"I think she'd deliberately tried to deflect police attention from herself by making it look as though the killer was someone trying to save the town of Rudolph. Someone like my dad, or any one of the business owners or town councillors."

"I noticed that little discrepancy, myself. You're good at this detective business, Merry."

I smiled, enjoying the praise.

"Don't let it go to your head," she said. "I can do my job on my own. Not that I expect we'll have any more murders to solve in this little town." Simmonds opened the office door. "I'd better see what damage Charlotte has done to your stock. We're going to the park. I've registered us in the snow sculpture contest. The mother and daughter category."

"Good luck," I said. "Competition is going to be fierce."

Her green eyes twinkled. "I've been known to be a mite competitive myself."

I had absolutely no doubt about that.

I was beginning to think about lunch, when one more person came in wanting to talk about events of the previous evening. She burst through the doors, spotted me arranging tree ornaments, and headed over with her gloved hand outstretched. "Dawn Galloway, *Muddle Harbor Chronicle*."

"I know," I said.

"Can you make a statement for the press?" Her voice boomed. Customers glanced up from their browsing, Crystal stopped ringing up purchases, and heads popped out of the alcoves.

"No," I said in my firmest voice.

"Are you sure?"

"Of course I'm sure."

She stepped closer. "You see, Merry—may I call you Merry?"

"I guess."

"I need this job, and I need an article for tomorrow's paper. Right now, I got nothin'. No one will talk to me." Her look was plaintive.

"I'll give you a statement," Jackie said, abandoning the gray-haired lady who had spent the last ten minutes vacillating between the ornament that said "Baby's First Christmas" and the one that proclaimed "Santa's Newest Helper." "If there's a picture to go with it," my assistant finished.

"Sure," Dawn said.

"You have one minute," I said, "starting now. And I don't want a mention of my name or this shop."

"I always thought something was off about Betty Thatcher," Jackie began.

She kept to the one minute and then beamed while Dawn used her cell phone to snap a picture. Instead of leaving, the intrepid *Chronicle* reporter spotted a white ironstone turkey platter and pounced on it with an excited squeal.

"Lunch is on me," I said to Jackie and Crystal after Dawn had left proudly bearing not only the platter but a full set of matching serving dishes.

I jotted down lunch orders and left the shop. I stood outside for a moment watching the activity. The air was crisp and cold, but there was no wind and the sun shone warm on my face. Smiling people strolled by, laden with bulging shopping bags, the Clydesdales headed for the inn to pick up another load, a lineup stretched out the door of Cranberry Coffee Bar, and another line was forming at the hot chocolate table outside the Elves' Lunch Box. "Are we going to see Santa now?" an excited little girl asked, and when her mom said, "Yes," she squealed in delight.

A rusty Dodge Neon drove slowly down the street, searching for a parking spot. It was in luck, as the SUV outside the dark storefront of Rudolph's Gift Nook pulled away at that moment. The Neon took its place with a great deal of inching back and forth and wheels striking the curb. A woman stepped out of the driver's seat and slammed the car door. My breath caught in my throat.

Betty Thatcher! Wasn't she in jail? Surely she didn't get bail?

The woman saw me watching and scowled. It wasn't Betty, but darn close. She was slightly heavier than the scrawny Betty and the hair peeking out from under her wool hat was an unnatural shade of dark brown, not Betty's steel gray. The beady black eyes were exactly the same, as was the hawk nose and the expression on her face—like someone had slipped a lemon into her eggnog—when she spotted me. She marched over.

"Hi," I said.

She looked me up and down, not liking what she saw. "I guess you'll be Merry."

"Uh, yes."

"You look ridiculous in that getup."

"It's my costume."

"If anyone expects me to dress in costume, they'll be sadly disappointed."

"And you are?" I asked.

"Margaret Thatcher. And no, I am not the former prime minister of England. I'm called Margie."

"You must be Betty's sister. How . . . nice to meet you."

"Twin sister. The eldest by two minutes, if you must know."

I refrained from pointing out that I hadn't asked.

"I've come to run the store until Betty gets herself cleared of this unpleasantness. She told me all about you. I'll be keeping my eye on you, so don't you try anything."

"I won't."

Margie looked around. If anything, her scowl deepened. "Christmas Town. Humbug."

Connect with Berkley Publishing Online!

For sneak peeks into the newest releases, news on all your favorite authors, book giveaways, and a central place to connect with fellow fans—

"Like" and follow Berkley Publishing!

facebook.com/BerkleyPub
twitter.com/BerkleyPub
instagram.com/BerkleyPub

Penguin
Random
House